AWAKEN

THE CURE CHRONICLES, BOOK TWO

K. A. RILEY

For those who always look for the good in the world.

SUMMARY

Leaving behind the people she loves most in the world, Ashen sets off into the wilderness in hopes of finding the elusive group of rebels know as the Consortium.

But when she finds herself among strangers in the former ski town the locals call the "Bastille," secrets begin to reveal themselves, friendships prove as fragile as glass, and Ashen begins to understand just how terrifyingly powerful her enemy really is.

When her brother, Kel, goes missing, Ashen is forced to return to the place she despises most in the world, where she'll be faced with a cruel and heartbreaking choice.

This is the second book in the Cure Chronicles.

PREFACE

Tessa, Ashen, Kel: I love you more than you know.

39.48968, -105.920279

My father's words and a series of mysterious numbers, carved as they are into the deepest reaches of my mind, are all that's keeping me from losing the last morsel of hope still clinging to my devastated heart.

The message is my only guide, the only clue to the whereabouts of allies who may or may not exist—who may or may not be hiding in a stronghold deep in the Colorado wilderness.

The only people who can possibly help me defeat the Directorate.

Fleeing for my life and desperate to find those allies, I chose to leave the Arc behind. I left my brother, Kel, in the clutches of the enemy. I left Finn, who means everything to me, in a place that would eat him alive if its inhabitants learned he was responsible for helping me escape.

Now, I have only to venture west and make my way toward the coordinates my father scrawled at the bottom of his note.

It all sounds so comically easy. *A leisurely stroll through the woods.*

But I'm not naive.

I know what's hunting me.

What I don't know is what I'll find when—or *if*—I reach my destination.

I have no idea when my father wrote the note or how much has changed since then. I can't begin to guess how many Dregs escaped the Mire in the early days before the Arc was complete.

I don't know how many survived, how many have been taken down over the years by the Blight—the biological weapon created in a lab by my father, stolen by the Directorate, and covertly used against our own people.

The very weapon the enemy used to kill my father seven years ago.

As I make my way through the wilderness in hopes of finding a hidden group of rebels known as the Consortium, I may well be making my way toward a whole new enemy.

But the truth is, I have no choice.

The unknown, as terrifying as it may be, is better than the certain death I left behind.

1

DAY ONE

I WAKE to the sound of birds chirping.

It's a peaceful sound, one I've heard thousands of times over the course of my life. But this morning, it's music. Pure, innocent, simple. In its quiet way, it tells me there's still some beauty to be found in the world.

More importantly, it tells me there are no predators nearby.

I'm still wearing the flowing cloak Finn crafted for me via some kind of extraordinary technology I'll never entirely understand. When activated, it masks me from enemies' eyes and from heat-seeking drones, rendering me all but invisible.

My silver dagger is sheathed at my waist, traces of my enemy's blood no doubt still darkening its blade. It's a fine weapon, and sharp. I'm sure no one meant for me to keep it after last night's battle with Randolph, the arrogant son of the Arc's so-called King and Queen—the man who was *supposed* to murder me.

No one expected me to live to see this morning's light.

Decked out as I am, I've evolved into some sort of

medieval rogue. I slip stealthily from place to place, adeptly evading any pursuers.

Except the notion of rogues seems romantic, and there's no romance in fleeing for my life. The act is nothing but a powerful blend of adrenaline, terror, and rage, all stirring frantically together inside me until I feel like I'm on the verge of implosion.

The enormous structure known as the Arc—the pretty Hell I left behind—is home to an exclusive club of sadists who want to see me killed in the most brutal manner possible. Entertainment for the wealthiest among them, a chance for their kind to revel in my downfall even as the masked cowards hide behind a veil of anonymity.

It's a good thing the Aristocracy can't be bothered to raise dogs inside the Arc, or they'd no doubt have an army of pure-bred murder-hounds after me. As it is, the worst I'm likely to encounter are weaponized drones, their laser-like red eyes ready to burn into my skin on sight.

Which, let's face it, is bad enough.

As I begin the day's long hike, my mind turns to thoughts of Kel. I wonder with the faintest trace of hope if Finn will manage to find him and tell him I'm still alive. That one day soon, I'll find my way to him and we'll flee the Arc and its horrible inhabitants for good.

Close to the city, most of the forest's trees are hollow, leafless corpses, collapsed against one another, seeking moral support in their final days. But as I distance myself from the Mire's outer wall and approach the mountains, the woods come alive, their limbs bursting with green leaves as if breathing a sigh of relief to be far from humankind.

Low-hanging branches slice at my face as I move, but I don't mind a few scrapes. The pain keeps me alert and serves as a reminder of the torture the Elite would have subjected me to had I failed to escape their grasp.

My mind spins with dark thoughts as I walk, my cloak pulled over my head to conceal me from any Directorate drones that may pass above the trees. I hear one or two of them as the day wears on, but surprisingly, when I dare the occasional glance upward as they soar overhead, I notice they're simple, unarmed surveillance drones like the ones I used to see in the Mire.

I could tell myself my enemy has given up on me, but I know better. The Duchess—the woman who accepted me coldly into her home inside the Arc with the express intention of watching me like a hawk—is no doubt doing everything in her power to locate me. She's desperate to find the Consortium's hiding place, if indeed such a place exists...and I'm her best chance.

But as the hours pass and no soldiers come at me with their weapons drawn, a renewed sense of peace begins to replace the terror I've felt since escaping the Arenum, the fighting ring where I left the King's son bleeding on the ground.

I soothe myself with thoughts of Finn, of his voice, his face. The touch of his fingers on my skin. I allow myself, for brief moments, to fantasize about walking hand in hand with him through these woods, leaning against him, the warmth of his body a much-needed security blanket.

As if the trees themselves are hoping to contribute to my mood, dappled sunlight has begun to flicker between the billowing leaves high overhead to dance magically on the ground before my feet. It's a sort of light that doesn't exist anywhere other than in nature, and I inhale deeply, relishing the temporary, fragile sense of calm it grants me.

Holding my breath, I tell myself how lucky I am simply to be alive.

"If only you were with me," I whisper as I exhale, sending the words to Finn, wishing that somehow he could hear them. "If only I hadn't had to leave you behind. We could start a new life out here. A new *world*."

I'll see him again. I can feel it in my skin, in my bones, with a certainty that's become as much a part of me as the blood in my veins. Whatever fate may have in store for us, I vow to press my hands to his chest again. My lips *will* find his and I will kiss him hungrily, needfully, and he'll utter the three words that are a balm for every conceivable wound.

I love you.

Incredible how three brief syllables can heal so thoroughly.

After a time, a surprising sound pulls me out of my reverie, drawing my eyes to the treetops before it comes a second time. The low, sustained hoot of an owl.

As I scan my surroundings, I spot him perched several feet above me in the boughs of a maple tree. Silvery-white, his feathers gleam in the sunshine. His eyes, bright and alert, seem to stare into my own. They blink once as our gazes meet.

"Hello, friend," I whisper. "Are you hunting?"

He twists his head to the side as if something has drawn his attention, spreads his wings, and takes off.

"I guess that answers my question," I chuckle.

Something about the owl gives me a jolt of bliss. If he can survive out here, if he can still thrive in this wretched world, maybe there's a chance for the rest of us.

But when I stop at a spring a few minutes later seeking clean water to drink, any fleeting joy fades as quickly as it came.

The snap of a twig meets my ears. Then another, and another.

A deer, maybe?

The frantic swarm of insects in my stomach tells me I already know the answer.

That's no deer.

I freeze, shrinking into my cloak to further conceal myself from any eyes that may be searching for me. That's when I see him: a young man with sandy-brown hair, dressed in the black uniform of the Directorate Guard, sneaking his way past me through the trees.

He doesn't spot me, but I have no doubt he knows I'm close. These woods are probably crawling with his kind, hunters quietly seeking me out so they can drag me back, kicking and screaming, to a woman who will delight in watching me suffer, alongside her monstrous allies.

When the man has passed and I can finally exhale, I consider pursuing him. I could easily sneak up behind him and cut his throat. I could end him here and now, and leave his bloodied body for the Duchess' people to find. A warning.

Stay away, or there will be more corpses.

No.

I remind myself that he was probably once like me. A Dreg

from the Mire who likely only trained to become Directorate Guard because his one other option was death. Like so many of us, he had no choice.

Wrong.

There's always a choice.

Always.

Still, I refuse to kill him. I've watched two classmates die, as well as an old friend from Sector Eight. The very thought of more needless death steals away pieces of my soul as I crouch, hidden, telling myself to let it be.

I wait until the sound of snapping twigs fades into the distance then move along the edge of the stream, heading west, the soles of my shoes sinking silently into the soft mud.

When I've hiked until my feet are burning, I force myself to seek shelter for the night. I find a rocky overhang at the base of a mountain, just high enough off the ground for me to stand under, forming a perfect little cavern. As a precaution, I choose not to hunt or build a fire. For now, I'm content to sleep hungry and cold.

After all, I'm still alive, aren't I?

A low *Hooo* meets my ears as I slip down to sit on the cool ground. I lift my head and peer out into the trees that surround my small shelter, scanning until I spot a pair of bright eyes. The owl is back, his talons locked around a thick branch, those shining eyes fixed on mine for the second time today.

"Are you following me?" I ask with a yawn.

I close my eyes, pleased by the thought of a keen-eyed new friend watching over me.

My mind fills once again with nebulous images of Finn as I will myself to sleep. The tactile memory of his arms around me, the intensity of his expressive eyes, which tried so hard to speak to me when we first got to know one another. I was too stubborn to read them, unable or unwilling to decipher his coded messages. I failed to understand when his eyes told me of the secrets lingering in the air between us, of so much hidden pain behind the pristine walls of the Arc.

It seems like madness now that I once thought of him as an enemy.

I command my mind to conjure dreams of him, but on this night—my second night in the wild—as I drift off to sleep, I only see images of violence. The life draining from my classmate Luke's face as other Candidates beat him to death. Maren's terrified eyes as she drowned in front of a sea of masked, cheering monsters.

Harrowing events that occurred mere days ago are lodged inside the prison of my memory, still as real as they were when I witnessed them.

In my nightmares, I see my brother Kel's face. Frightened, pale, helpless, crying out as he watches the Directorate's miscreants murder my mother.

His face contorted in fear as he's marched into the Arc.

I hear his voice calling my name. I try to respond, to shout, but my own voice catches in my throat and nothing comes out.

Just...air.

I jolt awake to the sound of heavy breathing and the sensation of someone yanking me violently to my feet.

I'm still dreaming, I tell myself. *This isn't happening.*

But a hard slap to my face tells me I'm dead wrong.

2

CAUGHT

POWERFUL HANDS SHOVE me against the jagged outer wall of my shelter, my head slamming hard against solid stone.

I should be terrified, but for some insane reason I snicker. My addled brain finds it hilarious that I've been out of the Arc less than forty-eight hours and the enemy has already managed to snare me.

Some stealthy rogue I am.

In the early morning light, it takes me a moment to make out the faces of three people standing before me. The closest is the young man who's pressing me to the wall, a look of pure rage contorting his features. He appears to be nineteen or so, with dark hair, light eyes, and a jaw coated in thick stubble. Through his grimace, it's impossible to fully assess his features, but something tells me he might be handsome if he weren't seething with murderous rage.

Behind him, standing at each shoulder, are a woman of thirty or so and a girl who looks my age, maybe a couple of years younger. *Yes,* I think. *She's got to be about fifteen.*

Wait—the Directorate is sending fifteen-year-old girls to hunt me?

***That's** new.*

"You're not Directorate Guard," the young man snarls from between clenched teeth as he pulls my dagger from its sheath and hands it to the woman, who tucks it into her belt. "Are you some kind of spy?"

"I'm no spy," I reply with a sneer. "But I'd sure like to know who the hell you three are."

The teenage girl lets out a high-pitched giggle, as if my reaction is shockingly amusing. I manage another glance in her direction, eager to size her up. She's pretty, with black, curly hair and green eyes, and has a white flower tucked into her hair by her left ear—an accessory that might seem sweet under any other circumstance. There's an impishness in her face that tells me she can't possibly be affiliated with the Directorate; she would hardly fit in with that band of sadistic creatures.

Then again, her companion *did* come close to splitting my skull open a few seconds ago, so maybe I'm not the best judge of character.

The red-haired woman next to the girl elbows her in an obvious attempt to wipe the grin off her face.

"You're in no position to ask questions," the woman says, stepping toward me. She pulls the cloak away from my body to examine my clothing. I glance down and immediately see why it was so easy for the trio to spot me. The cloak has reverted to a deep purple shade, which means I must have accidentally deactivated its camouflage setting sometime during the night. "You're definitely wearing a Directorate uniform," she says, eyeing the white outfit underneath. "But you're not a Chaperon or member of the Guard. You look like a Candidate. How on God's green earth did you end up out here?"

I wonder for a moment how she knows what Candidates' uniforms look like, but the thought flits away like vapor as I try to formulate a strategic answer.

"I escaped from the Arc," I finally blurt out, aware as the words emerge how insane they must sound. Still, I hold my chin high and force myself to look the woman in the eye.

"No one escapes the Arc," she scoffs. "We all know that by now."

"Yeah, well, I guess I just have useful friends," I snap before correcting myself. "One friend in particular. He helped me get out alive."

The woman narrows her eyes as if to tell me wordlessly that my story is unfathomable, and I can't blame her for her skepticism. Alliances between Dregs like me and those who live inside the Arc are rare, to say the least. The thought of someone powerful helping one of us is ridiculous at best.

"Look," I continue, clearing my throat. The young man is no longer pressing his arm into my neck, but he's still holding onto me tightly, like he's convinced I'll bolt. "I'm assuming you three are part of the Consortium. That means we have a few things in common."

The three exchange a look, but no one confirms my theory. "It doesn't matter," I tell them. "Either you're with them, or you're with the Directorate. If you're Consortium, it will mean something to you when I tell you I'm Oliver Spencer's daughter. If you're with the Directorate, it'll mean something, too. Just...probably not something good."

"Oliver Spencer..." the red-haired woman breathes. She takes a sudden step back, like I've just burned her.

Oh, damn.

This could be bad.

"How did you get here? What made you come west of the city?" she asks.

"A note I found," I tell her. "From my father. He left a message—a sort of coded one—and I followed the clues in this direction. Look, I need answers. I need allies. You must know that what's going on inside the Arc is..."

I stop talking, all too aware that I'm saying far too much far too quickly. I don't even know who these people are, and their clothing isn't helping me draw any useful conclusions. They're each dressed in khaki pants with olive green tank tops, like some kind of informal military uniform. At their waists, each of them has a belt with a sheathed blade of one sort or another.

There are no guns, at least. Though for some reason, I don't find their lack of sophisticated weaponry reassuring.

I do notice that none of them wears the symbol of the Consortium: a circle crossed by two swords. For all I know, these three are part of a band of nameless rebels... or worse, thieves. If they knew the value of the clothes on my back—of the specialized uniform Finn custom-made for me to enhance my strength—they might slit my throat, steal it, and leave my corpse for scavenging wildlife.

"What's happening inside the Arc isn't our concern," the woman finally says, her tone frosty. "We're just trying to survive out here, and there are enough obstacles in our way as it is."

"You're telling me it means nothing to you that the Directorate is killing Dregs?" I look her up and down. There's no question in my mind that she knows what I'm talking about. "How can you not care?"

She winces. "Of course I care. But what would you have us do? If we make the Directorate angry, we're all dead."

I stare at her, my thoughts braiding into twisted knots in my mind.

"You've *already* made them angry," I tell her. "They hate that they can't find you, for one thing."

The woman and the young man exchange a brief glance, but I can't quite decipher its meaning.

"The Directorate knows *exactly* how to find us, which is why we can't afford to anger them."

"I don't understand..." I stammer, baffled. "They don't let Dregs wander freely outside the Mire. How can you possibly survive out here if they know where you are?"

"It's...complicated. If you come with us, you can see for yourself." She lays a hand on the young man's shoulder and squeezes gently, nodding once.

The young man finally releases me and takes a step back. He looks at the woman, who seems to be the leader of their small group, and says, "What are we going to do with her?"

"She's Spencer's daughter," the woman replies. "We have no choice but to bring her with us. Veer will want to meet her."

"No way," he protests. "*They'll* be looking for her. There will be drones swarming the woods in no time. We saw three of them on the way here. If they think we're harboring an escapee..."

"We can't just leave her!" the dark-haired girl objects. "If their weaponized drones come for her, she's dead. She's safe in the—" She stops, looks at me, and says, "She's safe with us. But not out here, not in these woods. You know the rules."

"I don't care," the young man snarls. "If we bring her with us, she puts us all at risk. It's not our problem if we leave her behind and she ends up dead because she's literally too stupid to live."

"It'll be your problem if word gets back to Veer," the girl snaps.

"She's right," the woman says. "We can't leave Spencer's daughter in the woods to die, or Veer will have our heads—at least figuratively." She shoots me an *I hope you're worth it* look before saying, "Come on, then. We'll take you to the Bastille."

"Bastille? There's no place with that name around here," I say. "At least, there wasn't seven years ago."

"It's what we call Br—," the girl begins to explain, but she's quickly shushed by the others.

"It's fine," I mutter. "I don't need to know. Just tell me—*are* you part of the Consortium?"

"We're...part of what's left of it," the woman says.

"Wait—left of it?" A sick feeling begins to grow inside me. "What are you saying?"

The woman sighs. "There was a lot of fighting, years ago. Many died. Some among our ranks betrayed us. That's all you need to know. The Consortium isn't what it once was. It's basically gone."

Gone.

The word parches my throat, robbing my body of strength. I want to collapse, to surrender to the weight that's just overtaken my shoulders and is threatening to break me.

"There have to be more of you," I croak out. "There have to be more members out there..."

"I'm sorry." The woman lays a hand briefly on my shoulder. Her voice is kind, reassuring. "But it'll be okay. We'll look after you."

I fight back tears, unwilling to let the three strangers—especially the arrogant young man—see me cry.

"All right," I reply with a nod.

"By the way, my name is Piper. These two are Peric and Cyntra."

"Nice…to meet you." Weary, I gather my few things from the ground and begin to walk with my three captors. "My name is Ashen. How far is it to the…Bastille?"

Whatever the hell that is.

"A few miles," Piper tells me. "Shouldn't take us long to get there."

We begin the hike in silence, my mind spinning with horrible images of death and destruction, imagined scenarios of what could have happened to the Consortium.

I had such high hopes that my father's old alliance would not only be my salvation, but that of so many inside the Arc.

But if the organization is gone—truly gone—there's no hope for me, for Kel, for my friend Kyra, or for the other Dregs who have suffered for months on the inside.

With a heavy heart and slumped shoulders, I trudge along with the others, wondering if I'll ever see Finn or feel joy again.

3

THE BASTILLE

We hike along a series of barely visible paths that weave their way through the woods like twisting veins. My captors seem intent on cutting through the densest part of the forest, presumably to conceal themselves from the Directorate's ubiquitous eyes.

I can't exactly say I blame them.

But I'm still confused. Where are we headed? Do they have some underground dwelling, hidden from sight? Do they live in the location my father pointed to on his note?

Piper said they're what's left of the Consortium. I wonder how many of them there are. If they'll welcome me with open arms or burn me at the stake.

There's only one way to find out.

From the sun's position in the sky, I can tell we're still moving west, which is a relief. If the trio had turned and marched me back toward the Arc, I'd currently find myself embroiled in a fight to the death, and as impressive as Finn's suit is, I'm not entirely sure I'd come out of the brawl in one piece. The uniform doesn't compensate for hunger, and I haven't eaten a proper meal in over twenty-four hours.

My three escorts don't say much as we make our way through the woods. I notice Peric, who's in the lead, turning to check up on me now and then, his expression sullen. Piper is just behind me, with Cyntra following her.

After a time, Cyntra edges up to walk ahead of Piper. I can hear her breathing, and once or twice I'm convinced she's on the verge of saying something, but she stops herself before she starts. Finally, she whispers something to Piper, who says, "Fine. Go ahead."

Cyntra lets out a little squeal before poking my shoulder and asking me, "What was it like?" as we squeeze through the underbrush, snapping brittle branches as we go.

"What was *what* like?"

"The Arc! I mean, what was it like living inside it? I want to hear everything." Her giddiness tells me she knows nothing about the horrors beyond the Arc's walls—or worse, if she does know, she doesn't care.

Didn't she hear me telling Piper they kill Dregs?

"I've only ever seen video," she adds when I don't reply. "It looks so...*perfect*."

Turning my head, I try to offer her a smile, but it comes out as more of a wince. I understand her curiosity—I felt hopeful, too, a few months back when Kel and I used to watch the Directorate's propaganda videos. I'll never forget the look of excitement on his young face as he tugged at my sleeve and pointed to the seemingly euphoric Arc residents. Though I never said it out loud, it was my dream, as well as his, to one day glow with that same perfect bliss.

Of course, back then I had no idea it was all a façade, an

illusion, just like the Arc's multitude of phony windows and concealed doors.

As I ponder my reply to Cyntra, I'm not convinced I should go into graphic detail about what I lived through while I was in that hideous place, so I choose my words carefully.

"It was…very clean," I tell her, reaching for my earliest memories of stepping off the train on my first day in the Arc. "Immaculate. And huge. Every level felt like a new world."

"And the residences? What are they like?"

"I really only saw one. But I know the Wealthies who live on the upper levels own immense amounts of property. It's like they own entire palaces, all inside one giant building. The residence where I stayed—the Duke's place—"

"You lived with a *Duke*?" Cyntra chirps, her voice rising several pitches. I can tell it all sounds like a fairy tale to her.

I was once naive too, I think. *I hope for your sake that you never see the truth for yourself.*

"He wasn't a real Duke," I assure her. "The Aristocracy—that's what the richest of them call themselves—is completely bogus. It's a bunch of obscenely wealthy people trying to seem more important than they are by giving themselves titles."

"But they *are* important, aren't they? I've heard they built the Arc. They run it. They saved so many people by bringing them into that place."

Irritated, I glare at her. She sounds like a victim of the same propaganda the Directorate used to hurl at us. *The great and benevolent Arc. Paradise on earth. The perfect home for perfect people.*

"They didn't save anyone!" I snap before I have a chance to tell myself not to. "They convinced rich people to pour all their money into the Arc, then herded them in there like prisoners."

"But they're *not* prisoners, are they?" Cyntra says meekly. "The Directorate is only keeping them in the Arc to protect them."

"The Directorate wants to protect only itself. They're not the generous overlords you seem to think they are. They're terrified of anyone learning the truth about them. Besides, weren't you three just talking about the Directorate drones coming to kill us all?"

"Yes, because they don't like us being out in the woods. But they take people into the Arc all the time—they literally saved all those people from the Blight!" Cyntra protests, and with a shock, it hits me that she doesn't know the truth about the Blight or the Directorate's role in killing so many of the Mire's adults.

No. Of course she doesn't.

Very few people are privy to that toxic information.

I want to ask how Piper survived the Blight—how their home, wherever it is, is exempt from the slaughter of anyone over eighteen. But something tells me to wait.

I see Peric turn his head as if he's listening to the conversation, and I clench my jaw, resolving to keep the ugly details to myself. I have no idea how much these people know about my father's destructive biological invention, about how the Directorate used it so effectively against our own.

If they learned the truth, they might kill me on the spot.

"What do they look like?" Cyntra asks, thankfully changing the subject slightly. "The Directorate, I mean."

I take a deep breath, trying to calm myself down. "I haven't seen most of them. They wear masks when they're out at social gatherings, and at trials and...other things. They don't want people knowing who they really are, because it could come back to haunt them. There are a lot of people in the Arc who would be disgusted if they found out what the Directorate does to people like me."

"I've heard they punish Dregs who deserve it," Cyntra replies with a shrug. "Is that so wrong?"

"*Deserve*," I tell her, "is a relative term. It seems the Directorate has a different definition than I do."

I want to ask her if she thinks the death penalty is appropriate for someone who's spoken ill of the Directorate, but conjuring grisly memories doesn't seem like the most prudent idea at the moment.

With another shrug, she asks, "What about socializing? What did you do for fun?"

I turn to stare at her, puzzled by her numbness to the topic of the Directorate's cruelty. All I can guess is that she hasn't seen a lot of death in her young life—that she hasn't had to make difficult choices or sacrifice anything of herself. I almost envy her innocence. It's like someone has shielded her from the reality of the enemy that roams these very woods, and given her a pair of rose-colored glasses.

Even now, as she hikes along with a blade at her waist, she seems carefree, oblivious to threats.

"Sometimes I left the residence," I tell her. This time, my smile is genuine as memories of the hours spent with Finn float through my mind. "There was a secret place I went with the...friend...I mentioned earlier. We could swim and be alone there. Honestly, I sometimes forgot where we were. I felt...I don't know, free, I guess. It was pretty amazing."

"Oh my God," she sputters. "You had an actual *boyfriend*?"

Peric's head briefly turns to the side once again, though I can tell he doesn't want me to know he's listening.

"He was a *good* friend," I retort, feeling suddenly protective of Finn. I don't want to say anything that could give away his identity, his betrayal of his parents, of the Directorate. But I do wish I could say more about his kindness toward me, his...*everything*. I've never had the luxury of telling anyone how I feel about him. How much he's come to mean to me, how deep my affection truly runs.

But until I know exactly who my captors are, something tells me I'd do well to keep it to myself.

"What else did you see in there?" Cyntra asks.

"There was an amazing marketplace. And beautiful Royal Gardens. And apparently, huge shopping malls and football stadiums, but I never saw those. I mostly just stayed at the Duke's residence. It was tiring, being a Candidate. I never had much energy for anything else." I'm about to tell her about the Training Sessions, but I stop myself.

As we continue to walk in silence, more memories surge through my mind. Of Finn, of Kyra and Marsh, of our horrid instructor, Piotr.

But someone else infiltrates my thoughts. Another face, another voice, one that used to mean so much to me.

My former best friend.

Rys.

The living, breathing reason I've lost my ability to trust anyone.

Not only did he betray me, but he betrayed my mother, my brother. All because of some lies the Directorate threw his way to convince him my father was a murderous monster.

As I push the thought of him from my mind, I vow to be wary of everyone, to have faith in no one. The only people in the world I trust right now are Finn and Kel.

That is, if my little brother is even still alive.

He has to be.

With a shudder, I tell myself the Directorate will keep Kel

from harm. They have to. He's leverage, a bargaining chip in their war against the Consortium. A means to get me back into their clutches.

Until I'm dead, they'll keep him alive.

After a time, Piper says, "About twenty minutes until we reach our destination."

Peric, up ahead, seems to have stopped checking on me, and instead has tensed like a prey animal wary of his surroundings. He keeps shooting glances toward the sky like he's waiting for something to come flying down at us.

"What's wrong?" I ask. I'm grasping the edges of my cloak, feeling my way to the pressure points that will put me into stealth mode should the need arise.

"Drones," he whispers. "Approaching from the east. They don't usually come out this far. They must be looking for *you*."

Even through his whisper, I can hear the sharp jab of disdain in his voice. I'm nothing more than a liability, a thorn in his side. If it were up to him, he'd tie me to a tree and leave me for the Directorate to find.

And I can't say I blame him.

We stop walking, and I hear what he's talking about—the low, crescendoing buzz of one or more drones heading our way. I don't know if they're weaponized or simple surveillance models, but it doesn't matter. Both are equally dangerous—it's just that one will kill us on the spot and the other will summon armed humans to take our lives.

"Quick!" Piper hisses.

Without another word, she and Peric throw themselves to the ground, pushing their way under brambles, damp foliage, and anything else they can find. I'm about to activate my cloak when I think better of it and follow Cyntra under a half rotten, hollowed-out tree trunk that's lying on its side. Its edges crumble to chalky dust under my touch, so I stay as still as I can while the buzz overhead grows louder then gradually fades into the distance.

"Guess they didn't get close enough to read our heat signature," Cyntra whispers.

I'm tempted to reply *So much for the benevolent Directorate, huh?* but I manage to control myself.

"Good thing for us they haven't figured out how to make silent drones yet," Piper says when we finally dare to venture out of our hiding spots.

"Maybe they have," Peric replies. "Maybe they're just lulling us into a false sense of security." With that, he shoots me another accusing look. "Maybe *she's* the silent drone, coming with us so she can spy on us and report back."

I glare at Peric. If only he knew how much I loathe the Directorate, what I would give to see every last one of them hanging by their necks from the trees in these woods.

I'm the farthest thing from a Directorate spy. But I'm not exactly convinced you're one of the good guys.

"The Arc has eyes everywhere," Piper says mysteriously. "There's no need to send spies into the Bastille. Peric, you know perfectly well the Directorate is aware of our affairs."

I want to know what she means—how the enemy keeps such close tabs on them yet still allows them to exist. But I keep my mouth shut until we finally reach the outer edge of the woods. In front of us is a broad road. Its rough surface is pitted, cracked, and overgrown with tall weeds like so many of the streets in the Mire. It's clear that no vehicle has driven on it in some time, which, I suppose, is a good sign.

Still, I'm confused when our feet hit the uneven asphalt and we begin to walk. It feels suddenly like we're both heading in the wrong direction and making ourselves far too visible, too vulnerable to attack.

But once again, I resist the urge to ask questions. All I want is to get to our destination as quickly as possible. At least then I'll know my fate.

After a few minutes, I spot a weathered sign by the side of the road that's slipped off its supports and is hanging at a forty-five degree angle, its letters faded, its surface half-coated in winding vines.

Welcome to Breckenridge

"Wait," I say. "*This* is the place you were talking about?"

There's a bend up ahead blocking my view of the town itself, but I remember coming to Breckenridge with my parents when I was younger and Kel was just a baby. It was a charming little tourist town in the mountains, its Main Street lined with lavish shops and happy people sipping hot chocolate as they strolled along in expensive ski gear.

The coordinates my father left me pointed to a location not far from Breckenridge. But the town, exposed as it is, can't possibly be the Consortium's secret hiding place. There is nothing secure or hidden about Breckenridge, nothing covert. If this is where my father's former allies are concealing themselves, it's no wonder they're nervous about bringing me here.

We're sitting ducks.

"This is it, yes," Piper says. "But trust me—Breckenridge, or what we call the Bastille—is safe."

"How can it possibly be? The drones that flew over us a few minutes ago must patrol over it all the time."

"Actually, they don't, genius," Peric snaps.

"Why not? Are you telling me they just stay away out of the goodness of their hearts? Because I've got news for you—the Directorate doesn't know a whole lot about goodness."

"It may not be goodness that keeps them away," Piper says cryptically, "but they do leave us alone when we're inside the town. That's all you need to know, Ashen."

The look she throws me then prompts me to seal my lips. I glance over at Cyntra, who simply offers up one of her signature shrugs and raises her eyebrows as if to say, "Sorry, I don't know what to tell you."

When we finally come around the bend in the road, I begin to understand Piper's confidence.

What used to be the welcoming town I knew as a young child is now surrounded by concrete walls that must be fifty feet high or more. They remind me of the walls that surround the Mire, except for their grim lack of color. The desolate gray surface screams *prison,* and we're about to walk right in.

I stop in my tracks, my breath catching in my chest. The last time I willingly walked into a structure so forbidding, I nearly lost my life.

I'm not sure I want to make the same mistake again.

4

LEADER

WHERE THE RUINED road meets the wall, an enormous set of steel double doors swings open as we approach. I look up to spot a series of armed sentinels standing along the top edge of the wall, weapons in hand.

Snipers.

The Consortium—or *whatever* this is—is better equipped than I expected. Still, a few men with guns aren't enough to keep the Directorate away. I know how eager they are to take down every adult living outside the Arc.

None of it adds up, and I have little choice but to keep my mouth shut and trust that the answers I seek will come to me soon enough.

The steel doors slam shut behind us, and two uniformed guards stand at attention, their eyes on Piper.

"Where's Veer?" she asks.

"In the Bunker with some of the others," one of them says. "At least, she was a few minutes ago."

"Thanks." Piper turns my way. "Come on, then. It's time to meet the boss."

As we walk along what used to be the town's main strip, we pass old worn-down sporting goods stores, coffee shops, restaurants. My heart aches for the lives once lived in this place, for the joy the town long ago brought tourists seeking a simple weekend escape. Windows are shattered now. The insides of the shops are filled with wreckage and debris of various shapes and sizes, as if throngs of people long since rifled through the businesses to seek out anything of value before abandoning them to the elements.

The buildings' derelict façades remind me of movie sets for old western films. The street feels like part of a ghost town, and I find myself half-expecting to see a tumbleweed or two roll in front of us in warning.

"Who did this?" I ask. "Who attacked this place?"

"That's a huge question, with more than one answer," Piper says. "First, it was the Directorate. They dismantled every town in the area looking for supplies and electronics—anything they could use to contribute to the Arc's construction. They built the walls—they were contemplating using this location as an outpost. But they left after most of the Arc was completed, which meant the town was empty. There were...more conflicts after that."

Piper seems reluctant to divulge more, but I'm painfully curious. Are the guards positioned around the wall to defend against the Directorate or against something else entirely? Are they the only thing that keeps the drones from attacking?

No, I think. *Those guards wouldn't stand a chance against the micro-drones who killed so many of the Mire's residents years ago.*

If the Directorate wanted these people dead...they'd be dead.

The question of what happened here—how those who remain managed to survive—is almost enough to convince me to demand an explanation.

But once again, I tell myself to be patient. Clarity will come...but first I need to earn these people's trust.

On the way to the Bunker, something at once surprising and wonderful inspires a dash of quiet hope inside me:

Small children.

Toddlers waddling down the street, holding the hands of what look like parents or grandparents. The occasional woman carrying a tiny baby, even. I can't remember the last time I saw an infant, or the last time I was around anyone who announced joyfully that they were going to expand their family.

Come to think of it, the youngest children I've seen in recent years were Kel's and Merit's age, ten or so.

There's something so joyous about the sight, and it's more reassuring than words could ever be.

We walk until we reach the first intersection. To our right is an L-shaped yellow brick building that stretches around the corner, its windows boarded up. A sign that reads "Breckenridge Tourist Information" hangs precariously from two rusty screws above its door.

Piper presses a code into a keypad next to the door, and it swings open to reveal a surprisingly long hallway that leads not toward the back of the building, but slanting downward, as though we're about to descend into an underground crypt.

I follow her with Cyntra at my side and Peric behind me until we reach the bottom. Piper keys in a second code and we head through yet another door and down a dark hallway until we reach a large, open space lit from above with a series of bright Edison bulbs that dangle cheerfully from the ceiling.

A crowd of women is gathered in a circle inside the room, seemingly for a meeting of some sort. They're wearing dull-colored dresses with full skirts, long sleeves, and high collars.

I'm not accustomed to seeing women in dresses, other than the Arc's Aristocrats when they attend a fancy-dress ball.

But there's nothing fancy or flattering about the garments these women are wearing. They're wholly utilitarian, like dowdy uniforms.

Before us, the group of silent figures parts, and a tall woman with short-cropped silver hair comes forward. She's striking, with an angular jaw and high cheekbones. Her eyes are large and dark, her eyebrows arched and black. I can tell without asking that she's in charge around here. Unlike the other women, she's dressed like the three people who found me in the woods, in khaki pants and an olive green top. The outfit is accented by leather riding boots up to her knees and an olive-green suit jacket.

She raises an eyebrow to Piper, and I can feel Peric shifting uneasily to my left as though he's mildly annoyed not to be considered the most important member of our party.

"I'm going to assume you have good reason for bringing an outsider into the Bastille," the woman says. Her voice is measured and even, though I can feel a tension in its tone as if pushing her an inch too far might be enough to make her snap.

"We do have good reason." Piper looks around at the group of curious faces before us. "But I'd rather discuss it in private, if you don't mind."

"Fine. Come on, then."

We follow the woman through to the other end of the large chamber and down yet another narrow passageway. This one is lined with rough stone walls, and feels more cavernous than what we first came through when we entered the building.

The tall woman's gait is that of someone supremely confident. She has a presence, a sort of daunting air about her that reminds me some people are born to lead while others seem destined to follow. The Duchess—Finn's mother—has a similarly self-assured manner about her, an intangible quality that both intimidates people and draws them in.

But this woman feels more human than the Duchess. I know perfectly well that she could command the others to strike me down here and now, but I feel deep in my soul that she won't, regardless of what they say to her. She's too interested in me to want to hurt me. Too curious.

I wonder as I watch her if she knew my father, and if so, what he thought of her.

We finally come to a small room at the end of the hallway—an office with a thick steel door that only opens when the woman presses her hand to a dark pad on its right. The room we walk into is surprisingly bright, a strange circular skylight pouring sunlight into the space. "A solar tube," the tall woman says when she sees me eyeing it. "It's lined with silver metal that leads all the way up to the building's roof. This office is the only room in the Bunker with such a luxurious feature."

"The Bunker," I reply. "That's what you call this underground area?"

"Yes," she says.

"Is it fortified?"

"It's fairly secure—but not large enough for much of our population, which is why we have snipers at the ready up above. I'm sure you spotted them when you came into town."

I nod. *They're hard to miss.* "How do you keep the Directorate from attacking you?"

A direct question, but I'm here for answers.

The silver-haired woman lets out a snicker. "Right to the point, huh?" she laughs. "Let's just say we have our methods.

The snipers are well-trained and the Directorate knows it. But more importantly, the space above the Bastille is a no-fly zone for their drones. The woods are a different story entirely, but please know that as long as you remain within our walls—as long as we choose to keep you here—you're safe with us. If you decide to venture outside the Bastille, though, just know the drones will show no mercy."

The woman sits down in a wooden chair behind a beaten-up desk. Behind her on the wall is a series of maps, some hand-drawn, others the old folding type that my parents used to keep in the car despite the fact that they had full access to GPS when I was little. I can't help but smile when I see them. They feel like comfort, like home.

"So?" the woman says as she studies me from her spot behind the desk, pulling her eyes to Piper. "Is someone going to tell me what makes this young lady so special that you brought her here against strict regulations?"

"She's a Candidate," Piper says, pulling my robe away to reveal my uniform. "She's spent time inside the Arc. She knows how that place works."

"I deduced as much by simply looking at her. Tell me something more."

"She's Oliver Spencer's daughter."

At that, the woman's eyes go wide and her entire demeanor shifts as she fixes her gaze on me. "Oliver Spencer. Now there's a name I haven't heard in years."

5

VEER

"I SHOULD HAVE GUESSED who you were," the woman says with an approving grin. "Only Oliver's daughter would be resourceful enough to have found her way out of the Arc when no one else has managed it."

She rises to her feet and steps around the desk to lean back against it, arms crossing over her chest. "My name is Veronica Rolston. Around here, they call me Veer."

"Nice to meet you," I tell her, and I mean it. "Are you in charge here?"

She lets out a little chuckle, and I kick myself internally for asking the question. She probably thinks I'm being impertinent.

"I'm the Director of the Bastille, yes. As for whether I'm in charge, you'll have to ask someone else. One can only lead, after all, if one has the respect of those who follow."

She shoots a look at Peric, whose eyes instantly move to the floor. Meanwhile, Cyntra has a look of adoration on her face—one I've only ever seen in the eyes of small children worshiping heroic parental figures.

It's a look I used to see often on young faces in the Mire. Of course, that was before everything changed, and before those children's parents were murdered in cold blood.

"Veer is very much in charge," Piper tells me. "She's the whole reason we managed to take this town years ago. She has led us, instructed us, and kept us safe every step of the way."

"Did you have to fight the Directorate when you took the town?" I ask.

Veer's expression shifts into something vaguely cryptic before she smiles once again—a smile that doesn't quite reach her unreadable eyes. "That's a story for another day," she tells me. "Let's just say for a time, there was a certain amount of competition for this particular piece of real estate. So, there was a certain amount of...effort...involved in making it into a comfortable and secure home, and finding a way to keep unwanted parties out. We're quite pleased with our current situation. The Bastille is a safe haven—a quiet, peaceful place, as you'll learn."

"I see," I reply. But the truth is, I don't understand how there can be such a thing as a safe haven so close to the Arc. How there are adults living here, wandering the streets without a care in the world, when all the ones in the Mire were killed.

I want to ask a thousand more questions, but tell myself to pick my battles.

Veer looks at the other three and wordlessly nods toward the door. "I would like to speak to our guest alone," she tells them.

"But she..." Peric begins. He hangs his head when Veer gives him a stern look in response and heads for the door.

Piper pulls my dagger from her belt and hands it to Veer,

nodding my way. "This is hers," she says before accompanying Cyntra and Peric out to the hallway.

Veer hands me the weapon and strides around the desk to sit down, but not before gesturing to a small wooden stool sitting against the far wall. After I've sheathed my blade I step over and pick it up, carrying it back to where I was standing.

"Please, sit," she says with a smile. "*Ashen.*"

I return the smile, relieved to hear my name on her lips. If nothing else, it's confirmation that she knew my father, that she was indeed a member of the Consortium alongside him.

"Tell me something—why are you here?" Veer asks me. "Why did you choose to leave the Arc? From what I understand, it can be quite a tolerable place, if you find a way to fit in."

"Fit in? You think that's all it takes? The Directorate..." I stop, telling myself not to lash out at the one person in charge of granting me safety. "Let's just say it wasn't pleasant."

"I see."

I study her for a few seconds, still trying to figure her out. She has a strangely alluring quality—warm and inviting on the one hand, much like Breckenridge used to be. But there's something about her that feels broken, as if every hint of warmth exists solely on her surface while underneath, simmering quietly, is a barely concealed emotional stagnation. It's like she's a shadow of someone who was once both vivacious and ambitious—someone who's now trying simply to survive from day to day.

I feel for her. I saw the same look in my mother in the days after my father was killed. A sort of emotional emptying, a slow leak, draining her of everything that ever brought her joy.

But Veer has an energy that my mother lacked. She has

drive. She has a reason for being—an obvious desire to keep this place running.

"Do you have any family left?" she asks. "Anyone living in the Mire?"

I shake my head, a knot forming in my stomach. "They murdered my mother a few days ago, and took my younger brother. I…don't know where he is—only that he's most likely in the Arc."

I manage to say the words matter-of-factly, but as they ring through the air, my throat tightens. I haven't allowed myself the time to mourn my mother yet, to rage against Kel's kidnapping. The only emotion I've permitted myself over the last few days is a sort of numbness, as if my mind and body have shoved my pain aside so I could survive long enough to make it to this place.

"Your mother managed to stay alive until a few days ago?" Veer asks. "As sorry as I am to hear the news of her passing, that is impressive."

"She lived for years in our house, even after many of the other adults were dead. She lived quietly, peacefully."

"And you? Tell me, what happened to set you on a path in our direction?"

"The Directorate tried to have me killed, too, but they failed. I couldn't stay in the Arc, so I headed for the one place where I thought I might find allies. Only…" I'm about to tell her about my father's coordinates when a voice in my mind tells me to stop. As kind as Veer seems, I'm not yet sure I should divulge his secret to anyone. "Only, Piper and the others found me before I could make my way here."

"Clever girl," Veer says approvingly. "And truly, I'm sorry about your mother. Tessa was a kind woman. She didn't deserve any of this."

"None of us did," I say, thinking of all the other mothers who have died in the Mire over the last several years. Of all the children orphaned by the Directorate.

"That's very true." Veer sighs before adding, "That said, your father would be proud of you, you know. It's no small feat, escaping that place. I know how powerful they are. How daunting."

"I did have help," I say sheepishly.

Sensing my trepidation, Veer leans forward, her hands clasped on the desktop. "You can trust me. If you want to tell me anything, feel free. But I won't blame you if you don't after what you've been through."

I inhale deeply, look her in the eye, and decide to take a chance. "I lived with the Davenports. Do you know them?"

Veer nods, her lips downturned. "I know the Duke—or at least I knew him before he was *known* as the Duke. I know about his work as a biochemist."

I find myself wondering how much more she knows—if she's aware of the Blight's origins, of my father's involvement.

She partially answers my question when she adds, "I also know he and your father were somewhat at odds long ago. I assume it was no accident that you ended up in their residence."

I shake my head. "They thought I knew more than I did. The Duchess thought I could be useful to her, I guess. In the end, though, she was only too happy to see me die. But I didn't give her the satisfaction." I look around, my eyes locking for a moment on the solar tube. "I'm still confused—how do you feel so secure here, knowing what they're capable of?"

Veer ponders the question for a moment before replying, "Let's just say we have a sort of tenuous peace agreement with them. We stay out of their way, they stay out of ours, and no one gets hurt."

"So, the Directorate really does know you're here." It's a stupid thing to say; of course they do. Their drones could see this place from a mile away. "They know the Consortium is in what used to be Breckenridge?"

Veer's eyes go wide for the briefest moment, like I've either surprised or mildly amused her.

"Consortium," she says softly. "That's a word I haven't used in some time. A long-dead organization."

A wince of pain crosses my features. *Long dead?* Are they all gone? Is this small town all that's left of them?

"Yes," she says. "They know we're here. We've lived without conflict with the Directorate for years, though I suppose it's possible, now that you've come, they'll use it as a justification to attack. We need to brace ourselves for a potential conflict if you're to stay here."

"They don't know I'm here," I say. "I stayed out of sight when the Directorate Guard was looking for me outside of town. And the drones didn't see the four of us when we were hiking here."

Veer's expression shifts for the first time from docile to mildly irritated. "With all due respect, Ashen, you have no way of knowing if they saw you. They have eyes everywhere, and coming through the woods in a purple cloak isn't exactly making yourself inconspicuous. Chances are they watched you the entire time you were hiking." She stops there, seals her lips tight, and says, "Point is, you've put a target on all our backs. I'll likely be forced to do some damage control in the days to come, in order to keep the peace."

"I promise you they didn't see me," I insist, wondering

what she could possibly mean by damage control. Since when does the Directorate negotiate?

I can see by the lines on her forehead that Veer is worried, but she sucks in a breath and through pursed lips says, "Please explain."

I tense my jaw for a second, then reach for the cloak's hem, feeling my way toward the pressure point that will alter its appearance. When I've pressed it, Veer raises her eyebrows, impressed.

I know from experience that all she can see of me now are exposed bits of skin—my face, my hands. The rest of me is camouflaged like a chameleon, perfectly blended into my surroundings through a series of micro-mirrors that absorb and reflect everything in my vicinity. As I move, the illusion the cloak provides shifts and moves along with me.

"It also conceals my heat signature," I tell Veer.

"You *did* have help on the inside," she laughs. "That's some impressive tech. Far more advanced than anything we have around here."

I don't tell her about the custom-designed Candidate's uniform I'm wearing, about the modifications Finn wove into its fabric, or how strong it renders me. I want to keep a few cards, at least, close to my chest.

"A friend in the Arc gave me the cloak," I tell her. "He's been developing materials and uniforms that can help in the fight against the Directorate—if ever it comes to that, I mean."

"This friend must have serious money."

"Everyone in the Arc has money."

"True. But not everyone has access to the research facilities it would take to design and construct that cloak. And most would be killed for less. So, I can safely assume your friend kept his design a secret."

I don't answer. I like her, but she knows too much, somehow. Too much about the inner workings of the Arc, about the Directorate.

"Well," she finally says, "I'm impressed you've accomplished all that you have, given how many allies the Directorate has. You've proven yourself incredibly competent. I have a lot of questions for you, Ashen, and I do hope we get many chances to chat. But for now, I think you should get something to eat and some rest—not necessarily in that order. You are most welcome here in the Bastille. I'm glad you've come to join our little community…and our fight."

"Fight," I repeat, my voice filled with hope. "You're saying you do plan to take on the Directorate eventually?"

"Perhaps." Veer levels me with a curious look, her chin raised. "Tell me—how would you take on the Directorate if you were me?"

"I wouldn't. At least, not yet. The Arc isn't exactly a place you can just wander into. And a couple of hundred rebels aren't going to do much against the tens of thousands they have at their disposal. The only way to take them down is from the inside—unless we can find a lot more allies out here. No offense, but a few well-trained snipers won't cut it. You need a plan—and an army."

"Well, you probably won't be surprised to hear that I have no intention of waltzing into the Arc. Our goal out here is simple: we want long-term survival for our community. We have plans already in motion, and nothing will alter their course. But I'm hoping your knowledge will help us on the path to victory against any enemies who wish to take us on. You are of great value to us. I'm so glad Piper's small group stumbled upon you in the woods."

"Peric doesn't think I'm very valuable," I snicker. "I don't think he likes me much."

"Peric is a suspicious boy," Veer replies. "But he's smart, loyal, and a hard worker. He's also my son."

I nearly choke as she says those words, searching my memory for anything awful I might have said about him. "Oh...I'm...I didn't know."

Veer laughs. "Well, he's not my biological son. I took him in some years ago when we secured the Bastille—after his family was killed. He hasn't trusted anyone since then, and it's hard to blame him. He's a cold fish at the best of times, I know. My adopted son is, perhaps, overly prudent. Trust is not his strong suit, but he'll get there one day. You'll find there are others here who will be wary of you, too. People who didn't know your father as I did. Try to be patient with them. They've seen their family members die at the hands of our enemies, and it will be difficult to welcome a stranger into the fold without a little suspicion. It's been some years since we fought our way into this place, and the last thing my people want is renewed conflict—though something tells me it's coming sooner, rather than later."

"I came looking for answers," I tell her. "I was hoping to find a place where I could bring my little brother someday—if I ever find a way to get him out of the Arc. Your people don't have to worry—I'm not here looking for a conflict."

No, not a conflict.

The truth is, I want a war.

I want what remains of the Consortium, however small their numbers, to band together and help me defeat the Directorate...once I've figured out how the hell to do that.

But if all that's left of the organization my father was once part of are the people in this town—the women in their strange, plain dresses, the few snipers patrolling the wall, and the children I've seen wandering around—there's little hope for any sort of victory. A battle with the Directorate would amount to nothing more than an outright slaughter of these innocent people.

It's no wonder Veer seems so empty inside.

"I will do what I can to make you feel at home," she tells me. "On weekdays, you can attend classes with the other girls, if you'd like."

"Classes?"

The idea instantly horrifies me, and apparently Veer can read the fear on my face, because she laughs.

"Oh, they're quite harmless. Elocution, styling, behavior, that sort of thing. We like to give the girls something to look forward to, so we're teaching them to be proper ladies."

"Proper ladies? Shouldn't you be teaching them to defend themselves against attack? To shoot down drones?"

Veer issues a strange, mischievous smile when she says, "If they do well in their lessons, Ashen, they'll never need to defend against anything or anyone for the rest of their lives." She claps her hands together and adds, "With that said, let's get you settled in, shall we?"

She reaches under her desk and presses something, and a few seconds later, the office's armored door opens. Peric stands framed in the doorway, arms crossed, his eyes laser-focused on me.

"Please take Ashen to the empty apartment over the ski shop," Veer says. "It's as secure as any room in the Bastille. She'll sleep there tonight and every night, until fate chooses a new path for her."

Peric nods, and without a word, I follow him into the hallway.

As we begin to walk, I mouth the word "Fate," and wonder with a shudder what path it could possibly choose next.

6

CYNTRA

As we make our way toward my new home, I glance over at Peric. It turns out my very first impression of him was correct.

He's handsome, with the sort of sculpted jaw and angular features that used to irritate me in young men—a sort of antagonistic perfection.

Maybe it's part of why he's so arrogant, so aloof.

You're too good-looking for your own good, and you're convinced the world owes you for it.

With resentment oozing from his pores, Peric says nothing as he leads me back out to the street and down a series of short blocks until we reach a ski shop that seems less ruined than many of the Bastille's other buildings. Its façade is a combination of brick and reinforced steel, its door and windows protected by a grid of iron bars.

"It looks like a prison within a prison," I say with a nervous laugh.

"It'll protect you. That's all you should care about and more than you deserve."

Peric keys in a code before muttering, "Three-six-six-two. Remember it." The door clicks open and we enter the building to climb a set of steep stairs. He leads me down a narrow hallway until we reach a room with the number two on the door.

He pushes it open before speaking again.

"You'll find everything you need in here." His tone is curt, jagged, like it pains him to be civil to me.

"Thank you." I turn his way in the hopes of asking a question or two, only to see that he's looking at me now with a mixture of curiosity and irritation. At least he hasn't turned and left yet.

I tilt my head innocently to the side, making an attempt at charming naiveté. "Have I offended you in some way?"

A few months ago, I would have been afraid to ask such a question of anyone, let alone a guy with his particular brand of cockiness. But now, I find myself devoid of self-consciousness. My life has been threatened too many times for me to concern myself with anyone's good opinion of me.

"Why would you think that?"

"You've been hostile to me since the second we met."

"Did it ever occur to you that maybe you're just not all that likable?"

"I suppose that's possible," I tell him. "Not that you even bothered to get to know me before deciding I'm the devil."

This makes him pause, flummoxed, for a few seconds. But instead of answering, he asks a question. "Do you know why we call this place the Bastille?"

"The walls, I assume. The Bastille was a prison in Paris." I remember hearing about the Parisian fortress that was stormed in 1789 during the French Revolution, though I can't say I recall any details except something about eating cake and beheadings.

"Partly," he tells me. "But there's more to this place than just walls. We don't lock people in—we lock them *out*. There are rules here that don't apply outside the town's perimeter. We have a set of ethics and morals that may surprise you. Outsiders aren't welcome here, because outsiders don't understand what we need to do to survive. So, until you get it into your head that I am under no obligation to like you, I'd suggest you keep your mouth shut and your head down. You don't belong here, and you never will. So don't make yourself at home."

With that, he smirks, turns, and walks away without another word.

When he's gone, I let out a sigh of surrender and spin around to inspect the bedroom, which is sparsely decorated. A narrow bed is pressed against the far wall next to a nightstand with a small lamp and a solitary drawer. A dingy off-white dresser sits against another wall, and when I open the drawers I find them empty, except for a small photo of a boy who looks like he may be twelve or thirteen.

One window looks out over the town's rooftops toward the mountains, and I'm grateful for the view. In the distance I see snow-capped peaks, unfazed by the mayhem that's erupted down here in recent years.

A quick fantasy flits through my mind of building a cabin in those mountains and escaping with Finn to live undisturbed, away from everything and everyone.

This room is a far cry from my luxurious white bedroom in the Arc, with its soft bedding, plentiful wardrobe and room service.

But at least here, I won't be stalked by mechanical spy-insects hanging on my every word, or shadowed by a woman who's constantly thinking of new ways to kill me.

At least, I hope not.

I'm hungry, and my eyes are drawn to a couple of wrapped granola bars sitting on the dresser. But my exhaustion compels me to throw myself onto the bed, pull my arm over my face, and close my eyes tight.

Just for a few minutes. I just need a little rest.

I drift off, my mind reeling with fleeting thoughts of Finn, of Kel, of my mother. I hear their voices as I fall asleep, a mixture of cries for help and soothing reassurances, sending my consciousness spiraling into a vortex of fraught dreams.

I'm not sure what time I jolt awake to the sound of a fist rapping on the door. I look over to see Cyntra's face peering at me, her body tucked behind the open door, an apologetic smile on her lips.

"You awake?" she asks, though I'm quite sure she knows the answer is *Hell no.*

"Sort of," I tell her, wiping the sleep from my eyes. "What time is it?"

"Eight p.m. You've slept a long time. I didn't have the heart to wake you for dinner, but I thought maybe you were hungry, and the Mess closes at nine, so I figured I should come get you."

"I *am* hungry," I tell her gratefully. "Thanks."

"I'll take you to down and show you where the Mess is," she says. But instead of waiting in the hallway for me to join her, she steps into the room, closing the door behind her.

Her khaki pants and white tank top are gone, and instead,

she's wearing a yellow dress with short, ruffled sleeves. It looks like it's made of expensive silk taffeta, its skirt ballooning away from her body as though lined with crinoline.

It's the sort of dress a young mother might put on her baby or toddler when tempted to dress them up like a little doll, but hardly the sort of thing I would expect to see on a resident of the Bastille.

I suppose she reads the surprise on my face, because she grabs the dress' hem, twirls around and asks, "Do you like it?"

I bite the inside of my cheek to force my face into a serious expression, and nod. "It's very…pretty. Are you going out or something?"

"No. I always dress like this. In the Bastille, anyhow. A lot of the girls do, at least until their Finishing."

"Their what?"

She reddens slightly. "I shouldn't have said that," she replies. "I'm not sure I'm supposed to tell you about it. It's… sort of private." She lowers her chin and looks up at me. "But I guess you're one of us now, right? Veer seems to like you. I suppose she wouldn't mind if I told you a little about it."

"Is the Finishing when girls start dressing…differently?"

"Oh, you mean like the Matrons?"

"Matrons?"

"The mothers, I mean. The older women."

"Yes, I guess that's what I mean. The way they dress—it seems sort of old-timey."

"It is. I totally hate it. I'll never dress like them," Cyntra insists, twirling around again. "Not in a million years. But then, I don't plan on growing old in the Bastille."

My brow furrows. "Where *do* you plan on growing old, then?"

Cyntra lets out a strange giggle that would better suit a young child than someone trusted to patrol the woods with a weapon at her waist. "That's for me to know and you to find out, Ashen!"

"Fair enough," I say, stretching my arms above my head and rising to my feet in hopes of finally going out in search of food.

But it seems Cyntra isn't as eager to leave. "Can I ask you something?"

"Of course."

"How did you *really* escape from the Arc?"

She leans in, her expression that of a co-conspirator. I almost expect her to arch her brows and rub her hands together as if we're hatching a clever scheme to break others out.

I'm still not convinced I should reveal any secrets, though I can't deny that I like her. Something about her naive innocence makes her seem more trustworthy than the others.

"I had help, like I told you in the woods. From someone amazing."

"The boy!" she replies, leaping over to perch at the foot of my small bed. "Tell me all about him."

Ah, so that's what you really want to hear about.

It's almost a relief to be invited to talk about my love life with someone close to my age. I may be a fugitive, an escapee from a powerful government entity...but I'm still a seventeen-year-old girl. Still young, still a little lost when it comes to my emotions. I've been to hell and back more than once, but I must admit I crave normal interactions. A carefree life. Socializing, parties, living an existence filled with blissful irresponsibility, like teenagers did in the times before the Blight.

But surrounding every craving for a normal life is a thick

layer of scar tissue. My potential joy is blocked on all sides by impediments; walls made up of deep wounds, some of which are beginning to heal, others that are still wide open.

I smile at Cyntra. There's a perpetual sweetness in her that assures me she's managed to avoid some of the pain so many of us have endured. I see hope in her eyes. Excitement for a future that lives inside her mind like a bright, shiny gem.

I only wish I could find a way to feed off her optimism.

"I need details," she insists.

"His name is Finn," I say. "He's the son of the people who took me in."

"The Duke, you mean?"

"The Duke, yes."

"Is he hot?"

"Finn?" A laugh escapes me at the bluntness of the question. "Yes, he is. Though that's not really what makes him so attractive. He's smart. He's kind. He's protective. And if it weren't for him, I would be dead right now."

"Why didn't he come with you? You could have run away together—it would have been so romantic..."

"It would have been a terrible idea. The Directorate can tolerate losing someone like me if they have to. But losing Finn would have the hounds biting at our heels. His parents are very high up in the food chain inside the Arc."

"That's too bad. I would have liked to meet him. There are no boys my age around here. There was one I liked a few years ago—his name was Raleigh." She blushes as she says the words.

"What happened to him?"

"He was a couple of years older than me. He went through training, like all the boys do in the Bastille, in case they want to become snipers. But he headed out on patrol one day with some of the others, and didn't come back."

"Oh my God. Do you think he was killed?"

"I don't know. Killed or taken, I suppose. The men who were with him said he went off to check out a sound he'd heard, and just...disappeared."

She says the words calmly, as if it's not a trauma to know a boy she liked might have been brutally murdered in the woods.

"Peric is gorgeous, of course," she adds. "But he's such a cold fish. And he doesn't even know I'm alive. I guess I'm too young for him or something."

"What's his deal?" I ask, glad I'm not the only one he treats with disdain. "Why's he such a...?"

"Self-righteous butt-face?" Cyntra says with a smirk, and I laugh at the oddly childish insult. "It's in his DNA. To be fair, most of his family was killed a few years back—his parents, his sister, and his younger brother. He *lives* for the day when he can get revenge. I honestly think it's the only thing on his mind. In the meantime, he doesn't trust anyone—not even Veer. I can't say I blame him. A lot of the people around here are on edge all the time. I wish they'd just lighten up. We're safe here. We've been safe for years."

"This place doesn't seem safe at all to me. It's so open, so vulnerable to attack. I mean, the Directorate knows you're here. They could show up at any moment and take out every single person in this town."

"The Directorate isn't a threat to the Bastille," Cyntra says defensively, twirling a lock of hair around her finger. "They've done a lot of good for this town, actually."

"Good?" I ask, and it's all I can do not to grab her by the shoulders and shake her. "How?"

"Oh, crap. I forgot." Cyntra looks down at the floor. "I... I'm not supposed to talk to you about them. I shouldn't have said anything."

That's probably good advice, I think. *Because I'm about to blow a freaking gasket.*

I suck in my cheeks for a moment before asking, "Do you go on hikes in the woods often?"

Cyntra hesitates before saying, "This morning was my first time. But Veer goes out almost every day to check the woods for threats. She's so brave. You couldn't pay me to risk my life over and over again like that. She takes her life into her own hands every time she leaves the Bastille."

"So, the rest of the Consortium stays here?" I ask. "I mean, when she leaves?"

My choice to use the C-word is deliberate, and I hold a breath in my lungs as I wait for her reply.

Cyntra bites her lip, hesitating. "I don't know how much I'm allowed to say..."

"I don't want to get you in trouble," I tell her, cocking my head to the side and smiling. "I'm just curious."

"No, it's fine. It's just...we don't use that word, not anymore. Something happened a long time ago, I guess. Veer said we're never to call ourselves the Consortium under any circumstances. Or else..."

"Or else what?"

She seals her lips tight and shakes her head. "Nothing. She'd just get a bit mad. She can be scary when she's angry."

"I'll bet." I grimace, frustrated that no one in this place is willing to give me a straight answer.

"Oh, doodles!" Cyntra blurts out. "I almost forgot—you're still starving! Come on, let's see if we can find you some leftovers."

At the mention of food, my frustration fades a little. Maybe I'm just cranky because of a combination of low blood sugar and exhaustion.

Cyntra has an energy that reminds me of Kel or Merit—quick, manic bursts of youthful exuberance, unencumbered by tragedy. I feel old in comparison to her, my own energy sapped by a chronic, prolonged pain. But as Cyntra reaches for my hand, the smallest spark of joy ignites inside me. A flash of bliss, a frisson of something I haven't felt since the hours I spent alone in the Arc's Grotto with Finn, swimming in the darkness without a care in the world.

I suppose that's all life is, in the end. Sustained periods of worry, interrupted here and there by snippets of beauty and light.

It's almost as if all the bad exists to make us appreciate the good.

As we make our way out to the street and Cyntra guides me toward the place known as the Mess, I wonder how much good I'll manage to find in this strange, ghostly town.

7

THE MESS

CYNTRA TELLS me as we head down the street that the Mess is an old restaurant on the main drag that was once called "Maurice's Chalet." It was designed to look like an old log cabin from the outside, and when we arrive, I see that inside, the decor is suitably dark and a little musty. Heavy wood beams support an A-frame ceiling, and a large stone fireplace sits at the center of one wall, its ancient contents soot-black and neglected.

Above the fireplace is a large mounted head—an elk, I think—and surrounding it are other trophies: a wolf, a couple of deer, a mountain lion. I've always found it odd that people mount animal heads like morbid works of art, but as I study the collection, it occurs to me how badly I'd like to see the Duchess' severed head on similar display.

The restaurant, ancient and abandoned though it is, is warm and welcoming, with a series of beaten-up old wooden tables and benches lining its walls. At full capacity, I'd guess it can hold up to two-hundred people, though I have no idea if there are that many here in town.

At the moment, though, I don't really care. I'm happy just to feel moderately safe for the first time in days.

Even as Cyntra heads toward the kitchen at the back of the restaurant, I walk over to the fireplace, where something catches my eye. Carved into a stone in the middle of the mantel is a familiar sight:

A circle, crossed by two swords.

The symbol of the Consortium.

It's faint and dusty, and I have no idea how long ago it was scratched into the surface. But there's no mistaking it, and it strikes me for the first time that I haven't seen it on a single uniform, door, or anywhere else in the Bastille, for that matter. It's like Cyntra said: the town's residents have simply erased their former association with my father's organization.

But why? What happened to make these people despise their former alliance so much? What could they possibly hate about the group of rebels who very likely kept them alive as they fled the Mire?

"Hey, Ashen!" Cyntra calls from the back of the room, pulling me out of my thoughts. "Food's over here!"

I head over to a long table covered in a stained white tablecloth and an array of silver serving dishes. "You can call me Ash," I tell her. "No one calls me Ashen except people who don't like me much...and authority figures."

"Ash," she replies. "I like that. Come on—have some grub."

As I approach, my nose picks up the smell of cooked meat, and Cyntra leads me to a large side-kitchen, where a dozen or so roasting pans are sitting, leftovers half-stewing inside them still.

"Wild turkey," she tells me, grabbing a plate and loading it with meat, mashed potatoes, and what look like green beans. "We grow the potatoes and beans in town. Don't ask me where—I hate gardening. It's so…dirty. Plus, the gardens are under lock and key, protected by the snipers."

"Why's that?"

She shrugs, leans in, and whispers, "There's a pretty serious lack of trust around here," she says. "Among some of the adults. The food is limited, and if any were to go missing, it would cause a civil war."

"Lack of trust is probably wise," I reply. "My mother always said more people are bad than good. In my experience, she was right."

"Some people are more bad than others." The voice, coming from somewhere behind me, is deep, rich, and cynical. "My guess is that you're in the former category…*Ash.*"

I spin around, aware that I've still got my dagger sheathed at my waist, and wondering if I may have to use it.

Peric is standing in front of us, a half-smile, half-frown on his face. He's assessing me again, like he's trying to piece together just how serious an enemy I might actually be.

"Stop trying to intimidate the new girl, Per," Cyntra says, her tone a mixture of flirtatious and irritated. I get the impression she's never learned quite how to talk to a boy she finds attractive.

"Just trying to figure out what makes her tick," he says, never taking his eyes off me. "Dagger at her waist. Directorate uniform. She doesn't exactly scream *One Of Us.*"

"Okay, once and for all, it's not a Directorate uniform," I tell him. "It's a Candidate's uniform. Which means I'm a Dreg."

"Not all Dregs are our friends," Peric says with a sneer. "I know that better than anyone." I wonder what he means by that, but he neglects to expand on the thought. "Either way, you should put on something that doesn't make you stick out so much. You look like a hostile."

"Sorry, but I prefer to keep the uniform on." *For more reasons than one.*

"Why?" he scoffs, grabbing a bun off the counter next to him. "It doesn't make you look nearly as badass as you think it does."

In one lightning-fast motion, I reach out, grab his arm, and squeeze. With a yelp, he opens his hand and drops the bun into my other hand.

"I have my reasons," I tell him, taking a bite.

He takes a step toward me, and for a second I wonder if he's planning an attack.

"The last man who fought me didn't fare too well," I say, staring straight into Peric's eyes. "I flung him to the ground like he was a seven-year-old, and I'll do it to you, too."

I'm convinced he's going to try to take me down regardless. I've wounded his pride, hurt his tenuous grasp on his concept of masculinity.

But his lips twitch into a smile.

"You really think you have something to offer this place, don't you?" he asks.

"She knows things!" Cyntra snaps, drawing his eyes. "She's seen a lot more of the Arc than *you* have. She has tons to offer."

"So what? It's not like she can change the world. She's as much at the mercy of the Directorate as we are."

"We're not at their mercy," Cyntra insists. "We're—"

Peric issues her a glare of warning, and she stops talking.

"I *may* be able to change the world," I tell him with a scowl. "Eventually."

"Eventually," he chuckles. "That's such a convenient word, isn't it? I could say the same. It's awfully easy to make promises to do something *eventually*. The question is, what can you do for us now? Can you improve our lives? Can you tear down the walls around this town and still offer us protection?"

I glare at him, but say nothing.

"That's what I thought."

"Come on, Ash," Cyntra says, her nose in the air. "Ignore him. Let's sit down."

I follow her and take a seat at one of the long wooden tables. Surprisingly, Peric follows and seats himself with us. He looks like he's about to ask more questions when Veer and Piper walk in through the Mess's front door.

"Settling in all right, Ashen?" Veer asks me when they've reached our table.

"Fine, thank you." *Except for the fact that your son is a douche-canoe.*

Her eyes move down to my weapon. "You'll want to keep that out of sight while you're here. It could end up freaking out some of our residents. You've probably noticed no one carries weapons in town, other than the snipers. Many of our residents are pacifists."

"Right. Yes. Sorry, I forgot I had it on when I left my room. I'll be sure to put it away."

"It's fine. Most of our people are in their quarters by now." She pauses before adding, "Listen, Ashen—I was wondering if you'd be interested in joining us on a surveillance hike sometime?"

My eyes widen. "Sure."

"Great. We'll be heading up into the mountains in a few days, and I thought your eyes might be helpful. You know what to look for—patrols, drones, that sort of thing. I thought maybe you could help us identify any threats."

"Anything I can do to help," I tell her with a smile, grateful to be trusted enough to be invited—*and* grateful that I now have something to look forward to.

"Superb, thanks. Cyntra, see to it that our guest gets some rest, would you? Don't keep her up talking all night."

"I won't," Cyntra assures her.

"And Peric—" Veer says.

"What?" he asks sullenly, and it occurs to me for the first time how funny it is to watch him interact with his mother. Only surly offspring dare to speak to authority figures in that tone.

"Be nice."

"I'm always nice, Mother," he says in a faux-formal voice.

"You're always a pain in the butt," she replies. "Good night, all. Ashen, we'll see you in the morning."

When Veer has left us, Peric finally takes off, apparently just a little too obedient to stick around and make threatening noises any longer.

He's not a particularly charming person, yet I find myself curious to know more about him. Despite—or possibly because of—his obvious loathing for me, something about him feels oddly honest—a rare and crucial trait. I get the distinct feeling he'd do anything to protect this place and its residents. Even if it meant killing me in my sleep.

I can respect that.

8

SETTLING IN

AFTER I'VE EATEN, Cyntra asks if I'd like to see her room. I shrug and tell her that would be nice, despite the fact that I'm dead tired and all I want is to be alone.

She leads me out of the Mess and down the street toward the building that contains my quarters. But before we get there, we enter an old store on the right—what looks like it might once have been a chocolate shop—and head down a long series of narrow hallways until we come to a stairwell leading to the second floor. At the top, she pushes the door open and guides me down another corridor until we get to her room.

I don't know what I was expecting, but what's inside throws me for a loop. Her bedding is like that of a little girl—the same yellow as the dress she's wearing, with narrow pink stripes. It's punctuated by jaunty flounces, pretty flowers, and butterflies. On the wall beyond the bed are cut-out paper butterflies and photos of faraway places that look like they were torn out of tourist magazines.

Her dresser is painted pink, and on the floor is a pink and

white fluffy rug in the shape of an animal skin. Sitting on Cyntra's bed is a stuffed dog, its tongue lolling out cheerfully.

"Wow," I breathe as I step inside. "This is..."

"It's a bit much," Cyntra says apologetically when I fail to finish the sentence. "I know. But it's my comfort place. My special retreat. It makes me calm." Her tone has deepened into earnest territory, and it strikes me that maybe she isn't as ceaselessly perky as I'd thought.

"I get it," I tell her. "It's...happy. Like, *really* happy." I step forward to stare at a photo stuck to the wall, of an ancient-looking stone house sitting on a hill overlooking what look like vineyards. "Where's this?" I ask.

"The south of France. I pulled it out of a magazine I found years ago. It looked so pretty—so open and free." She sighs. "I wonder if France still has houses like that, or if everyone lives in Arcologies over there, too. Like, did the Blight hit Europe, or just America?"

It hits me like a fist—the realization that I have no idea what the rest of the world actually looks like anymore. I've heard there are other Arcologies—that the Directorate's reach is vast. But it's been so long since I've had access to a regular television or newspaper, let alone browsed the internet, that I'm not entirely sure if there are any free areas in this country anymore. It's possible every major city's population has divided itself, with the Wealthies moving into massive, luxurious structures while the poor languish in sickness and death on the outside.

When I was younger and the Directorate began building walls around the Mire, we were told the Blight was everywhere. That we were being separated from others for our own good to keep the spread at bay.

But it was all lies, of course.

"I don't know about France," I tell Cyntra, "but my house in the Mire is still standing. As for the Blight, I don't know how many people it's killed, but I'd like to find out."

"I'm glad your house is still there," she sighs. "I haven't seen the Mire in years."

"How old were you when you came here?"

"Seven. I mean, I was seven when I left my home with my parents."

"Your parents are here in the Bastille?"

She shakes her head. "No. They left the Mire with me, but..." She stops, looks over at another photograph, and shakes her head. "All I remember is a fight—a big one. It was more like a war, really, with guns and screaming. Fire and bodies everywhere. My mother told me to run, so I did. After everything got quiet again, Veer found me in the woods and took me in. I...don't know what happened to my parents. Part of me doesn't want to know, honestly. I can only hope they're safe somewhere."

"I'm sorry. I know how hard it is to lose family members."

"Things were hard for so many people. But I have a new family now, here in the Bastille. Veer has kept us all safe. I don't know what would have happened to me if it weren't for her. She's a saint."

"Is she?" I'm still not entirely sure what to think about the Bastille's fearless leader. But between adopting Peric and taking Cyntra in, it's hard to deny she does sound somewhat more saintly than the adults I've grown accustomed to meeting.

"She is." Cyntra smiles. "She's been so good to us. She negotiated the peace. She's secured happy futures for every one of us."

Once again, I find myself envying Cyntra's innocence. She

seems so utterly believing, entirely trusting, the way most children are with their parents until they reach an age of disillusionment and realize the people who raised them aren't living gods after all.

For me, that day came when my mother closed herself off from us, isolating herself in the back of our house. It was the day she ceased to be a parent to Kel and me. The day my mother revealed her utter vulnerability, her hopelessness. She was no longer my protector, so I was forced to become hers.

When I've yawned one too many times, Cyntra laughs. "I'm sorry—I've kept you up against Veer's wishes. You must be so wiped out. Come on, I'll walk you to your quarters."

"Thanks. I *am* tired. Spending two nights in the woods while the Directorate Guard may or may not be coming to kill you doesn't exactly make for great sleep. But I need a shower before I consider resting. I smell like death."

"I didn't want to say anything, but yeah, you kind of do," she laughs, holding her nose.

Cyntra accompanies me to my building. On the way, we pass a few men dressed in muted colors, and I ask her about the townspeople's clothing.

"Most of it was taken years ago from abandoned homes. A lot of the men's clothes—and the Matrons'—used to be brighter colors, but it's faded now. They save the expensive textiles for the younger people, like me. We're the ones who need to make a good impression."

"Who are you trying to impress?"

"No one, yet," she replies with a smile and a wink. "But soon enough, it'll be my turn."

I side-eye her, trying to work out what she could possibly mean. For a girl who talks far too much, Cyntra adeptly manages *not* to convey a lot of information. She's impressively good at keeping secrets when she wants to, which I find both admirable and frustrating.

"I've heard the clothes in the Arc are amazing," she adds.

"There's no lack of color in the Arc. I've seen Aristocrats dressed in every shade there is. But they're also obsessed with white. White walls, white ceilings, white everything. It's like a color of prestige or something—like the shininess of it all means everything is perfect."

"What about the Directorate? Do they dress in white?"

"No," I reply through gritted teeth. "They like black and gold. It's all about wealth for them. And power."

"Are the Aristocrats nice?"

I wince. Finn is, of course. And Merit. But they aren't exactly true "Aristocrats." They're simply unfortunate enough to have been born to sociopathic parents.

"Not really, no. Not that I ever saw, anyhow."

"That's too bad." She seems genuinely saddened by the revelation. "But maybe there are some good ones you just haven't met."

"There are millions of people in the Arc," I tell her. "All of them have money—at least, almost all. And I'm willing to bet a lot of them are good people who don't know what the Directorate is capable of. How cruel they can be. They think it's paradise in there."

Ignoring my condemnation of the enemy, Cyntra flicks her hair back and says, "One day, I hope to find my own paradise."

"I hope you do, too."

When I've said goodnight to her and made my way into the bathroom, I find myself thinking about my time in the woods. About the feeling of freedom, of openness. Of how I wouldn't trade the Arc's best qualities for nature's worst in a million years.

Better to dwell in nature, for all its dangers, than to be locked inside an enormous prison.

When I return to my bedroom after my shower, I turn the crank on the window, pleased to realize it actually opens. I lean out, inhaling the night air and staring at the silhouetted mountain peaks in the distance.

Somewhere out there, Finn is probably sitting in his room in the Davenport residence. I find myself wondering if he's thinking about me, if he misses me as much as I miss him.

I would give anything to feel his palms cradling my cheeks, his arms around me, his lips on mine. I make a silent vow to some unseen entity that one minute of his touch would sustain me for a year.

Somewhere in the distance, I hear the low hoot of an owl, and I smile.

Well, I may not be entirely at home here, but at least I have a friend.

Over the next few days, I find myself relaxing into a comfortable pattern: Wake up in the morning, head to the Mess, eat with Cyntra and sometimes Piper—or if we're really unfortunate, Peric, who continues to scowl at me every chance he gets.

Piper is friendly, at least to a point. She asks me the occasional question about my time in the Arc, though sometimes it feels more like she's interrogating me than being casually curious.

How did I know to go west out of the Mire? What exactly did my father tell me in the note he left? Did he leave any more details about location he hinted at—is there any risk the Directorate could have seen the information?

I keep my answers short and detail-free. On the surface I like Piper, but I can't say I entirely trust her. Something about her seems laser focused and eager, but I haven't yet figured out what her endgame is. Sometimes it feels like she's more intent on dissecting me than defeating the Directorate, and I can't entirely figure out why.

She asks me at one point if I think there's a chance a small army could take on the enemy. It's a question that fills me with hope that behind their strange reverence for that organization, Piper and the others are true allies...and that they genuinely want to formulate a plan.

The one thing I know for certain is that there's no way in hell we'll be able to go to battle without help from someone on the inside of the Arc, and right now, I have no way to communicate. No way to talk to Finn, to find out about my brother, about the Directorate's thwarted hunt for me.

I find myself craving technology. A communication hub. Any way of signaling Finn that I'm alive and well, and I've even managed to make a few friends.

Most of all, I want to let him know how much I miss him.

Veer comes by the Mess each day and asks how I am, how I'm settling in, if everything is to my liking. On my third day in the Bastille, Peric issues me an angry glare, apparently irate that I'm receiving special treatment from his mother. "She's not a hotel guest, Mom," he snaps. "At best, she's a leech, eating our food and drinking our water."

"She's an asset," his mother tells him, her tone final. "In more ways than one. You of all people should understand that."

The thing is, I don't want to be an asset, or to receive special attention. All I want is a place to rest, to think. I still have a brother to rescue. I have Finn to think about—I need, somehow, to find my way back into his arms. I'm desperate for it. And with each night of restless sleep, I become more acutely aware of how much I miss him.

The Bastille is a place of secrets and tight-knit alliances. Though its residents nod hello to me as I pass, they've made it all too clear they don't want to get close to me, to welcome me deep into the fold. And as nice as most of them seem, I'm perfectly happy to stay out of their way.

I have no desire for friends.

What I want is to stay alive long enough to see my brother and Finn again—and to figure out if the Consortium truly is a thing of the past.

9

COMING OF AGE

On the morning of my fourth day, Cyntra comes to find me in the Mess at breakfast. She's wearing a soft, flowing dress of light purple whose diaphanous fabric looks almost lighter than air. At its waist is a dark purple ribbon made of rich velvet.

"That's pretty," I tell her with a smile.

"Thank you so much!" she beams, spinning around so the dress's full skirt twirls away from her body. "It's what all the Maidens—that's what we call the girls under eighteen—wear on the day of the Finishing."

"You never did tell me what the Finishing was."

"You still don't know?" she asks, taking a seat next to me.

"Nope."

"Well...I suppose you've been here long enough that I can tell you. It's the moment every girl in the Bastille looks forward to all her life. It happens the day we turn eighteen—it's when we start the next phase of our lives."

"Wait—next phase? What does that mean?"

Cyntra laughs. "You should come with me and learn about

it for yourself. It only lasts a few minutes. I'm sure I can find you a dress! You're a Maiden after all, just like me."

My immediate reaction is to balk at the suggestion. By "Maiden," I'm assuming she means I'm pure and virginal, an innocent girl untouched by men. Or something equally creepy.

But part of me is morbidly curious to see the ceremony, to be an insider in the workings of the Bastille.

Another part feels deeply apprehensive, like this is a rabbit hole I don't really want to fall into for fear I'll never make it back out.

"I'm not sure..." I say, but Cyntra laughs and grabs my arm.

"Come on, you'll love it. The ceremony is beautiful. Besides, you're one of us now. You should know what goes on here. When you turn eighteen, you will have a Finishing of your own, Ash...If you're still around, I mean."

"Fine," I sigh, letting her drag me to my feet.

Cyntra does a little hop, claps her hands together, and lets out a squeak as only she can. "You'll look so good in the dress! Come on, we have to go to the Shop."

"Shop?"

I've wandered around the Bastille enough to know there are many shops here, but none of them is functional—which I assume is because no one has money. Every building that used to house a business is now run-down and decrepit, and most have been repurposed for other uses. There are bakeries that hand out free bread and pastries, a pottery studio, a tailor, a weaver.

Small efforts have been made here and there to beautify the businesses—flowers in planters, painted signs. But it's clear the Bastille lacks the resources to replace shattered windows or broken brick. It's not as though they can import the building materials they'd need; every piece of steel or glass was long since claimed by the Directorate.

"You'll see," Cyntra says, guiding me down the main street until we come to an intersection where she turns left, taking me by the hand.

"The Shop is just down here," she tells me. "It's run by one of the Matrons."

"She sells things?"

"Not exactly. But the ladies in town like to go there and rifle through the clothes, like we did in the old days. It's the only place in town a girl can go and try on new outfits. It's as close to shopping as we come."

We walk for two more blocks until we reach a wooden house whose exterior walls are crawling with densely braided vines. Its front door is wide open, and there's a hand-painted sign out front that simply reads, "Welcome, One and All!"

Cyntra skips her way up the stairs and inside, and I follow, still not sure this was a good idea.

"Magdalene!" Cyntra calls out when we're inside. "I brought you a new customer!"

A few seconds later, a short woman who looks seventy or so comes waddling out from a room at the back of the house. She seems to have a little difficulty walking, but she smiles when she sees me, her face instantly morphing into a younger version of itself.

"The new girl," she says. "Welcome."

"Thanks," I reply awkwardly.

"Ash needs a Maiden dress," Cyntra tells her, her tone vaguely bossy. "Right away."

"Ah, do you now?" Magdalene asks, looking me up and down. "Well, it just so happens I have a few lying around."

"Are you sure? I don't want to be a pain."

"My entire existence is about making clothing. I quite literally live for it. So there's no such thing as being a pain in my shop."

I smile. I like her—she reminds me of my grandmother on my father's side who died years ago, before the Blight. There's a natural generosity in her that can't be taught or faked. A joy derived from giving to others—the sort of personality I haven't encountered in a very long time.

She disappears into a side room only to return a few seconds later with a dress the same color as Cyntra's and a pair of shoes to match. "You can keep them," she tells me, handing them over. "Consider them a welcome gift."

"Thank you. Um...how do you know what size I am?"

"Decades of scrutinizing customers," she replies with a wink. "I can tell a good deal about you just by eyeing you."

Not too much, I hope.

"Well, thanks again."

"You should get changed," Cyntra tells me. "The ceremony is in half an hour. There isn't really time to go back to your place."

"Oh. Okay." I look apologetically at Magdalene. "Is there somewhere I could..."

"Yes, there are change rooms," she tells me, nodding over to a doorway on her right. "Just head on in."

I make my way through the door into what looks like an old dining room divided into narrow, flimsy-walled cubicles with curtains that can be drawn across their openings. I step into one and seal myself inside.

Seconds later, I'm out of my Candidate uniform and feeling uneasy about how vulnerable I've suddenly become.

But I fold the uniform and put on the purple dress, which fits like a glove, as do the matching shoes.

I study myself in the mirror for the first time in a long time. I look rested, my cheeks rosy. I pull half my hair back, tying it into a loose knot before tucking the uniform under my arm. I head back out only to be met with a whistle from Cyntra, who's smiling from ear to ear.

"You look so beautiful!" she shrieks. I let out a chuckle, amused by how excited she is.

"Thanks. But this isn't about me, it's about the girl who's coming of age."

"Indeed. The Finishing is a sacred day for that young woman," Magdalene says with a solemn nod. "Tomorrow, she becomes whole. It's the most important day of her life. Today, though, we prepare her for her Change."

"Change?" I ask, still confused about exactly what this ceremony is.

"When the Finishing is complete, she will become a part of something larger than herself," Magdalene offers cryptically. "As she opens her mind and body to her future, a new world will present itself to her. One far greater than ours."

I find myself feeling queasy at the strange sincerity in the woman's voice. Maybe I'm too cynical to believe a ceremony with pretty dresses is enough to change any girl's life. I went to my own Introduction Ceremony, after all, dressed in the most beautiful gown I've ever seen. In the end, I was introduced to a fake king and queen and then herded away with my fellow Candidates like livestock headed for the slaughterhouse.

I can only hope the girl who's coming of age today doesn't suffer the same fate that I did.

10

THE FINISHING

"Where are we going?" I ask when we've left the Shop.

"To the Clearing," Cyntra says.

"Clearing? Outside the Bastille's walls?"

She shakes her head. "It's within the walls. Come, I'll show you."

I'm grateful to hear we're not about to embark on a trek. My shoes may fit, but they're not made for hiking through dense underbrush.

I've still got my white uniform tucked under my arm.

"Do you want to leave that somewhere?" Cyntra asks. "No one will take it, I'm sure."

"No," I tell her, my tone sharper than I intend. "I mean, I'd rather have it with me, in case I need to change."

"Okay," she says with a shrug. "But they won't let you bring it all the way. No one carries personal items to the Finishing."

I contemplate telling her I've changed my mind, or that I'm tired and can't go. Any excuse to avoid being parted from my uniform—my one protection from enemies. "I'll bring it as far as I can, then."

"Suit yourself," she chuckles before asking, "So tell me, is this town everything you expected it to be?"

"I wasn't expecting a town at all. I guess I figured Breckenridge was just totally gone."

"You said your father left clues before he died. They pointed you here, right? That's why you were close?"

"Not...exactly."

"Where, then?"

I look at her sideways, trying to work out if she's asking out of idle curiosity or something more sinister. "I honestly don't know," I finally reply, struggling to make my voice sound light as I lie through my teeth. "There were a bunch of numbers but I can't remember them. It's why I ended up in the cave where you guys found me."

"Your father wrote down a bunch of numbers, and you're telling me you didn't even memorize them?" Something in Cyntra's voice has altered, like an underlying anger is straining the words. But as if trying to compensate for it, she lets out a little giggle and says, "You're so flaky!"

"I guess I am. But at least I found you. Or you found me, rather. By the way, no one's ever quite told me how you three stumbled upon me."

"It was Veer," Cyntra's eyes are focused on the distance as she guides me down the main street.

"Veer?" I ask.

"She sent us. Woke us up in the middle of the night and told us we needed to go on a hunt."

"Veer was looking for me?"

"Oh, no. I'm sure she didn't know you were out there...but she was looking for *someone*. Veer's always hunting. Her whole life is about finding people. I suppose she had a hunch that some poor soul needed our help."

"Impressive hunch."

"You're telling me!" With that, Cyntra breaks into a jog, grabbing my arm and dragging me along with her.

Over the last few days, I've wandered the streets of what used to be Breckenridge, exploring the more public areas. The town square, known as the Piazza. A small park two streets over, and several residential streets...but there are certain areas I haven't explored for fear of finding myself in conflict with the Bastille's snipers.

One such area is the southwestern corner of the town, which is guarded at all times by two men with rifles. It seems we're headed for that zone now, and I'm grateful to have Cyntra with me as we approach.

The two guards stand side by side, blocking the entrance to a narrow dirt path that leads between two small houses. As we step toward them, one of the men nods to the house on his left.

"Leave any belongings on the porch," he tells me, eyeing the folded uniform under my arm. "And put on the masks."

"Masks?" I repeat, looking at Cyntra.

"Oh, yeah! It's fun. No one sees our faces during the Finishing. It's all very secret."

I follow her onto the house's porch, lay my uniform on a chair, and watch as a Matron in a gray dress hands Cyntra an eerily familiar silver mask.

She slips it on, pulling a long piece of elastic around her head to secure it.

"Where did these come from?" I ask, my voice tight.

"We've had them for years," the Matron says as she hands me one. "It's tradition."

"Tradition," I echo. I stare into the shiny silver surface for a few seconds. At the distorted reflection of my face, gazing back at me from what looks far too much like the sort of mask the Directorate wears.

Coincidence. It has to be. These are made of plastic; the Directorate's are made of metal. These probably came from a costume shop in the city years ago, back in the days when the Consortium was still meeting in secret.

I slip it over my head, telling myself not to be so paranoid.

When we head back toward the guards, they part to let us through, and Cyntra takes my hand to guide me along the narrow path that leads between the houses to a small wooded area just this side of the Bastille's outer wall.

"The Ceremony takes place up ahead," she says. "Just a little farther along." As we walk, I spot other girls up ahead, wearing the same purple Maiden dresses that we have on. They move silently, solemnly, like they're heading to a funeral, and I begin to wonder why Cyntra is so giddy about the whole thing.

"Should I be worried?" I ask.

"Not at all," she whispers with a shake of her head. "Look."

Through the woods I can see people moving around. Maidens and Matrons alike are shuffling into position, seemingly with purpose. As we advance, quiet music begins to surround us—a sort of delicate humming that seems to move on a cool breeze that's just risen up, blowing strands of my hair this way and that.

We keep walking until we come to the edge of the Clearing. I can see now that the Matrons—ten of them or so—have positioned themselves around its perimeter. Like us, they're wearing silver masks.

At the center of the Clearing are the Maidens, stepping into formation as we approach.

Leaning in close to Cyntra, I whisper, "Which one is..."

"The girl who's coming of age?" Cyntra replies under her breath. "There, with the red hair."

The girl's back is turned our way, but I spot her immediately. Her long red hair is twisted around her head in a series of thirty or so narrow braids. Like the rest of us, she's dressed in lavender. But when she turns our way, I see that her mask, unlike the ones we're wearing, is pure white.

We join the other Maidens in the circle and, without a word, begin to pace slowly around the girl, who must be seventeen or eighteen. As we move, the Matrons' soft humming begins to crescendo as the women close in around us, creating a sort of double circle of bodies, all surrounding the red-headed girl.

I feel disturbingly as though I've become part of a religious ceremony, some ritual I don't entirely understand or want to participate in. But I tell myself it's too late now; having been invited, it would be disrespectful to leave.

Just as I command myself to relax, one of the Matrons breaks off from the others and moves to another spot in the Clearing, several feet from our circle. With her mask concealing her features, it's hard to guess her age, but I'd estimate about fifty, two long gray braids streaming down her chest like orderly waterfalls.

"Samantha Collins," she says from her spot in the clearing. "Come to me."

Our circle stops moving and the red-haired girl steps between two Maidens, who part to let her through. When she reaches the Matron who summoned her, she kneels before her in a rehearsed, elegant move.

"The gown," the Matron says, thrusting her arms out as if awaiting an offering.

Two Matrons I hadn't spotted earlier approach from the

edge of the woods, one holding a white gown, the other holding a veil.

"Wait—are those...?" I whisper.

Cyntra nods silently then squeezes my hand as if to tell me to be quiet.

"Undress her," the gray-haired Matron commands.

I watch as the girl called Samantha rises to her feet. Two other Matrons from the circle step toward her and strip her down until she's naked aside from her white mask. For a few seconds she stands in the clearing, her eyes to the sky, before the Matrons help her into the lavish-looking gown. It's beaded with curling vines of pearls and sequins, its skirt so full that it seems to take up half the clearing. Its bodice is exquisitely tailored and strapless, and fits Samantha perfectly.

The image is stunning as the Matrons back away to look at her. Still, it's disturbing to see such a young woman dressed in a wedding gown. Much as I love Finn, I can't imagine marrying him—or anyone—this young, particularly with our world in a state of utter mayhem.

But Samantha looks euphoric as she removes the mask to reveal her face, beaming as one of the Matrons comes forward, the veil in hand. Whoever the girl's future husband is, she must be madly in love with him to look so pleased about the whole affair.

Finally, the Matron secures a flowing white veil to Samantha's hair and slips its translucent white fabric over her features.

"Samantha Collins," the Matron says, "you have come of age, and your Finishing is complete. Tomorrow, in this very dress, you will wed. In the years to come, you will bear your husband children. He will protect you from harm and provide you with all the earthly possessions you could possibly desire. He is your savior. Your guide in life. Your master."

Wait—Master?

Surely the Matron isn't serious. This has to be some kind of role-playing farce.

I glance at Cyntra, but she's unreadable behind the reflective silver of her mask.

"The bride is ready for you," the gray-haired woman announces, turning to face the woods. A few seconds later, two figures step out from between the trees and approach. Each is dressed in dark gray, with matching gray masks covering their faces. "She is leaving, and she will not return to the Bastille. Her time with us is at an end."

I reach for Cyntra. "Where are they taking her?"

Cyntra takes me by the hand and pulls in close. "Isn't it wonderful?" she asks in a whisper.

"Where is she going?" I repeat. My heart is pounding, my breath shallow.

"Her new home," a voice says. I turn around to see one of the Matrons standing behind me. "An idyllic place filled with wonderful things. Samantha is about to begin a perfect life with a doting, handsome husband."

I feel myself on the verge of hyperventilating. *A perfect life. One where she's expected to call her husband Master.*

"Don't worry, Ashen," Cyntra assures me with a hand on my shoulder. "She's safe. She's going to be so happy."

"Who is she marrying?" It's clear that no one intends to answer my previous question. "Does she even know?"

"She knows all she needs to," the Matron replies, "which is that her husband is worthy, and he will do everything in his power to grant her every wish. For most girls, the Finishing is a dream come true."

It sounds like a nightmare, I want to retort as two of the Matrons come over to congratulate each other on their latest success.

"Does this Finishing thing happen a lot?" I ask Cyntra when we've stepped away from the crowd.

"Every few months, depending on who's turning eighteen," she tells me. "Mine won't happen for almost two years, not unless Veer grants me special privileges and lets me come of age early."

"Would you really want to get married before you're eighteen? To a complete stranger?"

"You say it like it's a bad thing," she chuckles. "When actually, it's the best thing in the world. Veer chooses our husbands for us—with some help from a council of Matrons. I trust them completely. Look, Veer has known me half my life. She'll choose someone suitable. I know it."

"But what about love? What about getting to know each other? Don't you care about any of that?"

"I already love the man I'll marry," Cyntra tells me with a shrug. "I haven't met him yet, but in my mind, he's perfect."

"Cyntra—" I say, but her sweetness fades when she pulls off her mask and glares at me.

"Stop," she snaps.

"Look, I'm only protecting you..."

"By telling me you think our ways are wrong?" Her tone is dagger-sharp. "We brought you here as a guest. As an outsider. And you step into our town and tell us we don't have a right to be happy?"

"I didn't say that."

"You didn't have to."

"I just think it's weird that your fate is being dictated like this, by a bunch of women who have no idea what you really want."

"*Your* fate was dictated for you. You were a Candidate, which means you were taken from your home by Chaperons when you turned seventeen. You had no idea what would happen to you, yet you still went with them."

"And look where that got me. I'm not exactly the girl you should aspire to be."

"Don't worry, you're not. The girl I aspire to be is the one in the wedding dress who just left for a better life."

Without another word, she turns her back and heads down the path that leads out of the woods.

I follow a few seconds later, baffled that any girl can hope for such a life—to offer herself up as little more than a smiling servant to a man she's never met. A man who, for all she knows, could be cruel or vicious.

Cyntra is young. She's naive. She hasn't seen or experienced what I have. She'll realize, with each day that passes, each wretched event, the world is a far cry from the place she dreamed of when she was a child.

But maybe she's right—maybe it's best to let fate guide us through our time on this earth. Maybe it's too much to hope we can change anything for the better.

Maybe life is just a constant struggle for survival. No more, no less.

I follow a line of purple-clad "Maidens" back down the path, my eyes turning to the sky, where I spot the silver underbelly of a large bird gliding elegantly overhead. As I watch, he swoops down toward the girls walking ahead of me and banks sharply toward the edge of town, as though he wishes to remind me of his existence.

Finally, casting off all the wretchedness brewing inside me, I smile.

Some things in this world are still beautiful.

And some creatures are still free.

11

HIKE

On the morning of my sixth day in the Bastille, Piper comes knocking at my door before breakfast to tell me she, Veer, and Peric are about to hike up the ski hill to an abandoned chalet above town, and they'd like me to come.

"I've brought you some clothing," she says, handing me a neatly folded pile of the same tank top and khaki pants she was wearing the first time I met her.

"If it's all the same to you, I'll wear my uniform and cloak," I tell her. I've hand-washed the garments twice since my arrival, and tested the uniform in private to make sure it's maintained the strength-enhancing properties Finn wove into its fabric. I was worried at first that water would cause some sort of short-circuit, but remarkably, the garment doesn't seem to have been affected in the least. It's as though any wiring hidden away within the fibers is insulated against the elements. Even the slash in one sleeve from my fight with the King's son doesn't seem to have hurt the suit even a little.

Most importantly, my not-so-refined surgical removal of the implant the Directorate injected into my wrist doesn't seem to have hampered the suit's effectiveness. It's like it's learned to read my thoughts and intentions, all through some sort of miraculous psychic osmosis.

"The cloak," Piper says. "May I see it?"

"Veer told you about it?"

She nods.

I reach for the flowing piece of fabric, which is sitting draped over the dresser. I slip my fingers down to the pressure point and activate its camouflage setting, pulling it around my shoulders.

Piper looks stunned.

"Holy crap," she says, stepping toward me. "You look like a disembodied face, floating in the air." As she moves forward I unconsciously take a step back, protective of the precious garment.

Piper simply stares at me and asks, "Did you get it in the Arc?"

I nod, pulling the fabric away from my body and deactivating it. "It was a gift," I say. "It's saved my life on at least one occasion."

"If only we had some of this material..." She reaches out to touch the cloak. Instinct tells me again to pull away, but after a moment's hesitation, I step forward and allow her to examine it. "I can only imagine what we could do," she adds, seemingly awestruck. "If we could actually find a way to take on our enemies, I mean."

I watch her eyes as they move over the intricate fabric. There's a sudden hunger in her, a sort of quiet bloodlust that sends a shiver skittering over the surface of my skin.

"By our enemies," I say, "I assume you mean the Directorate."

She doesn't reply immediately. Her jaw tenses and she

steps back. "Yes. Of course that's what I mean. I...I can't get over that tech. It's incredible."

"I just wish I could talk to the person who gave it to me. He's got so many resources at his disposal. He could probably supply us with a ton of useful gear."

"It still wouldn't be enough to accomplish what we need to. But it sure as hell wouldn't hurt. The truth is, we need *people.* Manpower. Fighters. You've seen most of our population—we aren't exactly building an army here. But we'd like to. It's one reason we want to—"

"Want to what?" I ask when she fails to finish the sentence.

Piper looks uncharacteristically frazzled, like she's said too much and it's pained her. "Never mind," she replies. " Let's head down to the Mess. You can get some breakfast, then it's about a three-mile hike to our lookout spot."

"I'll meet you in a minute," I tell her with a nod. "I just need to get washed up."

When she's left, I take my sheathed dagger out of the top drawer of my dresser and strap it around my waist. If all goes well today, I won't need it. But if the Directorate's drones come for us, we'll need all the help we can get.

When I'm ready, I head to the Mess, passing half-familiar strangers on the way who smile and nod at me warily. I always get the urge to speak to them, to tell them who I am—that my father was Oliver Spencer, the man who helped create the Consortium. That I'm an ally, a supporter of their cause.

But somehow, I don't think that would reassure them in the least.

As I head to the restaurant formerly known as Maurice's Chalet, my mind swims once again with thoughts of Finn. Every morning when I wake up, I miss him more than the previous one. I miss the comfort he brings with his presence. I feel as safe as can be expected in this place, but I also feel lost, like part of my mind, my body, my soul, was left behind in the Arc.

As much as I despise that place, the two people I love most are still trapped between its walls. And with each day that passes and each breath I inhale, I'm drawn back.

I wonder with a tentative swell of hope if today's expedition will bring me any information, any updates on what's happening in the Arc.

When I get to the Mess, I immediately spot Veer and Piper sitting together in a far corner. Peric is nearby, chatting with a man of about thirty. He's smiling and laughing, and actually looks approachable for once. But the second we lock eyes, his smile fades and he skulks over to Veer's table.

Cyntra is sitting with a few other teenaged girls at a table in the far corner. I hesitate for a moment before striding over.

"Hey," I say, crouching down next to her.

"Hey," she replies with a curt nod.

"Listen—I'm sorry for the things I said to you in the Clearing. I had no right to be so judgmental. It's not my place to say how things should be done around here. I...I know how hard it can be to find happiness in this world of ours, and if it makes you happy, then I'm not going to try and talk you out of it—no matter what *it* is."

Her face lights up and she throws her arms around my neck and squeezes me tight. "Thanks, Ash," she says. "I knew you didn't mean those things."

Oh, I think, *I definitely meant them.*

But that doesn't mean I should have said them out loud.

Leaving her with her friends, I grab some food from the nearby buffet—eggs, turkey bacon and dry toast made from a sort of flavorless bread the Matrons make in the bakery down the street—and head over to join Veer and Piper. My purple cloak is draped over my right shoulder, and Veer gives me a nod when I sit down, but says nothing.

"I see that you got the memo about concealing yourself in the woods," Peric says sarcastically.

"I'll be more camouflaged than you will," I reply with a sneer.

"Right—because as everyone knows, trees are purple. Very clever of you."

"Peric," Veer growls. "Ashen escaped the Arc, and no doubt more than a few pursuers. She made it this far. Give her a little credit, will you?"

"She'll get us all killed," he retorts. "You know she will."

"Somehow I doubt it," Veer says. "That's enough of your griping. If you'd rather stay behind, I'm sure Cyntra would be only too happy to take your place."

"It's fine," Peric mutters, glaring at me. "Just don't blame me if we get shot by—." He stops short of saying who our executioners will be.

"We'll keep an eye out for Directorate Guard and anyone else who may be a threat," Veer tells him. "We'll be fine."

I make a note to avoid Peric as much as possible today and to keep my mouth shut, my eyes peeled. I have no interest in arguing with a petulant child.

Once we've all finished eating, Veer leads us toward the restaurant's back exit, which takes us along a dirt path squeezed between two other buildings.

After a few minutes spent making our way between derelict houses, we arrive at a single, narrow steel door embedded in the town's wall. At its center is a rusty-looking wheel, which Veer grasps with both hands and turns with some effort.

"This is what we call the escape hatch," she tells me. "It's solid and secure, and can't be breached from the outside."

Once she's finished cranking the wheel and inputs a series of numbers into a small panel to the door's left, I see why she says it's secure. The code is eleven or so digits, but I'm unable to watch closely enough to memorize the sequence of numbers.

When we've all stepped through the door, Veer closes it and seals it from the outside. She then looks up toward a sentry guard standing on top of the wall, who nods down to her.

"We'll enter through the main gates when we come back."

She gestures to me to walk close behind her and I do, my cloak activated, my eyes scanning the landscape around us warily as we head toward the trees.

Peric walks next to me for a moment, staring at my face, but I ignore him. I know he wants to ask about the cloak, but I have no intention of telling him anything. He can stew in his envy, for all I care.

"I'm sure you still have some questions for me," Veer tells me over her shoulder as we advance. Her voice is hushed but not quite a whisper, as though she's relatively confident there are no listening ears close at hand. "We haven't had a chance to talk much since your arrival."

"I do have questions," I admit as I pick up my pace to walk beside her. "A lot of them, actually. Like, the girl I saw yesterday at the Finishing Ceremony...Samantha."

"Yes? What about her?"

"Where did she go when she left here?"

She stares straight ahead when she says, "You may think you want that answer. But trust me when I say you don't. Now, I believe we're done with the questions."

12

THE CHALET

We hike for some time, mostly in a tense silence. I catch the occasional glare from Peric out of the corner of my eye, but I don't really care at this point if he despises me. I don't need to be his friend, and I sure as hell don't need him to be mine.

We arrive at our destination after an hour and a half spent pushing our way through thick, overgrown woods leading up the side of the mountain. The landscape is a sea of lush green, which is both refreshing and soothing in stark contrast with any wariness our small group is feeling. It's like this part of the world has ignored the entropy that's taken over the Mire and so many other places, and instead has opted to flourish in its own quiet isolation.

The treetops are a shield, a fragile barrier between us and the Directorate's watchful eyes. I'm grateful for their gift—though unsure how effective they really are. My cloak hides my body heat, but the others are sitting ducks if a heat-seeking drone chooses to fly directly overhead.

Fortunately, we don't hear the familiar buzz of patrol drones. The only thing that greets our ears as we climb is the pleasant sound of birds chirping, which *should* relax and comfort me. But instead, a warning has begun to churn through my insides, as though I can feel someone watching us from afar.

Apparently Peric isn't so worried, though.

"I'm confused about something," he tells me, his breath heavy as he hikes up the steep terrain beside me.

"What's that?" I ask.

"Why *aren't* they looking for you? The Directorate, I mean."

It sounds like an innocent enough question, but I can tell without asking that it's an accusation. The fact that I'm not being stalked at every turn is proof, in his mind, that I'm in league with the enemy. "I thought you were some precious commodity. The daughter of the great Oliver Spencer should be worth something, but it looks like they've just discarded you like trash. Why do you think that is?"

"I guess because I'm trash," I reply under my breath, my eyes scanning our surroundings warily. "Now you know the truth."

He snickers. "I already had my suspicions. It was good to hear you admit it, though."

When we get to the edge of the woods, Veer hushes us and tells us to duck down behind some shrubs. We do so, edging forward, where I realize we have an excellent view of what looks like a large, multi-building ski resort.

We're greeted by a series of what probably used to be pretty wooden buildings, which are now covered in invasive, snaking vines. The dirt road leading to them, no doubt once overrun by luxurious SUVs, is now overgrown with dense weeds.

Veer leads us along a winding path until we reach the main

building, whose windows are shattered like so many in the Bastille.

"What's the plan?" I ask her. "Why are we here?"

"This place served as a lookout of sorts for the Directorate until quite recently. The main building is filled with surveillance equipment, and I want to see if it still works."

"It can't possibly. Why would they leave it behind for other people to use?"

"Much of it is useless to them at this point," Veer says. "The tech's not very advanced—not very valuable to the Directorate, but useful for us. From here, we have eyes all over the country."

As my vision adjusts to the darkness inside what used to be a ski shop, Veer makes her way over to a long desk covered in flat screens of various sizes. She reaches out and presses a button, and the screens flare to life.

"They're solar-powered," she tells me. "The roof tiles above us are the power source."

She inputs a series of passwords, and I find myself curious to know how she has access to information only the Directorate should know.

"I have my ways," she says as if reading my mind as she scans the images in front of her.

I've grown used to the holographic screens in the Arc, so these old-school ones look ancient and unwieldy in comparison. Still, the images they show us are crystal clear.

Veer stares for a long moment at the screens, and I ease behind her to peruse them over her shoulder. At first, I only see a view of the Bastille from above, no doubt from a camera set up on the mountain.

But as she moves through a menu on the right side of the main screen, more images pop up. I gasp when I see the familiar multi-colored wall surrounding the Mire. In its shadow, houses like my family's sit abandoned and hopeless while the Directorate's patrols wander the streets.

But it's when Veer types a few words in and a new image crops up that I find myself stunned into silence.

Another set of walls appears, surrounding another city. These ones aren't solid concrete like the Mire's, but a sort of tightly-woven metallic grid. Warning signs hang here and there that seem to indicate the wall—or is it a fence?—is electrically charged.

"Where is that?" I ask.

"Manhattan," Veer replies. "It's quite something, isn't it? I've heard the wall is a hundred feet high."

I step back, horrified to realize the rumors are true: as far away as the east coast, the Directorate has taken control. The sight disturbs me more than I can say. New York is a city known for its residents' rebellious natures, and the idea that the Directorate has conquered their spirits is soul-crushing.

As Veer navigates her way through more camera views, I see an enormous arcology rising in the center of the city in what looks like old Central Park. The building takes up almost the entire landscape—the entirety of what used to be open, lush green space.

"How..." I stammer. "Is that..."

"Another Directorate stronghold? Yes, it is."

"You really didn't know about New York?" Peric asks, his tone mocking. "There's an Arc in every major city. I would've thought the almighty Oliver Spencer's daughter would be aware of that, at least."

"Hush, boy," Veer says in a patronizing tone. "Can't you see she's in shock?"

"I guess I suspected it," I reply. "I just...I didn't know the Blight had made it that far east. I was hoping..."

"The Directorate has spread its power far and wide," Veer says. "Their reach is immense. Perhaps now you can see why we can't afford to take them on. Why we have to find ways to appease them. They're simply too powerful, Ashen."

"I *know* they're powerful. But if no one challenges them, how will anyone ever overthrow them?"

"Maybe no one will. Maybe we shouldn't. The fact is, the Arcologies have proven a benefit to our world in many ways. They keep people from destroying the land. Look how this mountain has healed and flourished—how the forests, the streams are healthy now. There are no cars on the roads. No factories belching out smoke. Maybe this is all a blessing in disguise."

I stare at her, taken aback. Surely she can't mean this. The Directorate, good for society? Keeping people convinced of a destructive lie and planting fear inside them, convincing them to abandon their homes and leave their lives and friends behind...

How can these be *good* things?

"Do you see anything?" Piper asks when Veer shifts the screens to views of the chalet we're standing in.

As she scrolls, I recognize the entrance we came through and the destroyed road outside, as well as the pathways leading to the neighboring buildings.

At first, all looks quiet and peaceful, and I'm beginning to wonder what she's expecting to see.

But a flicker of movement on the second screen from the right grabs my attention. I move over and stare, certain at first that I've imagined it. Then I see it clearly: One figure, then another, moving in a crouch toward our location, rifles in hand.

"Directorate Guard?" I ask in a whisper as Veer joins me.

"They're wearing the Guard uniforms," she says, reaching into her backpack and withdrawing a handgun. "See the rose?"

I squint at the screen, noting something small and shiny on the left side of each man's chest.

Damn it.

Veer turns to the others and whispers, "We need to get out of here. If they find us, we're as good as dead. Understood?"

Piper and Peric nod. Veer shuts down the screens and heads for the front door.

"Isn't there a back exit?" I ask, trying to keep my voice down.

"No," she replies. "There used to be, but it was welded shut years ago by the bastards out there. We have no choice but to head out the front."

I follow the others, my cloak pulled around my body and face, its camouflage setting activated. As my three companions slip out the door and around the building, I turn to face the two men who are still headed slowly in our direction. They're young—maybe twenty—and look frightened. They're dressed in faded black uniforms that don't entirely fit their bodies. One is too baggy, the other too tight, like they accidentally swapped them this morning when they got out of bed.

For a moment I stand still, staring, wondering if I should talk to them, try and convince them to let us go.

You were once Dregs.

Weren't you?

But Peric's hissed whisper breaks me free of my idealistic fantasy.

"Ash! Get over here!"

I turn toward him, and even as I do, one of the men picks up his pace and begins jogging in our direction.

When I've joined Peric beside the building, I ask where Veer and Piper are.

"Gone," he tells me. "Headed for the woods, probably."

"Why did you wait around?"

"Because I'm an idiot. Now come on!"

We begin to run, our legs carrying us toward the edge of the woods that lead down the mountain. We're almost under the cover of the trees when I hear shouts behind us and the nauseating sound of a buzzing drone.

Peric grabs me and pulls me under a coarse shrub, pushing me down toward the ground. Thinking fast, I pull my cloak around him, squeezing him tight to my body. It feels strange and forbidden, touching him like this. We don't like each other. We can barely *tolerate* one another. But I'm not about to let any Directorate bastards hurt someone who's as close to an ally as I've got.

I hardly dare lift my chin off the ground as a large drone—bigger than any I ever saw inside the Arc—flies directly over us, pausing only for a few seconds before proceeding.

"I think it's gone," Peric whispers after several seconds. His face is millimeters from mine, his breath tickling at the loose hair around my ears.

"It's not," I reply, pointing. "Look."

The drone is some distance away, maybe a hundred feet, its rounded eye-like lens pointing toward the edge of the woods.

As I shift my gaze, I catch sight of Veer. She's standing at the forest's border, but as the drone approaches, she steps out, exposing herself entirely to its line of sight.

"What is she doing?" I ask, pushing myself to my feet. "She'll be killed!"

Without thinking, I take off in a sprint, pulling my knife from its sheath and preparing to hurl it at the flying mechanical predator. But I've only run a few feet when Veer holds up a hand, palm facing me. She's shaking her head slowly, as if issuing me a warning.

She says something then, eyes locked on the drone's camera. Holding up two fingers, she continues to talk as though she's conveying information, then backs away once again.

The drone rises into the air and takes off over the woods.

"What the hell…?" I ask.

Peric, who's behind me now, replies, "I don't know what that was about. But we've got a problem." He nods toward the resort.

I turn my head to see the two uniformed men crouching behind a half-shattered window in one of the smaller buildings. Their eyes are locked on the drone, and as it disappears, one of them says something to the other, who nods before they both duck out of sight.

"Why didn't the drone attack Veer?" I ask. "Why did those men look like they were scared of it?"

"I have no idea. My mother is a master negotiator, but even *she* knows how dangerous the Directorate's drones are out here. They don't care who we are—if you're not wearing Directorate uniforms, you're dead. We should get out of here before those two men have a chance to come after us."

With a relieved exhale, I start jogging toward the place where Veer disappeared into the woods. Peric shoots me a look—I can't tell if it's one of gratitude or annoyance—as he joins me.

We're nearly at the tree line when a deafening gunshot rings through the air, echoing off the mountainside, and Peric slams face-first into the ground.

13

TROUBLE

I CAN'T TELL if Peric has been hit or not—only that he's lying in the dirt, groaning in pain.

I twist around to see the two men in Directorate gear sprinting our way. One, a man with dark, shaggy hair, has a handgun pulled, his rifle slung over his shoulder. The other looks like he wants to punch me in the face or strangle me... or both.

What I can't figure out is why they didn't just shoot us both from where they stood.

Then I remember: *The Directorate wants me breathing.* I'm no good to them dead, after all. There's no sport in bringing a corpse back to the Arc, not when they can toy with me instead.

I thrust myself between the attackers and Peric, who's trying in vain to push himself up with his left arm. His right shoulder is bleeding, though from the looks of it, not badly.

"Stay down," I tell him. "Don't move, whatever happens."

"What are you—" he begins to say, but I hiss at him to be quiet.

The first of the two men runs at me, clearly expecting the ensuing collision to knock me off my feet. I thrust my arm out, stopping him easily with the heel of my hand to his chest. As he gasps for breath, he aims his gun at Peric's head. Shouting a panicked cry, I grab him by his loose-fitting jacket, throw him to the ground, and kick the gun out of his hand.

The other man, shocked, freezes for a second before lunging at me, his fist flying at my face. Kicking my leg out, I catch him in the torso before he can make contact.

He goes flying backwards, landing hard on the ground next to his companion.

Even now, I'm astounded by Finn's remarkable suit, by how much it amplifies my meager strength. But I don't have time to revel in the surge of power; the first man is back on his feet and, convinced my first victory was a fluke, he leaps at me.

This time he catches me off guard and I go tumbling backwards with him on top of me, his fingers clutching my uniform by the collar as my robe twists around me.

He's just yanked his arm back, preparing to slam his clenched fist into my face, when I hear Peric's voice.

"Get off her. Now."

He's standing behind the soldier, the gun in his hand. I watch in horror as he presses the weapon to the man's temple and cocks it.

Raising his hands in the air, my assailant climbs off me and slowly turns to face Peric.

I leap to my feet, nodding to let Peric know I'm okay. The man I kicked is on his back on the ground, still trying to catch his breath.

"Why are you here?" I ask the intruders. When both men fail to answer, I step toward the one who's lying on the ground and place my foot on his chest, slowly increasing the pressure. He looks up at me, terror written all over his face. "Did they send you to look for me?" I snarl.

"To look for you?" the man on the ground croaks. "We don't even know who you are."

"Then why are you here?"

"We're—"

Before he can say anything more, he's interrupted by the startling ring of a gunshot cracking through the air. He freezes, tightening under the oppressive sense of danger.

"Shut your mouth," a woman's voice snarls from somewhere behind me. "Don't you say another word, or the next bullet will land between your eyes."

I spin around to see Veer emerging from the woods just ahead of Piper. Veer's face is twisted into a look of determined rage, the gun pointing straight at the soldier's face.

"These two will be our prisoners," she tells Peric and me. "We'll bring them back to the Bastille with us."

"That's insane," Peric protests. "The drone's long gone. We should just kill them. What good are they to us?"

"They possess vital information."

"Are you kidding me? We don't even know if they're even—"

Veer steps forward and issues her son a stern look of warning. "We're bringing them to the Bastille," she repeats. "Do you understand me?"

Peric pulls his eyes to the ground and nods, his mouth clamping shut.

Veer grabs one of the young men and tells Peric to gag him. She keeps the gun aimed at the prisoner, and judging from the hatred in her eyes, I have no doubt she'll follow through on her promise to shoot both soldiers if they dare speak another word.

"Gag him with what?"

"Anything. Doesn't matter."

Peric takes off his jacket, which is stained with blood, and stares at it, lost.

"Here," I say, handing him my blade. "Use this to tear the stitches and rip the sleeves off."

He obeys, tearing the first sleeve into two pieces before tying them around the man's head, the fabric cutting at his mouth like a horse's bit. He does the same to the other man before ripping off more strips to bind their hands behind their backs.

I watch the young men with more sympathy than I probably should as I recall what the Directorate does to many of its foot soldiers. *Drugs them to keep them compliant. Trains them to hunt people like me down, to drag us to the Hold to be punished in a private show of brutality.*

I want to feel a smug satisfaction at watching these two young men being taken captive, but I can't. They're probably former Dregs, like me. Probably scared, both of what Veer might do to them and what the Directorate will do if they ever see them again.

Peric grabs hold of one of the men's bonds with his left hand. Piper grabs the other.

"You three, take them back down to the Bastille," Veer tells us when the two prisoners are secured. "I'm going to stay behind and double-check the monitor feeds again, in case they tell us what these two were doing here."

"Shouldn't you ask *them* that?" I blurt out, disturbed that Veer would leave us to herd two would-be killers down the side of a mountain while she lingers behind.

She levels me with a hostile look. "You think these men would tell us the truth? You're more naive than I thought, Ashen."

"You shouldn't stay here alone, Mom," Peric protests. I can see the fear in his eyes. "There could be more. That drone...I thought it was going to..."

For the first time since I met him, Peric seems wholly human and vulnerable. A boy concerned about his mother's safety. It's almost—*almost*—endearing.

"I'll be fine," she tells him with a reassuring smile before turning to me. "Ashen, would you give us a moment, please?"

I nod, glancing at Peric to make sure he's all right before moving out of earshot. I watch as Veer puts a hand on her son's good shoulder and whispers something in his ear. He replies, then nods.

Silent as usual, Piper is standing nearby, but I have no idea if she's heard the interaction. All I know is that when Veer summons me back over, she and Peric both look more at ease than they did a minute earlier.

"I won't be far behind you," Veer assures us. "You know the drill, Per. Just signal the guards when you're close to the main gates, and they'll open them for you. I'll follow soon, I promise."

Peric looks like he wants to say something more, but he shuts his mouth and nods.

I watch Veer, puzzled when I see her shoot a final, cryptic look of warning Piper's way. But I tell myself I must be imagining it, because a minute later, Veer's whistling happily as she heads back up toward the chalet and we're striding into the woods with the two silent prisoners in front of us.

As we begin our downhill hike, a low hoot greets my ears. I look up to see the silver owl soaring overhead, his face pulled down unnaturally toward mine, like he's issuing me a warning of his own.

I'm not sure if it's a trick of the light when his eyes flash red for the briefest moment before he flies away, disappearing over the treetops.

14

RETURN

BACK IN THE BASTILLE, Piper sends Peric off to get his shoulder bandaged and then enlists the help of a few of the snipers to secure the prisoners in what she calls the "Sub-Bastille," a narrow corridor in the same Bunker that houses Veer's office.

I follow them down until we reach a steel door embedded in the thick stone wall, which Piper opens with a key she carries on a chain around her neck. The corridor where we end up is narrow enough that we have to walk single file. It's lit only by a single, flickering bulb dangling from the ceiling.

To one side are a series of small doors, also made of steel. Piper has a sniper open one before shoving the first prisoner inside. I can see nothing in the room but darkness, and the man goes tumbling in, landing on cold stone before Piper slams the door shut again without so much as removing the makeshift gag still strapped around his head.

"Will they have light?" I ask. "Food?"

"I don't know why you care," Piper tells me, her tone chilly.

"I care because they're human."

"Trust me. They're not."

She treats the second prisoner with the same disdain as the first, shutting him into a cell two doors down from the first one before leading us back up the corridor.

"These cells were here when we took over the Bastille," she tells me as we go. "The Directorate built them."

"Are there other prisoners in here?" I ask, horrified to think the answer could be yes.

"No." Piper shakes her head. "Taking prisoners isn't really our style. But if they might be in possession of valuable information, that's another story. Veer makes the calls."

"What information could these two possibly possess? The Directorate Guard's soldiers don't know anything. They're just sheep. They obey orders and barely think for themselves...and if they *do,* it's usually only about how awesome their overlords are."

Piper stops and turns my way, her jaw tense. "Veer has her reasons, and you'd do well not to question them. Now, if I were you, I'd head to the Mess and find some food. You must be hungry after that hike."

I nod silently, annoyed that I'm being kept in the dark once again.

I'm also confused.

It makes no sense for Veer to treat those men so badly, not if she's trying to stay in the Directorate's good graces. It's like she's *challenging* them to punish her.

But why? Why would she put this town and everyone in it at risk?

When we've reached the main corridor, I turn without a word to leave the Bunker and head to the Mess, hoping to find answers elsewhere.

When I arrive, I spot Peric sitting at a table with Cyntra. He's wearing a t-shirt with one sleeve cut away, his bicep and shoulder wrapped tightly in white gauze.

"Are you all right?" I ask as I sit down across from him.

He nods. "It's just a scratch. Two stitches. It'll be fine."

"I hear you risked your life to save him from those bastards," Cyntra tells me. "You're quite the badass, Miss Ashen."

"Not really," I chuckle. "I just did what anyone would have."

Peric shakes his head. "They would've killed me if you hadn't been there. You and I both know it."

Something in his voice has changed, softened, like his hatred for me has finally abated.

"I'm not so sure—they didn't seem to want to kill either of us. If they had, they would have stayed back and fired their rifles instead of running at us. They wanted something else entirely, I think."

"Well, whatever it is, I'm glad you didn't let them have it," Cyntra says. She puts an arm around Peric, who winces slightly. "This guy may be a jerk-face, but he's *our* jerk-face, and I want him around a little longer."

"Thanks, Cyn," Peric says, pulling away from her and rolling his eyes at me as if to say, "Kids, am I right?"

"Those prison cells in the Bunker," I ask, choosing to ignore their awkward one-sided flirtation, "have you used them a lot?"

Peric shakes his head. "I told you, you're the first outsider we've brought into the Bastille in years. Then again, we haven't been threatened recently. Not until you showed up." I expect him to sneer at me, but instead he chuckles. "You're quite the liability, you know."

"I know, and I'm sorry. I didn't come here to screw things up for any of you. But as I recall, you brought me here, so technically, this is your fault."

"Stop it, you two," Cyntra says. I'm not sure if she actually thinks we're bickering or is simply annoyed that we're getting along.

"Fine," Peric mutters. "Listen—those two men...If they're Directorate Guard, they're far from their usual patrol zone. Which means they're here for you, Ash, regardless of what they said up there. So you need to be careful."

"You said *if* they're Directorate Guard," I tell him. "If they're not, what are they?"

Peric looks like he wants to answer my question, but instead he tightens his jaw and looks away. "I'm just being stupid. Of course they were Directorate. My mother said they were, and she would know. Which only proves we need to be vigilant. We can't afford to piss the Directorate off."

"So much drama in the Bastille," Cyntra says with a laugh. "Ashen Spencer, at least you've brought us some excitement."

"I would have loved to leave all the excitement behind, believe me. I've had enough to last me several lifetimes."

"Yeah, well," Peric says, "I'd like to know why it is that the whole world flips upside down when you're around."

"It's simple," Cyntra says. "She's more important than we are. More interesting."

"That's not the reason," I reply as a flood of wretched memories comes surging back to me.

"Then what is?"

"I nearly killed the King and Queen's son, for one thing."

"What?" Cyntra gasps, her eyes going wide.

"I second that *what*," Peric adds. "I mean, what the hell?"

"There was a fight...on my last night in the Arc. One that

the Directorate forced me to participate in—a sort of gladiator battle. Randolph—that's the King's son—was supposed to kill me to prove the Aristocracy's supremacy over us Dregs. But I…sort of threw my knife at him. They weren't too happy about that."

Peric and Cyntra stare at me, their jaws dropping open for a few seconds before Peric bursts into hysterical fits of laugher.

Cyntra, on the other hand, looks horrified.

"You really did that?" Peric finally manages to ask. "Seriously?"

I nod. "Seriously. In my defense, he was a real ass."

"Of course he was. Rumor has it the King has always been awful. I'm not surprised to hear his son is a piece of work."

"Awful?" Cyntra snaps, her brows meeting. "The King and the Directorate are responsible for building the Arc, for saving millions of people!"

"Wait," I reply, too stunned by her reaction to think straight. "Are you really still defending the Directorate? The people who shot Peric in the arm? Are you serious right now?"

"It's not the King's fault Peric was shot! It's not the Directorate's fault, either. I know it and Veer knows it."

"Cyntra, I saw the roses on their uniforms," I tell her. "Whose fault do you think it was?"

She locks her eyes on mine, a strange malevolence growing in her glare. "If you had half a brain, you'd know perfectly well whose fault it was," she says under her breath, her voice feral. "But you see the world through this perfect little Ashen Spencer lens. You think everything is black and white, that there's one bad guy and everyone else is good and right. But you don't know anything. You're ignorant, and it's going to get you killed. Just you wait."

Cyntra has always seemed almost innocently sweet in her adoration of the Directorate and her idealization of the Arc. But right now, stripped of the mask of purity, I see another side of her, a spiteful edge that reminds me a little too acutely of the Duchess.

"Is that a threat?" I ask. "Because it sounded a lot like one."

"Not a threat," she retorts. "A guarantee."

With that, she pushes herself to her feet and storms out of the Mess, today's flouncy dress bouncing merrily in an almost comical contradiction of her rage.

"When did sweet little Cyntra turn into Satan's Little Helper?" I ask, sitting back in my seat.

"Don't mind her," Peric says with a wave of his good hand. "She's always had it in her head that the Arc is heaven and everyone in it is an angel. She *worships* the Directorate."

"You don't seem bothered by that. Which is weird, given what happened this morning."

"It's...complicated," Peric replies, to my surprise. "As is our relationship with those people."

"Well, you and I just helped make it a lot less complicated. We just took two of them prisoner, which means we can probably expect a drone attack at any moment. And I hate to tell you, but even the best snipers won't be able to stop it."

"I wouldn't worry about it," Peric says, leaning back in his seat, a smug look on his face.

"Oh? Why's that?"

"Like I told you up on the mountain, my mother is a master negotiator. She can talk her way out of anything. She'll find a way to send those men back to wherever they need to go, wipe her hands of it, and that'll be it."

I shake my head. "Whatever the weirdos around here may think, the Directorate is pure evil. They don't just forgive people who have taken their soldiers prisoner. They've killed my friends for far less."

"Like I said, it's complicated." Peric leans toward me, his eyes locking on mine. "Look, I wish I could tell you more—I really do. You deserve to know. It's just..."

"Just what?"

He looks around briefly before murmuring, "I don't know if you remember when we first brought you here, and I told you the code of ethics in this place is different from what most people are used to."

"I remember."

"That's the complication."

"Okay, you've lost me, Peric. What are you talking about?"

"Like I said, I wish I could tell you more." He inhales a deep breath, looks me in the eye, bites his lip, and pushes himself to his feet. "Thank you again for saving my life. I know I give you a hard time, but I am genuinely grateful for what you did. Someday I hope to repay the favor."

"It's fine," I mutter, irritated. *If you want to repay me, tell me what you were talking about. Tell me more about the Bastille's twisted relationship with the Directorate.*

Help me understand.

Peric is staring down at me with renewed interest, as well as something vaguely resembling admiration. I'm taken aback, confused and slightly disturbed by the affectionate expression that's taken up residence on his features.

But after a moment, he turns away and says he's going to go watch for Veer's return. "I'll see you, life-saver," he tells me with a wave as he walks away.

When he's about to reach the front door, a woman of about forty steps over to the table and takes a seat opposite me.

"Well, well. Somebody's smitten," she says.

My cheeks heat when I realize Peric has turned to look back at me. "*I'm* not smitten, if that's what you're implying," I retort.

"Not at all. I was implying that *he* has the hots for *you*."

I glance at the woman. She's pretty, her hair pulled back into a tight bun, her skin damaged from the sun. Like so many of the other Matrons, she's wearing a dress of a dull mud color.

I snort out an inadvertent laugh. "That's ridiculous. Peric hates me."

The woman shakes her head. "Hardly. I know worship when I see it."

I sit back, my insides tangling in confusion. Peric did risk his life today to help me. I suppose if he truly hated me, he could have just fled into the woods and left me to be captured, or worse.

"I have someone in my life," I tell the woman. "Someone I care about."

"Oh? Who might that be?"

"Long story," I reply, confused as to why she's showing so much interest in me. I don't even know her name.

She leans forward. "I have nothing but time. You don't have to say a word, of course. But if you'd like to talk about him—if you miss him..."

"I do miss him," I confess. *More than I can say.*

"Tell me about him, then."

I look into her eyes, amused at how genuinely interested

she seems. I don't think I've ever had anyone aside from Finn or Kel look so fascinated or curious to know what was going through my mind.

"I'm sorry. I don't know your name…"

"Norah," she tells me, holding out a hand. I shake it, a smile growing on my face in appreciation of the normality of this interaction. She has a calming presence and a warmth that make me feel like I'm sitting in front of a cozy fire, and it's nice to relax for a moment.

"Now tell me about him," she says again.

"He's…tall," I begin. It's hardly the most impressive thing about Finn, but it's the simplest. It paints the beginnings of a picture.

"Dark, handsome. Yes, yes. I know. Tell me about what's inside him."

"You mean like his digestive tract?" I laugh.

"His soul."

I take a deep breath. "He's kind, protective. He hates what the Directorate has done, even though he's very close to it. He wants to fight them, to change how things are. He's the reason I got out of the Arc. The reason I'm here at all."

"Then we owe him our thanks for helping you make your way to our little town."

"I owe him everything. I just wish I could talk to him."

"I'll bet you do," she says with a wink. "And then some."

I want to reprimand her for what she's implying. But the truth is I have been thinking constantly about Finn's lips. About their softness, the heat that floods my bloodstream when they caress my own. The weightlessness when he touches me, when he speaks softly, intimately.

Norah's not wrong—I want to do *much* more than talk to Finn.

But it's all a fantasy. A dream.

As much as it hurts to admit it to myself, I may never see him again.

Shaking off the thought, I push myself to my feet. "I'm going to head to my room. It was nice talking to you, Norah. Maybe I'll see you around."

"Maybe," she says with a smile.

When I get up to my room a few minutes later, Peric is outside my door, pacing the hallway as he waits for me.

"My mother made it back," he says. "She wants to see you in her office in the Bunker."

"Oh?" For some reason, I feel like I'm being called to speak to the principal. But I tell myself to calm down; Veer probably just wants to thank me for keeping her son from getting killed today.

"I...don't know what it's about." He seems nervous, restless. "I hope everything is okay. My mom can be a little intense."

"I'm sure it'll be fine," I tell him with a smile. "I'll head down there now."

He nods, bites his thumbnail, then turns and leaves, spinning around once like he's going to say something more...but he whirls around again and takes off down the stairs.

Within five minutes I'm at the Bunker's door. A Matron opens it for me and guides me down to Veer's sunlit office.

Veer smiles up at me when I enter and asks how I'm doing.

"I'm fine."

"Glad to hear it. Listen, I wanted to thank you for all you

did today—for taking those men down. My son could have received far worse than a simple flesh wound."

"It was the least I could do."

"Well, I want you to know what it means to me to see you in action like that. You proved your loyalty today in no uncertain terms. Not that I ever doubted Oliver's daughter, of course. Your father always did despise the Directorate in an almost pathological way."

"With good reason."

"If you say so."

My brow furrows. *How is she not more angry, more passionate about this? She just said those men would have killed her son on the mountain. How does she not hate their leaders just as much as I do?*

What grim hold does the Directorate have over the Bastille's population?

"Did you get what you needed when you went back into the chalet?" I ask.

"Hmm?"

"You went back in to look for something. I was wondering if you were successful."

"Oh—yes, thanks. Very."

"Good." I stare at her for a few seconds, biting my lip nervously.

"Was there something else?" she asks.

I tense up before exhaling. "The prisoners we brought down here today..."

"What about them?"

"They've probably been in the Arc recently, so they might know something about my brother Kel, about what's happened to him. I was wondering if I could speak to them."

Veer's jaw clenches before she offers up another smile. "I'm afraid that won't be possible. Those men are dangerous. They tried to kill you, not to mention my son—in case you've forgotten."

"But they're your prisoners," I protest. "They have no weapons. They can't hurt anyone. Please, it's important. I need to know Kel's all right."

"The answer is no." Veer's tone is icy cold and final, and I know better than to argue with her. "However," she adds with a strange little smile, "I have some good news for you and everyone else. Tonight, we're going to have a public dance in the Piazza at the center of town."

"A dance?" I ask, irritated. *You think a dance will make me forget my brother is in danger?*

She nods. "Today's mission, while risky, was successful, and I think we should celebrate. I hope you'll attend. Cyntra will be glad to lend you a dress, I'm sure."

I raise an eyebrow, shocked. What exactly do we have to celebrate, other than taking two men—who apparently aren't going to offer us any information of value—prisoner?

"With all due respect, I'm far more interested in my brother's safety than in a dance, Veer."

She balls her hands into tight fists, looking like she's going to bring them down hard on her desk. But instead, she opens them and forces another smile onto her lips. "I'll tell you what, Ashen—I'll talk to the men for you. I'll ask about your brother and glean any information I can. I suppose it wouldn't hurt."

"Really?"

She nods. "Really."

It's all I can do not to run around her desk and hug her jubilantly. "Thank you so much. I can't tell you what it means to me."

"Well, you saved my son today. I suppose we can call it even. Now go, have a nice time. I'll see you at the dance."

Nodding, I leave, practically skipping my way out of the room. It's entirely possible the men won't know anything, but at least there's a tiny morsel of hope working its way through my mind.

Hope—however slight—means more to me than any dance ever could.

15

DANCE

As Veer predicted, Cyntra comes to me after dinner with a pair of cream-colored shoes and a long dress. Emerald green and flowing, the garment looks like something out of a dreamy fairy tale.

"I'm sorry for how I acted earlier," she says as she holds out the apparent peace offering. "In the Mess."

What I want to say is, *For some completely unhinged reason, you think highly of the organization responsible for the deaths of thousands and thousands of people. You're a brainwashed drone.*

But instead, I simply tell her, "It's fine. You have your opinions, I have mine. I've seen things you haven't. But maybe someday, you'll understand."

"Maybe," she replies with a smile, seemingly relieved. "Anyhow, I shouldn't have said those things. It was unkind of me."

She utters the apology like an actress reciting rehearsed lines. But I nod my acceptance, unwilling to dwell on the matter any longer.

She bounces on her toes as she hands me the dress.

"It will look so good with your eyes and hair," she squeaks. "I absolutely love it."

"It's very pretty. But not really my style..."

"Oh, come on. You wear that stupid uniform every day. Have some fun. Let your hair down."

I take it reluctantly, knowing full well that putting on the dress means leaving safety behind. It means rendering myself vulnerable to attack for only the second time since my arrival in the Bastille.

But Cyntra looks so excited to have an excuse to doll me up that I surrender and grin back at her.

"I'll get ready, then," I tell her. "Promise you'll meet me at the dance? I find these things awkward, to say the least."

"Of course. And don't worry—it won't be much of a dance, really. It's not like there's anyone around to choose for partners. Except Peric, and getting him to dance is like getting a squirrel to..."

"*Dance?*" I ask with a laugh.

"Pretty much, yeah."

"Well, I don't expect Peric will want to dance with me. So he's all yours for the night."

"I *wish.* I may be in love with my future husband, but Peric is the one I'd be with if I could actually choose." She lets out a lovesick sigh. "Look—I'm going to my room to change. I'll meet you in the Piazza, all right?"

"Sure. See you in a bit."

She nods, bouncing up and down again as if possessed by an excitement she can't quite keep from exploding out of her every pore. "See you!"

When I've changed into the dress and shoes, I fold my uniform and cloak and put them into my backpack, along with my sheathed knife. After ten or so minutes have passed, I carry the pack with me down to the building's back door.

Outside is a series of old empty garbage cans and a rusty dumpster. I conceal the pack behind the dumpster and make my way toward the square at the center of town.

The Piazza is the site of a destroyed block of buildings, remnants of their foundations still visibly outlined along the ground. In the daytime, it's usually full of comfortable seating —bean bag chairs, old couches, all manner of soft furnishings so people can lounge around in the afternoons.

But on this night, Veer's people have transformed it into something else. Emptied of all seating and hanging with sparkling, solar-powered lights twisted around lamp posts, it's morphed into a sort of dreamy elfin paradise.

As I walk around its perimeter, my eyes find Peric, who's standing across the way, his gaze fixed on me. He's dressed up for once, wearing a pair of black pants and a white button-down shirt with the collar undone and the sleeves rolled up.

Much as he and I have always had a difficult relationship, I can't deny that he's a sight for sore eyes.

Between us are thirty or so Bastille residents, each of them consumed in conversation, their faces lit up joyfully. For some reason, I find it surprising and slightly off-putting to see a bunch of adults looking so thrilled about a dance.

But I suppose they don't exactly get many chances to celebrate small victories. Locked inside this town, it's not like they can travel or see old friends. This is probably the highlight of their social year.

His chin lowered, Peric walks over to me and on instinct I find myself shuffling my feet, bracing for whatever criticism he plans to level my way.

To my surprise, he stops a few feet from me and grins.

"You look…good," he says. "*Really* good."

"Um, thanks," I reply, trying not to sound baffled. Compliments from him feel unnaturally twisted, like they can't possibly mean what they *seem* to mean. "Are we really here to celebrate taking those men prisoner?"

He shrugs. "Sure. But it's probably not just about that. My mom's got something up her sleeve—I'm not sure what, though. She doesn't normally get this excited about *anything*."

As he's speaking, a few musicians begin to play behind us on a wooden platform. A fiddle player, a guitarist, and a singer have all gathered to improvise a jaunty Irish tune together.

"Want to dance?" Peric asks.

I look over to see that others are beginning to pair up and lock hands. Matrons dressed in brighter colors than usual, coupled with men in jeans and white shirts. It all looks oddly prim and proper, as if an informal gathering has turned into a strangely formal affair.

"I don't think…" I begin, looking around for Cyntra. "I…"

"You can just say no," Peric tells me with a chuckle.

"No, it's fine. Let's dance."

When he holds his hand out, I take it and let him guide me out to the floor. With the touch of his hand on mine, my vulnerability rears its head again. Peric has run hot and cold since the moment I met him—mostly cold. It's hard not to recoil at his touch. I still remember the looks he gave me that first day—the desire I saw in his eyes to take me down and show me who was boss.

But instead of aggression, he pulls me close as the fiddle breaks into a slow, lilting waltz. I feel his body heat in the air between us, his breath on my neck, his hand clasping mine tight—not possessively, but hungrily, as if human touch is something he craves as much as I do.

I'm just stunned that he wants it from *me.*

"I keep thinking about what you did for me up on the mountain," he tells me quietly, his breath stroking my ear. "I really think I would have died out there if it weren't for you."

I find myself shivering, which only seems to inspire him to pull me closer. For some reason I don't resist. Instead, I allow myself to melt into his warmth, to feel comforted by his words instead of wary of his intentions, for once.

But I close my eyes and think of Finn, of how much another man's touch makes me crave him—and only him.

A surge of guilt swells inside me, and I force my eyes open.

"Your mother took me in," I say quickly. "She could have left me out in the woods to die. I wouldn't be much of a human being if I'd let something happen to you."

He pulls away just enough to look into my eyes. "I've been an ass to you, Ash. This whole time, I've doubted you. If you'd asked me yesterday morning if Ashen Spencer would protect me with her life, I would've laughed. I was wrong about you, and I'm sorry."

A strange warmth rushes through my veins, and I understand for the first time why Cyntra is so smitten with Peric. He can be a cold fish, but in moments when he reveals his humanity, I get it. He's not just attractive, but perilously endearing.

Still, he's no Finn, I remind myself with another shiver. *Not even close.*

"It's all right," I tell him, my voice tight. "I've learned that trusting people is dangerous. I don't blame you for not having much faith in me."

"I hope you know you can trust me."

I chew on my lip. "I..."

I'm about to tell him my trust is hard earned when a bell

starts clanging somewhere near the band, bringing the music to an abrupt stop. I pull away from Peric and look over to see that Veer is making her way onto the small platform-stage. She's holding up a glass of something that looks like wine, raising a toast to the crowd.

"Earlier today," she says, "we caught two prisoners while on a surveillance mission on the mountain. At long last, my friends, we have taken two of *them*. Which means we are one step closer to our goal."

The crowd erupts in a chorus of joyful cheers. I look around, puzzled at their jubilance. *Closer to our goal?* There are still fewer than two-hundred of us. It's not like we can suddenly take on the Directorate. Two young members of the Guard won't even be useful as bargaining chips; the Duchess and her cohorts would laugh at the very notion.

So what goal, exactly, is Veer talking about?

"In three days' time, the Reckoning will take place here, in the Piazza, and I will announce our prisoners' fate. By then, I will have extracted any information I need from them. My friends...we *will* win this war yet."

I raise my eyebrows, skeptical. Veer has gone from cautious, protective leader of the Bastille to foolishly optimistic in the course of a day. What exactly did she see up at the chalet that changed her mind? Is there an army marching toward the Arc that I don't know about? Did the prisoners tell her something?

Veer steps off the stage and makes her way toward us, a bright, toothy grin on her lips.

"How are you two doing?" she asks.

"Fine," we reply in unison before I add, "Did you manage to talk to the two men?"

Her smile fades. She nods solemnly. "I did, and I'm sorry, Ashen. They don't know anything about your brother."

She presses a hand to my shoulder before walking away. The music and dancing resume, but I'm in no mood to dance, and apparently neither is Peric, whose eyes are locked on my face.

"Hey," he says softly, leaning in close, "I want to show you something. Some*where*, I mean. You interested?"

"Is it somewhere other than here? Because if so, hell yes, I'm interested."

Something in Veer's eyes, in her voice, set off a deep worry inside me, though I'm not sure what it is that I'm afraid of. My mind and body have melded into a sort of queasy unrest, and all I want is to get as far away as possible.

At a near-jog, Peric leads me away from the Piazza and toward the Bunker.

"You're not taking me to see the prisoners, are you?" I ask. "Because I'm pretty sure your mom would freak."

"No, she'd have my skin for less. I'm not allowed to talk to them either, for obvious reasons."

"Obvious?"

His smile fades as he keeps walking, and for a few seconds, he goes silent. "I mean, one of them *did* shoot me," he finally says with a smirk.

"Right. Fair enough."

When we get to the Bunker, Peric inputs the code and we slip inside. "I hope Cyntra doesn't kill me," I tell him. "I told her we'd see each other at the dance."

"Don't worry—knowing Cyntra, she'll just follow us. She's like a shadow, that one. Always lurking where she hasn't been invited."

"Wait—she knows how to get into the Bunker?"

With a roll of his eyes, Peric says, "She knows *everything*. Cyntra is a pet of my mother's, in case you hadn't noticed. She's the golden child around here. It's why she came on that patrol hike the first time we met you. My mother trusts her with the biggest of the Bastille's secrets. I swear, they tell each other everything."

We make our way into the depths of the Bunker, and Peric leads me along until we come to a sealed door beyond Veer's office, which he unlocks with another code.

I hesitate for a moment before asking, "Why do I get the impression you don't think Cyntra should be trusted?"

"I don't think *anyone* should be trusted," Peric replies, pulling the door open. "But the truth is, I think my mother—Veer—has more faith in her than in me. Make of that what you will."

"Why's that?" I reply as we walk along a long, dark hall with a series of small lights that spark to life as we move, as if detecting our presence.

"I suppose because I've questioned a lot of my mother's decisions over the years. I've challenged her. It irritates her to the point where she doesn't always keep me in the loop anymore. But she's kept us alive against all odds, so I've learned to keep my doubts to myself."

"Yeah, about that..." I reply, hesitant. "About your doubts..."

"Hold that thought," Peric tells me as he guides me through another door. When he opens it, I'm met with a gust of damp, cold air.

"What's this?"

"The tunnel."

"Tunnel?"

"Yeah." We step into darkness and Peric reaches for an

unlit torch on the wall to our right. He flicks a match along the coarse stone wall and brings it to explosive life. "Someone built this years ago—it used to link up with a whole network of underground passageways, they say. But not anymore."

"Why not?"

He shrugs, his shadow reflecting on the wall to our right as he carries the torch in his left hand. "Not sure, but the doors are all welded shut from the other side. All except for one."

We walk for some time in silence before we come to a set of steps leading up to the door Peric was talking about, which looks more like a hatch, embedded at a forty-five-degree angle in the tunnel's ceiling.

When we've climbed up, Peric clicks a small latch and pushes the hatch open. We emerge a moment later into a clearing in the woods, much like the one where the Finishing Ceremony took place. Above us, the moon shines bright, the world around us glowing a soft, decadent blue.

"Wow," I say, stepping out into the night air. I inhale deep, savoring the sensation of temporary freedom.

"Pretty amazing, right?" Peric says. "Only a few people know about this place. It's almost impossible to get here through the woods, but the tunnel makes it easy."

As Peric closes the hatch I turn to watch it conceal itself under a thick layer of dry leaves and long weeds that have attached themselves to its surface over time.

"Do you come out here a lot?" I ask, snickering when I realize it sounds like a cheesy pickup line.

"Only when my mother pisses me off…or when I have some special reason."

With that, he sets the still burning torch against a boulder-sized rock jutting up from the ground, its flame dancing in the air.

I seat myself on top of the rock, pulling my knees up under my chin.

"Can I tell you something?" Peric asks. "Something a little...personal?"

"Sure."

"I don't think my mother has ever told me the whole truth about the Bastille. About our enemies."

"You mean the Directorate?"

"No. I mean an enemy out there," he says, nodding toward the mountains. "One that we've been hunting for years. I think she's been hoping you'll lead us to them."

"Lead you? I don't know of anyone in the mountains, and if they're an enemy, I'm sure as hell not about to go toward them."

"When we found you, you said your father left you a clue—you said that's why you headed west from the Mire."

"That's true," I tell him, my body tightening. "But I've told you everything I can about that."

Peric's voice seems to lower an octave when he says, "No, Ash, I don't think you have."

16

QUESTIONS

A HIDEOUS THOUGHT enters my mind—did Peric bring me out here to threaten me? Was the charm he piled on earlier—the compliments, the intimacy—meant to give me a false sense of security?

Fear overtakes me as I pull my knees tight to my chin. I'm still vulnerable to attack in Cyntra's green dress. I don't have my blade or cloak with me. I have no defense out here against someone as strong as the boy who's staring at me right now, an unreadable expression on his features.

"I can't tell you anything more about my father's message," I say in the most forceful tone I can muster.

"I don't want you to," he replies, his voice softening, to my relief. A few feet away from me he begins to pace, and my eyes are drawn to movement in the sky above us. A glimmer of something shiny—the owl, flying over us in circles as if he's watching, listening, scrutinizing.

I can't explain why but I feel suddenly protected, as if by a force I don't entirely understand.

"Then why are you accusing me of concealing something?" I ask, pulling my eyes back to Peric.

"Because there was a time when I thought your reluctance to share would lead to your death or ours."

"What do you mean?"

"The men we caught on the mountain, the ones who shot at us...there's something you should know about them."

"What is it?"

A sudden noise a few feet away draws my attention and I leap off the boulder, tensing into a defensive pose.

A second later, the hatch flies open and Cyntra steps out, a friendly smile on her lips.

Just as Peric predicted.

"There you two are!" she sings. "Bad Ash, you said you'd hang with me at the dance."

"Sorry—I needed a break, and Peric convinced me to go on an adventure," I tell her with a quick, relieved exhale.

"I can't blame you for saying yes," she says, leaping over to him and grabbing his arm, pulling him close. "He's such a handsome thing, isn't he?"

If I didn't know better, I'd think she was tipsy.

"His handsomeness wasn't what made me want to leave the dance," I reply, glancing up at the owl who's still circling overhead. "It was something else entirely."

"Huh. What were you two talking about out here?" Cyntra pulls away from Peric to flit around the clearing. "Are you...conspiring?"

Even as she asks the question, the owl sweeps down into the clearing, dive-bombing her. She shrieks and leaps to her right, landing on her palms on the ground before her winged assailant flies off toward the peaks in the distance.

"What the hell was *that?*" Cyntra cries out, irate as she pushes herself to her feet.

I have to stifle a laugh as Peric asks if she's okay.

"No! That freaking bird tried to kill me!"

"It probably thought you were dinner," I tell her.

"Owls don't hunt humans, smart-ass."

I shrug.

"You're fine, Cyn," Peric says. "But we should probably all head back to the Bastille. It's getting late, and my mother will get cheesed off if she finds out I brought Ash here."

"Or we could send her back and you and I could stay," she tells Peric. "It's so pretty out here in the moonlight."

"I'll get my butt even *more* kicked if I let Ash head back on her own. Rain check?"

"Sure," Cyntra chirps. It seems she's over her owl-induced trauma; her voice has returned to its usual high-pitched sweet self, and she's reverted into a flirty teenage girl.

Heading back inside, we work our way through the tunnel to the Bunker and out onto the street. When we're back in the Piazza, Cyntra asks Peric to dance.

He shoots me a look as if asking for permission. "Go for it," I tell them both. "I'm going to head back to my room and get some rest. I think I've had enough excitement for one day."

Peric pulls away from Cyntra and holds up a hand. "I'll walk Ash to her place. When I get back we can have that dance, okay?"

"You really don't need to," I tell him. "I'm fine."

"Still, it would be my pleasure. Cyntra understands—don't you, Cyn?"

She scowls but nods reluctant approval as Peric and I begin the walk.

"She really likes you, huh?" I ask as we make our way along the street.

"She's a child," he replies coldly. "A volatile one. She'd throw almost anyone in front of a fast-moving train if it meant her rank in society would improve. If she likes me, it's only because I'm Veer's son."

"You think so?"

"I know so. Cyntra's not as sweet as she seems, Ash. You've seen the evidence for yourself."

"I can't deny that. So tell me—why does ambition always turn people into psychopaths?"

"Not always. Look at you."

"Me? I'm not ambitious."

"Oh, come on. You're calm, calculated, and nothing if not ambitious. But you're no psychopath. You're Ashen Spencer, the girl who wants to go to war against the Directorate."

"Hey—I've never said I want to go to war."

Not out loud, at least.

"On that one front, you're an open book, Ash. You wear your Directorate-hating heart on your sleeve—which is risky around here." As we stop in front of the ski shop, he turns to me and adds, "I know your heart's desire."

I chuckle. "Oh yeah? What is it that I desire, then?"

"Stability. Family. Safety. Happiness."

I raise an eyebrow. "Okay, but everybody wants those things. What else?"

"You want for the Directorate to pay for what they've done to you—even though you know it might get you killed."

At that, I turn away, averting my eyes, which sting all of a sudden with hot tears.

"I may not know the whole story," Peric says softly, "but I know they hurt you a lot. I just...I want you to know the

Directorate aren't the only ones out here who destroy families."

"What do you mean?" I manage when I've taken a deep breath.

"My parents' death—my biological parents, I mean—wasn't by the Directorate's hand." He turns to look toward the jagged, silhouetted mountains in the distance. "Like I said before, there are other enemies to be found in the wilderness. Dangerous ones."

As he speaks the last two words, his voice breaks. I know the pain he feels—it radiates through me even as I listen. It's the same pain I feel each time I think of my mother's needless death. Of my father's. Of Kel's abduction. It's a cruel, vicious agony, and I would give anything to find a way to numb it permanently.

I desperately want to know what—*who*—Peric means. But the tears in his eyes tell me it would be cruel to demand answers of him right now.

I tell myself I'll find the right moment, and soon.

"I'm sorry about your family."

"I know you are. You're very kind, Ash." He reaches for me, and in a moment of mutual sorrow, I let him take my hand in his. But when he steps toward me, I freeze, terrified of what's about to happen.

Failing to read my body language, Peric leans in to kiss me, and I turn my face just in time to spot Cyntra half a block away, a look of pure rage in her eyes.

I yank my hand away and step back.

"Ash…" Peric says. "I…"

"I need to get some sleep," I reply sharply, "and you need to go dance with the girl who's waiting for you. Goodnight, Peric."

17

THE RECKONING

CYNTRA DOESN'T SPEAK to me the next day, or the day after that. Every time I approach her or attempt to strike up a conversation, she meets me with a sneer of warning, like a cornered animal.

It's almost comical to think that after all these years spent living a far-from-normal existence, I'm finally getting to experience what it feels like to be a regular teenager. Jealous spats over boys. The silent treatment. Petty problems that used to dominate high school drama—at least in the days before life became a perpetual game of *Will I survive to see my next birthday?*

After she's rebuffed me more than a few times, I give up on the notion of having friends in this town, choosing instead to spend my days exploring the areas of the Bastille I haven't yet seen. Curious to learn more about what makes the strange little town tick, I wander every street and alleyway in what remains of the former Breckenridge.

Here and there, I stumble upon evidence of the Bastille's fraught past. Faded Consortium symbols painted on the wall of this or that alley, or carved crudely into cement while it was still wet. There are other symbols, too: a golden rose, sometimes on its own, sometimes twisting around a daisy. Some are stenciled on crumbling walls, some scrawled on the side of houses.

The golden rose, of course, is the menacing symbol of the Directorate.

As for the daisy, I'm not entirely sure what it represents.

Most of the symbols are faded, which seems to confirm what the others have told me: that the Directorate once occupied this place, but moved out when they'd stripped it of all useful materials.

But on one street in a residential area tucked away at the northern end of the town, I'm met with another story.

A tidily painted gray house sits on one corner. Its door is red, and at its center is a golden rose. It looks as if someone painted it mere days ago, its edges crisp, its lines delicate. Sharp thorns jut out from its stem, as threatening as fangs.

I seat myself on a bench not far from the house, waiting to see if anyone will emerge from its depths. But as the minutes —then hours—tick by, no one does.

"Can I help you?" a woman's voice finally asks just as I'm about to rise to my feet and head back to my small abode. I twist in my seat to see Norah, the friendly Matron who plied me with questions about Finn a few days ago in the Mess.

"Oh, hi," I reply with a slightly pathetic smile. I point to the gray house. "Yes—can you tell me who owns that residence?"

"None of the residents *owns* any of the houses in the Bastille. But I live in that one."

"I see. If you don't own it, who does?"

When I ask the question, her friendliness disappears, replaced by an icy hostility. "You ask a lot of questions, girl."

"Sorry. I'm just curious to learn more about the Bastille." Thinking quickly, I alter my voice in an attempt at Cyntra-level sweetness. "It's just that Veer has been so welcoming. I want to educate myself...out of respect."

"The Leaders own the properties," Norah says, her tone lightening a little. "They let us stay in them as long as we support the Cause. Those who don't show their support lose their privileges."

"I'm sorry—what do you mean by *the Cause?*"

"The reason we're here," Norah says, like it should be obvious. "The reason this town is allowed to exist." Her eyes narrow into a wince. "You don't have the first clue what I'm talking about, do you?"

I shake my head and smile. "No, not really. Like I said, I want to learn."

"Well, it's not my place to tell you, I'm afraid."

"Of course not. But could I ask—why is there a Directorate rose on your door?"

She glances at her house then back at me. "Because I like to remind myself who's really in charge around here."

With that, she turns and walks toward the house. When she reaches the door, she places a reverent hand on the rose then enters, leaving me with more questions than when I started.

Reluctant to return to my small room, I wander a little more, heading up one of the quieter dead-end streets away from the Bastille's center. The houses, like Norah's, are in good shape. Some are new-looking, like they've been recently renovated—which strikes me as odd, given the apparent lack of building supplies around here.

My plan is to turn back when I reach the end of the street.

But a sudden movement in a large bay window at the front of the house to my right draws my gaze.

A girl about my age, wearing a light blue, flouncy dress in the style Cyntra so often wears, is speaking to a man dressed in what looks like a white lab coat.

He asks her something and she nods, an enthusiastic smile lighting up her face.

He takes her right arm and jabs her with a needle, yet her smile remains. As I watch, the doctor extracts a blood sample.

Over the house's front door, I notice a small sign that reads:

Evaluation Center

Next to the words is the same combined symbol of a rose and a daisy intertwined that I've seen elsewhere in town.

As I'm staring at the sign and trying to sort out what it might mean, a young woman opens the door and steps out onto the porch, holding the hand of a toddler of two or three.

I can tell in an instant that the woman has been crying. When she spots me, she wipes the tears from her cheeks and mutters a curt greeting.

"Are...are you okay?" I ask.

She nods, sniffling. "Are you here for your Evaluation?" she asks.

"I don't know what that is. Is it why you're here?"

"For my son." She looks down at the small boy, who's intently watching a squirrel bounce along the sidewalk. "It's good news," she adds. "They say he's ready."

"Ready? For what?"

The woman is about to answer when the house's front door opens once again. The same doctor I saw taking blood from the teenage girl grabs the woman by the arm. "What do you think you're doing?" he shouts at the young mother, as if she's committed some egregious sin. "Get in here!"

Without a word, she scoops the toddler up in her arms and heads back inside.

The doctor issues me a look of warning and says, "You're an outsider here. What happens in the Evaluation Center is none of your concern."

"But I..."

"Get off this street or I'll report you."

The doctor heads back in and slams the door.

I turn and head back toward the main street, an ugly foreboding gnawing at my insides.

Around seven p.m. that evening, a distant bell clangs five times, commanding the town's inhabitants to meet at the Piazza for the event Veer referred to as "The Reckoning." The moment when the two men we took prisoner on the mountainside will be told their fates.

With my white uniform concealed partly by a gray canvas jacket I found in my closet, I head out to the street. Once again, I stash the pack containing my cloak and my sheathed blade behind the dumpster in a nearby alleyway. Something tells me emotions may run high tonight, and I want to be prepared in case the worst should happen.

I'm not looking forward to another strange ceremony, or to having to make eye contact with Cyntra—or Peric, for that matter. Each of them seems intent on filling my life with a drama I don't need or want.

As I approach the Piazza, I find my mind wandering once

again to thoughts of Finn and Kel—and how much I want to speak to Veer, to find out if she's learned anything more from the prisoners. I make a note to pull her aside later in the evening when she's finished making her announcement.

When I get to the Piazza, I tuck myself into a corner under a tree, pushing myself into the shadows beneath its branches. Wary, I scan the sky for the Directorate's drones, half expecting a swarm of them to come pouring out of the clouds to take down the crowd of vulnerable innocents gathering in the open.

The only flying thing I see, however, is my ever-present owl flapping slowly as he circles the area like a vulture scanning the ground below for death and decay.

"My winged stalker," I whisper to myself. I can't quite decide whether it's creepy or oddly endearing that he's still following me after all this time.

When I scan the crowd my eyes land on Cyntra, who's standing at the other side of the square, glaring at me. I could choose to ignore her, to pretend I don't care that she's staring daggers into my flesh.

But the truth is, I feel a duty to protect her feelings, to let her know nothing has happened between Peric and me.

"Enough of this high school crap, damn it," I whisper under my breath. I leave the relative safety of my tree and push through the crowd toward her, determined to put an end to the tension between us.

Shaking off the uneasy feeling that's settling in my gut, I march over, my eyes locked on hers.

"Do you have any idea what's going to happen tonight?" I ask, nodding toward the stage.

"I don't really care right now," she says, crossing her arms, her eyes locked on Peric, who's standing near the platform at the far end of the Piazza. A microphone is set up a few feet away, and I can only assume Veer will appear shortly to make her announcement.

A few seconds pass before Cyntra mutters, "You two were getting pretty chummy the other night."

"No. *He* was getting chummy. I was not."

"He tried to kiss you!" she hisses.

"Maybe he did. But if he ever kisses me, I'll slap his lips off. I'm in love with someone else, Cyntra. You know that."

"Well, that someone else isn't here, is he? For all you know, you'll never see him again. So it's no wonder you and the hottest guy in town are eyeing each other like rare steak."

"For one thing, I *will* see Finn again. I'm sure of it. But even if I wasn't, I wouldn't do anything to hurt you. I know you like Peric."

"Oh come on, Ash. Don't tell me you weren't enjoying the attention."

"There's *nothing* going on between us," I insist in a whisper. "I was as shocked as you were that he even so much as wanted to dance. I always thought Peric hated me."

"Yeah, well I'm beginning to regret loaning you that green dress. You looked too good." At that, Cyntra finally lets herself smile, and we both start laughing.

The thick wall of ice has finally begun to melt.

I put an arm around her and squeeze, just as a flurry of movement draws my eyes over to the mini-stage where Peric is standing. I focus my attention on Veer, who's making her way out to position herself in front of the microphone. Peric steps over to stand on her right, arms crossed over his chest. As I watch, he looks over at Cyntra and me and issues us a tight smile.

"Hey," I say out of the side of my mouth. "What's the Evaluation Center?"

"You saw it?"

I nod. "I don't think I was supposed to, though."

"No. You weren't."

"So what is it?"

Cyntra's got a strange smile on her lips as she replies, "It's where we're tested."

"For what?"

"To ensure we're suitable for our future families."

"Good evening, all," Veer says, her tone solemn as her voice rings through a set of old speakers. "Welcome to the Reckoning. Tonight, you will learn the fate of our two prisoners."

I keep whispering to Cyntra. "There was a little boy there...he couldn't have been more than two or three..."

"Right. That's the perfect age, don't you think?"

"Perfect for what?"

Cyntra shushes me as Veer gestures to two rifle-wielding men who part ways to reveal the two prisoners, bound and gagged and looking like they haven't eaten or bathed since their arrival in the Bastille. They're still dressed in their Directorate uniforms, but the gold roses have been ripped off their chests, leaving ragged holes in their wake.

"A new day is upon us," Veer bellows, "and it begins tonight. I intend to turn one of these young men over to our Leaders two days from now."

"Leaders?" I ask, my voice still low. "I thought Veer was the leader. What's she talking about?"

"The Directorate, of course," Cyntra says, beaming. "They run this place, Ash. Like you didn't know that."

My mind steers its way to my brief conversation with Norah earlier.

I like to remind myself who's really in charge around here.

Nervous, I glance over at Peric. He locks his eyes on me and smiles as if to say, "*We* did this. You and I."

"Tonight," Veer says, "we solidify our alliance. Tonight, we join with the Directorate to become one powerful force."

The arm that was hugging Cyntra drops to my side as if it's lost all strength.

"No. She can't be serious," I whimper. This place has always been too forgiving of those horrible people. But to form a formal alliance with them? Why would Veer want that? Why would a*nyone?*

To Veer's left, two men wheel a large object along the ground into the Piazza's center, forcing the crowd to part ways so they can get through. The wooden structure must be twenty feet tall, and is covered in a massive piece of flowing black fabric.

Veer gestures toward the strange sight, her arms in the air, and say, "It is time."

Four Matrons step forward to take hold of the fabric and pull it away to reveal a massive, terrifying weapon I've only ever seen in history books.

Its enormous silver blade gleams in the moonlight, menacing beyond words.

"A guillotine," I say under my breath.

"Surprised?" Cyntra asks, a strange glint in her eye.

"Shocked, actually."

"There's more than one reason this place is called the Bastille, you know."

"They're not going to…"

Cyntra replies with a shrug. "Here's hoping."

"It's been a few years since we've used the Blade to make an example of one of our enemies," Veer cries out to the crowd, who are now cheering heartily at the prospect of a beheading. "But tonight, we'll be using it once again."

I gasp, desperate for air. None of this makes sense. Everything happening before my eyes is a contradiction, and I'm slowly growing convinced I'm losing my mind.

The prisoners, still on the stage, are restless now. Even from a distance, I can see the tears staining their cheeks, their legs threatening to give out under them.

On Veer's signal, a sniper shoves one of the men forward, and I recognize him as the one who shot at Peric.

"What's going on?" I ask. "Why would she do this?"

"Because it's justice," Cyntra says. "That man is a traitor. He almost killed Per, or have you already forgotten?"

"Why would she kill one of the Directorate's men? How does this solidify an alliance?"

Cyntra lets out a laugh utterly unlike her usual girlish giggle. Full-bodied, deep and monstrous, it freezes the blood in my veins. "Those men aren't Directorate, silly. You of all people should have realized that the second you laid eyes on them."

"But Veer told us..." I stammer. "She *insisted*...They were wearing the rose..."

"They stole those uniforms, genius."

"If they're not Directorate, then...who are they?"

But Cyntra doesn't answer. Her eyes are focused on the guillotine, on the man who's being pushed toward it while his horrified companion looks on.

"Do you have any last words?" Veer asks him as he stands, shaking, beside the guillotine's glinting blade.

The man glances at her, then fixes his gaze straight ahead. In a shaking voice, he shouts, "The Consortium lives!"

I press back against the wall behind me, the friction from my palms the only thing keeping me from collapsing in a heap on the ground.

On Veer's signal, a sniper grabs the prisoner by the shoulders and forces him to his knees. The blade rises and the man is pushed into position, his neck pressed against a wide groove in the wood.

Sick to my stomach, I stare at the Bastille's leader whose eyes have found my own through the crowd.

"The Consortium lives," I whisper.

I finally understand why Piper was so intent on learning more about my father's note. Why Cyntra asked all those questions.

Why the drone didn't attack Veer on the mountainside.

The enemies in the mountains—the ones Peric began to tell me about. Maybe they're the allies my father pointed to—the ones I thought were long gone.

And the man who's about to lose his head is one of them.

When the blade crashes down, I pull my face away, my ears registering the agony that echoes through the air as the second prisoner lets out a wail of torment.

A split-second later, I hear the first man's head land with a sickening thud on the ground.

When I finally dare a glance back toward the platform, it's Veer alone that I see, her eyes fixed on mine. She raises a glass toward me, then nods to a man to her left, who's holding some sort of contraption in his hand that looks like a remote control.

He presses a button and a large holographic screen—tech the likes of which I've never seen in the Bastille—flares to life in the air before the crowd. At first, it flashes white, but as I stare an image manifests, bright and ominous at its center. Blurry at first, it grows clearer with each second that passes, as if a multitude of pixels are arranging themselves into a tidy, horrible creation:

A face.

One that I know all too well.

I stop breathing as our eyes meet across the crowd. I stare at her, sickened by the sight of her tight smile, her cold eyes, and the knowledge that somehow, she can see me.

18

UNWELCOME

"HELLO, ASHEN," the Duchess' voice says in the fake saccharine tone I've come to despise so violently. "It's *so* nice to see you again. I hear you've been well taken care of by our friends in the Bastille."

"She has indeed." Veer steps around the projected screen and faces it, her wine glass still in hand. "Two of my men will bring her to you," she tells the Duchess. "I trust that you'll hold up your end of the bargain."

"Of course."

I'm frozen, my breath a reluctant prisoner inside my chest. My heart is pounding so fast that I feel as though the world has come to a standstill around me.

"Cyntra?" I breathe, quietly wishing she'd tell me none of this is happening—that I'm in the middle of a nightmare and I'll wake up very soon.

But all I hear from her is the sound of amused laughter.

"Until you do send your men to the Arc," the Duchess says, her voice echoing off the walls of the buildings surrounding the Piazza, "lock Ashen Spencer up. And see to it that she's not treated with kid gloves, will you? She's more dangerous than she looks."

"It would be my pleasure," Veer replies, nodding to two men armed with rifles. They begin pushing their way through the crowd toward me, and I stand motionless, frozen like a deer whose eyes are locked on a set of bright headlights.

From behind Veer, Peric's eyes are fixed on me, a look of horror on his face that tells me he's the only other person in the Bastille who didn't see this moment coming.

Shouting, he lunges toward Veer. "What are you doing?" he cries. "You never said anything about this!"

But two of her henchmen stop him in his tracks.

"Ash!" he yells, twisting my way as they push him back. "Run!"

My eyes dart to Cyntra's. She looks for a second like she's grown sympathetic, but instead of offering help she reaches for my arm, grabbing it and squeezing. "Don't even think about it," she snarls under her breath.

Pulling my free arm back, I slam my fist into her jaw, throwing her backwards. I turn and flee down the street, zigging and zagging down alleyways until I reach the dumpster where I hid the bag that contains my dagger and cloak. Without stopping, I grab the pack, yank out the cloak, and drape it over my shoulders, pulling the hood over my head and squeezing the pack tight to my chest.

I don't know where to go, how I can possibly escape this place. The Bastille's main doors are guarded by sharp shooters. The door Veer guided us through is protected by an eleven-digit code.

Terrified, I sprint mindlessly toward the edge of town, hostile footsteps beating at the earth and concrete behind me.

When I hear a low hoot, I look up to see the owl I've

spotted so many times flapping wildly in the air overhead. Even as my eyes lock onto his underbelly, he drops something that hits the ground before me.

Not knowing why, I reach down to pick it up, skidding around the corner of a decrepit wooden building to dart down another narrow alley.

The object in my hand is a small metal sphere, made up of two halves that split open when I lay them in my palm. Inside is a note.

Southeast corner. Ladder. Get there now, Ash.

"What the—" I begin. "Where did this come from?"

But there's no time to think, to speculate. Someone is trying to help me, and I have no choice but to listen.

Finn? Did you do this?

I mouth his name, hopeful that somehow from his home in the Arc, he's got his eyes on me.

Putting all my faith in the owl's mysterious offering, I spring toward the Bastille's southeastern corner, the sound of my deranged pursuers growing steadily louder behind me.

I reach the high wall, slipping along it, hunting for the elusive ladder mentioned in the note.

Finally, I see it, ten or so feet above the ground.

Damn it.

It's too high for me to reach.

I leap up, trying in vain to grab hold. When my feet hit the ground again, I whirl around to see the angry mob from the Piazza running my way. Among them are Piper and Cyntra. Piper has a handgun drawn, but it's Cyntra—formerly sweet Cyntra, whose blood-stained face is now contorted into that of a wild animal—who frightens me more.

Veer, her features creased with determination, shouts, "There she is!"

The two armed men pause and lift their rifles, but Veer tells them not to shoot.

"Kill her and the Directorate will have all our heads. Just grab her!"

Desperate, I leap up again, and once again, I fail.

Focus, Ash. You're wearing a uniform that gives you super-human strength, for God's sake.

You can do this.

I jump again, and this time my fingers curl around the ladder's lowest rung. I pull myself up, climbing with an agility granted to me only by the grace of Finn's suit. Throwing the backpack strap over one shoulder, I will myself to reach the top of the wall, hoping I get there before Veer changes her mind and tells the snipers to land a series of bullets in my back.

When I reach the parapet, a nearby sniper falls to one knee, taking aim at me, but from below I hear Veer's voice once again shout, "Take her alive, idiots!"

Thinking fast, I pull the cloak over my face.

"She's gone!" the sniper shouts.

"She's not gone! She's cloaked!" Veer yells.

Crouching down to render myself as small as possible, I ease along the parapet away from the confused sniper until I come to a spot in the wall crawling with thick vines that have grown invasively over the top like grasping fingers.

My father told me once that some types of ivy attach themselves so strongly to brick and mortar that they're capable of tearing entire buildings apart. Putting my faith in the vines' determined grip, I slip over the wall's edge and climb down, grasping at the braided green cordons even as they pull away from the concrete in twisted clumps.

After what seems like an eternity spent challenging fate and gravity at once, the soles of my feet collide with the ground and I spin around to face the woods, springing away from the Bastille into the darkness. I don't turn to look, to see how many eyes are hunting me through the darkness. I don't want to know.

Above me, the owl soars toward the woods, while behind me, the sound of gunfire echoes off the Bastille's walls.

Before me lies nothing but dense forest and uncertainty.

19

ESCAPE

I've never run so far—nor so fast—in my life. With voices still shrieking commands behind me, I tear in a twisting zigzag through the woods, unsure where I'm even headed.

Trying desperately to control my rasping breath, I pull the cloak tight around my body, tripping and leaping my way over fallen branches and tree roots until the sound of voices in the distance fades to virtually nothing.

Finally spent both physically and emotionally, I sink to the ground with my back against the trunk of a tree, my lungs burning. This sickening feeling is familiar, harrowing. The sensation of being a prey animal pursued by predators who want to tear me apart for no other reason than for their own vile entertainment.

When I escaped the Arc—when the Directorate Guard was after me—I was fleeing a known enemy, one I'd grown to understand all too well.

But now, I'm running from people I thought I could trust, if only a little. People who assured me they had my back—that

I was part of their strange little community and that they'd keep me safe.

I want to kick myself for failing to listen to my instincts the first time I met Veer—failing to see that she was looking at me like I was a valuable commodity, one she could use to her advantage.

But even more vile is Cyntra's role in all this. Cyntra the deceiver, the liar, acting all along like an innocent, bubble-headed schoolgirl. For a time she had my trust, my friendship. As I catch my breath, I realize with horror how quickly I told her about Finn—who he was, what he'd done to help me escape the Arc.

If she told Veer, and if Veer told the Duchess...

Oh, God.

I barely muster the courage to conjure the words in my mind.

Finn could die because of my foolishness.

I wonder now if anything Cyntra ever showed me of herself was honest. Her feelings for Peric. Her hyper-feminine bedroom, her excitement over the Finishing Ceremony.

Staring into the darkness, my chest heaving, I tell myself I was confiding in a snake this whole time.

And then there was Peric.

Ironic that I never entirely trusted him, yet he's the only one who came close to telling me the truth about Veer's prisoners. But he held back, his mother's voice commanding him to keep the secret to himself.

If he'd just told me, warned me, I could have prepared myself. I could have planned an escape.

But even Peric didn't seem to know Veer would offer me up to the Directorate like some human prize. He looked genuinely shocked tonight, as if his mother had deceived him, too.

My breath bursts out of me in hard, violent gasps that turn quickly into sobs.

Hopelessness. That's what I feel. By some twisted, spiteful miracle, it turns out the world is even crueler than I thought.

I have nowhere left to run. Nowhere to conceal myself from the inexorable viciousness that pursues me everywhere I go.

When I have no tears left to shed, I inhale deeply.

The owl. The message in the small metal sphere...

Finn, I think again. It *had* to be him—which means he's okay.

It means he's still alive.

Are his eyes on me now? Has he been watching this whole time?

Whether it was Finn or not, someone saved my life back there—and managed to restore a sliver of my faith in humankind.

With each slow breath, my sense of security comes back to me, a feeling of strength taking over my mind and body once again. Finn's invisible arms are holding me, his flesh woven into my white uniform's fabric. I close my eyes and feel him out there somewhere, reassuring me from afar.

There is some good left in the world, Ash. It's just a matter of finding it.

I draw the cloak around my face once again and press my head back against the tree, asking myself what I should do next. I can't sleep out here in the open, not when I know Veer will be sending a patrol to scour the woods for me. *I need to find shelter.*

As the thought sits in my mind, a low hoot pulls my eyes to a tree limb high above me.

I scan the branches overhead until I spot my ally, his silver feathers sparkling delicately in the pale light. His eyes flicker and flash red, then blue, then silver.

"Who *are* you?" I whisper-hiss up at him.

The creature blinks and pulls his head down in a sort of nod.

"I don't understand," I say. "I need words. And if you say 'Who,' I swear to God I'll climb up there and punch you in the face."

As if in response, the owl drops something once again, an object that lands at my feet before rolling a few inches. Another metallic sphere, which I lean over and pick up.

Follow me to safety, the message inside reads.

Without a moment's hesitation, I rise to my feet. I may not know exactly who's controlling this intelligent beast, but whoever they are, I have little choice but to trust them.

As I move, my eyes shift between the tree branches that reach out like gnarled, skeletal hands above me and the dark sky where the owl is flapping northward, away from the Bastille. I follow as well as I can while pushing my way through thick brambles and dense foliage, losing my companion occasionally before catching up to find him hovering in the sky in wait.

My uphill pursuit of the bird lasts an hour or more, and by the end of it I'm exhausted. The owl finally comes to a landing on a rocky outcropping high above me, and I push myself under a stone overhang, slumping down onto the cold ground, my arms wrapping around my body as the cold night air settles in.

"I guess you're just going to watch over me tonight," I say

under my breath, though I can no longer spot my silver companion. The thought of his presence is reassuring, at least. A guardian with keen eyes to warn me if anyone should come close.

I find myself once again torn between weeping and laughing, wondering if anyone has ever experienced anything as absurd as my life. Ever since I turned seventeen, my entire existence has been a series of insane, unfathomable events.

But this night may just be the craziest of them all.

As my mind spins with a nauseating cyclone of horrible thoughts, it settles on the image of Peric's face.

The way he looked at me when he told me to run—it stunned me. There's a goodness in him that I'd never seen before that moment. An ability to care fiercely, to protect. He was ready to tackle his mother to the ground if it meant saving me.

I'm only sorry he didn't get the chance.

I wonder what he thinks of Veer now. How he feels, knowing she was about to send me to my death without a second thought.

I wonder, too, if he'll be punished for his insubordination.

My thoughts turn to Finn again. Yet another young man with a mother who wants me dead. I'm sure there's a lesson in there somewhere—though I refuse to believe I deserve to be so despised. It's unchecked power that makes those like Veer and the Duchess awful; the ability to reign over other humans, to control them. It's like I told Peric—blind, greedy ambition often turns people into psychopaths. It makes them forget what it is to feel empathy, to want to improve the lives of others. All they see is the potential of their own greatness.

All things considered, Finn and Peric both turned out to be remarkably well-adjusted young men.

As if I've summoned him, the silver owl flaps down and lands on a nearby log, head turning toward the woods for a moment before twisting back toward me.

His eyes glow bright blue in the dark, creating an ethereal ring of light around his head that looks like a halo.

"Who—what—*are* you?" I ask again, despite the fact that I know how futile the question is.

"I'm a drone," a voice replies, startling me enough that I reach for my dagger. "Of sorts."

20

FRIEND

THE VOICE CAME from the owl.

I'm sure of it.

If I were standing right now, I would collapse under the weight of my shock.

"Wait," I stammer, "did you really just say something?"

The owl's head shakes slowly.

"Great. Then I've lost my mind."

The voice comes at me again. "No, Ash. The owl didn't speak—*I* did."

The words are distant, like they're being fed through a long metal tube. But the voice is familiar, a fleeting memory of something I once knew intimately.

I contemplate it for only a few seconds before I recoil, my chest tightening.

No. It can't be.

"Rys...?" I gasp.

If the owl is controlled by Rys—if he's been watching me this entire time...

And if he's still in league with the Duchess...

I don't even want to think about it.

"Ash," he says, reading my thoughts. "It's okay. I'm trying to help you, in case that wasn't obvious back in the Bastille."

He has a point.

"Fine," I reply. "You saved my butt back there. But..."

"You're still angry with me for what I did. I know." I can hear Rys sigh on the other end. "Think of this as me trying to make amends. I know it's impossible to make things right, but I do want to help you."

I go silent for a moment, my jaw tightening. I want to scream at him. To tell him to leave me the hell alone, that I don't need his help.

But that would be a massive lie.

"The owl," I finally say through clenched teeth, "what *is* he?"

"Something I've had in the works for a long time. Since before I left the Mire. I designed him at home in Sector Eight, believe it or not—him and a lot of other prototypes. I studied birds' flight for years, read old books, watched videos when I had electricity. Their bones, their wings, how they push off into the air, all of it. I also studied the Directorate's drones—their cameras, how they run surveillance missions, how they keep their charge for hours on end. I never had access to the materials I needed to build a drone of my own until I got to the Arc, but now I have everything I could possibly want—enough to build an army. The owl's name is Atticus, by the way."

"Atticus," I repeat. It suits him, somehow. "Does the Directorate..."

"Know about him? Not exactly. They've seen sketches of him and others—but as far as they know, my drones aren't yet functional. I mostly operate Atticus at night from my quarters or in secret, using a program disguised as surveillance tech."

"The Directorate isn't watching you?"

"No. They give me a lot of freedom, ever since..."

He stops just short of saying, "Since I betrayed you, got your mother killed, and Kel taken."

"They trust you because of what you did to my family," I say bitterly. "If they knew you were doing this—that you helped me tonight—they'd kill you. You know that, don't you?"

"Well, then, I have to make sure they don't find out. Don't worry—I told you ages ago, I'm smarter than they are."

For a millisecond, a pang of nostalgia assaults my chest. A moment of wistfulness, a craving for what used to be, for a friendship I was once sure would last my entire life.

He made a horrible choice—one that cost me everything. Because of him, Kel is imprisoned in some secret location. Because of him, I'll never be able to attend a funeral service for my mother.

I may never be able to forgive him...

But I'm still human.

The truth is, some part of me has missed Rys.

"Okay, then." I exhale. "What do we do now?"

"You stay where you are. Atticus and I set up a couple of misdirects for the Bastille's hunting party. They'll head southwest and won't find you tonight. After a while, they'll give up and head back to their demented prison-town, and if all goes well, Veer will get chewed out by the Duchess until she cries like a little boy."

"Then what? I can't just live in the wild for the rest of my days. I mean, I *wish* I could, but..."

"I've sent someone from the Arc to find you," Rys says. "An

ally, someone I trust. When they arrive, you can work out what you want to do. You have choices here, Ash. You need to decide your own fate. But in the meantime, I want to make sure you have food and supplies, everything you need to stay alive. You may need to lay low for a few days."

"I don't need anyone to find me," I tell him, moderately irritated that he's sent someone without asking my permission. I have no idea if this person is a member of the Directorate Guard or some friend of Rys' from the tech sector. Either way, I seriously doubt if I can trust them. "And you're wrong—I *don't* have choices. Everyone I thought I could trust has betrayed me. So my options are pretty damned limited." Icicles dangle on the air as I utter the last few words.

"Look," he tells me, his voice a disembodied entity as the owl's head twists and turns, his eyes searching in every direction. "I've turned over a new leaf, Ash. I've learned a hard lesson—one that cost me the best friend I've ever had. I'll never stop trying to make up for it. I know you won't believe me when I tell you to trust me—but please…try."

I clench my jaw, fighting back a new swell of tears forming in my eyes.

Damn you for saying the right thing, Rys. I so want to hate you.

Just let me hate you.

"There's something I want to show you," he tells me. "Something that will hopefully make you feel a little better."

The owl swoops down and lands on the ground before me, his silver talons digging into the earth. He pulls his head up to look at me and his glowing eyes disappear, as does his entire face. In its place, a blank, shimmering screen flashes to life.

After a few seconds, my eyes are met with a sight I've craved for weeks without fully comprehending how desperate I was for it.

Kel.

My little brother is sitting on a rug, surrounded by a sea of children's toys and games.

"I know that rug," I say, stunned by the sight. "It's in Merit's room, at the Davenports' residence. I don't know how you got video of him…I…" My lip quivers.

"He's in their care, Ash. He's well looked after. That's all you need to know."

"Care? They don't care about anything, least of all my brother. You know that as well as I do."

Still, I'm relieved beyond words to see Kel safe. As I watch, Merit approaches and sits down next to him. They begin to play with a couple of toy trains, smiling and laughing as they joke around—probably, knowing Kel, about the fact that he's convinced he's far too mature for toys.

Tears stream down my cheeks as I watch, euphoric to see that my brother has a friend for the first time in his life. Even if that friend is the son of two of the worst people I've ever met, the fact remains that Merit is Finn's brother.

Which means there has to be some spark of goodness inside him.

"I wonder if I'll ever see him again," I say softly. "If I'll ever get to hug him."

"Like I said," Rys' voice streams through the air, "you have choices, Ash. If you want it to happen, something tells me it will. And I'll help you."

I take in a deep breath and push it out. "Fine. I'll wait here for your ally. But if he or she tries to drag me back to the Arc, just know I'm not going unless they present me with the most ingenious plan that's ever been concocted. I refuse to die before I get a chance to see my brother."

"You won't die, I promise. Not while Atticus lives. He's

more than just a pretty face and a weird, creepy screen." With that, the image of Kel and Merit fades away and the owl's face returns. "He can protect you in ways you haven't seen yet."

A reluctant smile makes its way over my lips. "So, the mechanical owl-drone really is my bodyguard. He's felt like that from the start—I just didn't know he wasn't real."

"Oh, he's real. Just not in the way you imagined."

"Fair enough."

"My ally will be there sometime in the early morning hours," Rys tells me with an audible yawn. "For now, you should try and rest. And...try to trust me a little, would you?"

"I'll try." I nod at Atticus, who spreads his wings and takes off into the night sky. I'll admit, if only to myself, that I'm exhausted. This evening was too strange, too gruesomely disillusioning, and it robbed me of every meager bit of joy and energy that had managed to make its way into my bloodstream since I first found myself in the Bastille.

I lie down, curled into a fetal position, pulling my cloak tight around my face. Exhaling, I stare out at the calming silhouettes of the trees that line the mountainside.

When I close my eyes at last, I tell myself that at least tomorrow can't possibly be worse than today was.

21

WELCOME

SOMETIME IN THE middle of the night while darkness still falls in a thick blanket over the forest, the nearby crack of a brittle twig startles me into consciousness.

I pull myself into a sitting position then scoot backwards, cowering in the shadowy depths of my rocky shelter. Fearful of discovery by malevolent eyes, I look down to ensure the cloak is still activated.

Somewhere above me, Atticus lets out a low *Hooo.*

He heard it too.

The intruder could by Rys' ally. But it seems far more likely this close to the Bastille that it's one of Veer's snipers hunting me down.

I wait, my breath trapped tight inside my lungs as another twig snaps, then another. A mere few feet away, branches part and a figure pushes its way out into the small clearing before me. Shielded as my eyes are by my drooping hood, I can't see details at first—only that the stranger is a man. When I dare pull my chin up a little, I discern that he's dressed in a dark uniform of some sort.

Yes, it's definitely a uniform, with something small and shiny accenting the left side of his chest.

The Directorate rose.

He steps closer, like he knows I'm here. Though it's possible I'm being paranoid. I hold in my breath, unwilling to make a single sound for fear of discovery.

I can see his feet now, encased in dark leather boots that are scuffed at the toes. His breath huffs out from between his lips.

He's so close I swear I can feel each exhalation on my skin.

He knows I'm here. He has to.

"You know," an exquisite, deep voice says, "you're far too beautiful a woman to hide your face like that."

Those words—that voice.

It can't be. It's not possible.

In a split second, my racing heart goes from panicked to euphoric. Fumbling and shaking with excitement, my fingers pull the cloak away from my face and shoulders. It drops to the ground as I slip out of the shelter and rise to my feet, leaping at the visitor.

"Finn!" I breathe against his skin, hardly daring to believe he's real.

His arms are around me, squeezing me tight, our chests heaving in a mutual excitement approaching pure bliss.

"Rys said he was sending an ally. He was talking about you?"

He pulls back, his palms cupping my cheeks in the affectionate gesture I've been craving as desperately as a suffocating person craves air. Without answering the question, he kisses me, and I instantly forget where I am. I can't recall my own name, even.

But nothing matters right now. Nothing except that we're

together out here in the open air, our heartbeats pounding in a perfectly synchronized rhythm.

"Yes, Rys was talking about me," he finally replies when he pulls back. "He came to me after you left, wanting to make amends. He told me he had a way to keep an eye on you out here. He said he knew where you were. At first, honestly, I wanted to kill him for what he'd done to you, but I chose to listen to him. I was desperate to know you were safe. And when he told me about your little trip up to the chalet—that you'd nearly been killed—I almost lost my mind. I made him show me video of you that he'd taken with his drone, and insisted that he tell me what he knew about the Bastille and the people in it. Finally, I began to feel desperate, and said I wanted to come find you. He told me to wait, that something was coming—that he'd get you out of the Bastille soon. So I held on as long as I could until he gave me the go-ahead."

"How did you get here? How did you get out of the Arc?"

"The same way you did, through Sector One," he replies, pulling the end of a long cloak from his bag. As I watch him, I note that there are several identical garments inside the pack. "Except no one was chasing me. I got my hands on this uniform as an extra layer of protection from drones, but my parents think I'm in the lab for a few days, pulling all-nighters while I work on my latest project. They won't miss me."

"Your implant won't give you away? Isn't it tracking you?"

He holds his right arm up to reveal a wide silver bracelet that covers the implanted chip that so many of the Arc's residents have under their skin. "Inhibitor bracelet. I have it programmed to tell the Arc's surveillance systems that I'm in the lab and all is well. Eventually, they may figure it out and look for me, but it won't be here. Not that I'm too worried about my parents even *thinking* about me. Something's up with the Directorate. My mother has hardly been home in days."

"Well, yeah. She's been getting ready to bring me in and torture me."

Finn shakes his head, his expression grim. "There's something else going on. Something bigger. Not that anything is more important than you, of course."

"You think they're planning something?" I ask, thinking of Veer, of her intention to hand me off to the Directorate along with one of the soldiers that she took prisoner.

"Believe it or not, I don't think it's the Directorate who's planning something. I've heard quiet talk about rebels inside the Arc. Disgruntled Serfs and Dregs, finding ways to communicate under the radar. The Directorate is going nuts trying to figure out how they're managing it."

"Really?"

Serfs, those who live in the lowest level of the Arc, are the Directorate's work horses. Those who were rich enough to buy property inside the enormous building, but who now live as servants to the Aristocracy in order to make ends meet. They're at the mercy of the Directorate, just as the Dregs are.

"Really," Finn replies. "Someone has been helping them—providing them with ways to evade the Directorate's surveillance system. Don't get me wrong—I'm glad it's happening. But it's dangerous for them. I can only see this ending in a civil war, and we know whose side will inevitably win. But look—I didn't come here to speculate about the awful things my mother might do." With that, he pulls me close and kisses me again. My body goes limp as a swarm of delighted butterflies dances around inside me.

Suddenly, I no longer care about the Duchess, about the Arc or the Directorate. Right now, all I want is to whisper desperate words to Finn, to beg him to stay out here with me forever.

We could go deeper into the mountains. I know how to hunt, to survive. We could live together, hidden from the cruel world...

But with one simple thought, reality assaults me once again.

Kel.

I can't abandon my brother to the cruelty of the Duchess and her band of psychopaths. Kel is my first priority, regardless of how pleasurable Finn's touch may be, how delicious a thought it is that he's risked his life and come all this way to find me.

As if reading my mind, he caresses my neck with the gentlest touch of his lips, pulling me out of the abyss. I let my head fall back as his lips brush my skin, moving down to my shoulder and sending goosebumps trailing along my flesh in their wake.

I take hold of his jacket. "I can't believe I'm holding onto a man in a Directorate Guard uniform," I chuckle, pulling back to examine it.

It's form-fitting and well-tailored, and he looks remarkably glorious within its confines. Still, it's disconcerting to see him in the clothing of traitors.

"It's not my first choice of wardrobe, I'll admit," Finn says.

I reach for a gold clasp at his neck, undoing it and unzipping the garment. Pushing it off his shoulders, I press my hands to his chest, stone-hard and taut, as the jacket falls to the ground. The thin white t-shirt that's left is a vast improvement.

Finn wraps his fingers around my wrists and brings my hands, palm first, to his lips, kissing them. I slip my arms around his neck and our lips meet again. Before I know it, we're on the ground, his body forming a perfect, protective shelter over mine.

We're now vulnerable to anyone who might be in the woods searching for us. All too visible to the naked eye, to patrolling drones, to any and all enemies.

But for a few minutes, I permit myself the luxury of pretending we're alone in paradise, and that nothing can touch us.

When dawn begins to break, I have no concept of how many hours have passed since Finn's arrival. Nor do I particularly care. I want time to stand still, to halt entirely, to allow us to remain in this moment forever.

But Finn, it seems, has other priorities.

"Ash, your brother—you know he's—"

"With your family? Yeah, I know. Have you spoken to him?"

"I've tried, but..."

"But what?"

"My parents won't let me. They keep us apart, like they're afraid I'll say something. Maybe they're worried I'll tell him what happened to you—what they've done."

"You mean to tell me Kel doesn't know your mother is responsible for our mother's death?"

Finn shakes his head. "I'm pretty sure he doesn't even know she's Directorate. Honestly, it's probably best to keep things that way. He's been through enough."

"He has. But there's part of me that wants him to know what she is. I don't want him to trust that bi— "

I stop myself before I can finish saying the word,

reminding myself that as much as I loathe her, the Duchess is still Finn's mother.

"Sorry," I mutter.

Finn takes my hand. "It's all right. I hate what she did to you—what she and her Directorate allies have done to so many. I don't trust her. Most mothers would take a bullet for their children, but I'm not sure mine would take so much as a paper cut."

Finn pushes himself to his feet and steps over to rifle through the pack he brought with him. He pulls out a khaki jacket made of a fabric similar to that of my uniform, and I wonder if it has the same miraculous enhancements. He slips it on before coming back to sit next to me again.

"What are we going to do?" I ask. "How do we get Kel out of there?"

"With a little patience. All I know is you need to stay away from the Arc. Kel is a lure—a pawn in my mother's game. I'm going to stay out here for a day or two. We'll try to figure things out. But for now, I'm exhausted. I've been hiking for hours on end, and I need to close my eyes. Tomorrow morning, we'll wake up, you and I. It will be a new day. I'll kiss you a thousand more times." He presses his forehead to mine, hands cradling my neck. "I'll tell you I love you so many times you'll get sick of it."

"I love you, too," I whisper back, tears in my eyes to think how much I needed those words.

I can think of nothing better, except spending a few hours lying next to Finn, his reassuring breath coming at me in slow waves. "We can fit into the shelter, if you don't mind getting close to me."

"Mind?" He laughs, then kisses me again. "Do you have any idea how much I've missed you? How often I've thought about you? How much I want to..." He stops there and issues a wicked smile. "Someday," he says, half to himself.

Delight sweeps through my body and mind to know he's been as desperate for me as I have for him. He's the one thing in this world that keeps me from shattering like fragile glass.

"I've thought about you, too, every moment of every day. I knew we'd see each other again, though I didn't know how or when. There were times when I nearly lost hope..."

"I know. Me, too."

Silently, we sit down on the cold slab of stone. Finn leans back against the shelter's wall, and I press against him and close my eyes, devouring the perfection of his arms around me.

I escaped to the wilderness days ago, looking for a place that feels like home.

It took a second brush with death to realize Finn's touch is the only home I'll ever need.

22

MORNING

When I stir awake after a few hours of mercifully peaceful sleep, Finn is still holding me tight, his breath teasing my neck and shoulder.

In my contented fog, I've forgotten where I am. All I know is I'm safe and happy in a quiet utopia, a perfect set of muscular arms taking possession of my body and soul at once.

But my eyes have been open only a few seconds before a renewed dread sends adrenaline coursing through my body.

They're still hunting me. They're still out there.

I can feel them.

As if my racing heart has woken him, Finn stirs behind me.

Without a word, we pull apart and ease our way out of the shelter, our eyes watchful. "We have a task this morning," Finn says quietly, stretching his arms over his head.

"What do you mean?"

Looking far more relaxed than I feel, he reaches out and pulls me close to kiss me. "The coordinates—the ones your father left. Did you ever figure out where they lead?"

"Not exactly—but I'm pretty sure there's nothing out here

but forest. On the first day they found me, the Bastille's team hiked me through the woods right past the location those coordinates pointed to. If there was a compound or a town there, I would have seen it."

"Maybe," he concedes, "but maybe not. The Consortium has always been good at hiding itself, ever since the Directorate declared them enemies of the people years ago. There must be something, some clue in the woods. I think it's worth looking, don't you?"

"I'm really not sure. Peric—that's Veer's son—said something about dangerous enemies in the wilderness. I suppose it's possible he was talking about the Consortium —though I'm not sure why they would be dangerous to the people in the Bastille. Veer's got the Directorate on her side."

I never did get a chance to ask Peric what or who he was talking about, who the enemies in the wild really are. Which leaves the possibility that the Consortium, if indeed they still exist, may just prove to be another violent foe.

If the prisoner Veer killed was one of them, it would only prove my theory. I felt visceral, terrifying rage in that man's eyes as he ran at me on the mountainside. I *saw* the hatred on his face.

"You're not sure my plan is a good one, then," Finn says.

"No, I'm not sure at all. But my father left those coordinates behind for a reason, which means somewhere out here, there may be people he trusted. And as terrified as I am, you're right—we should at least look for them."

"Excellent. First, though," Finn says, pulling his large pack out from its hiding place and unbuckling one of its pockets, "I think we should have some breakfast."

He extracts a container with a couple of delicious-looking

muffins, a thermos of still-hot coffee, and an impressively fresh-looking fruit salad.

I laugh, my mood instantly lightened. "How did you manage this?"

"Keeping food fresh while hiking through the woods is the least of my latest technological innovations, Ash." He winks, and I get the distinct impression he's got a few new tricks up his sleeve. "I figured if I found you, a romantic picnic in the woods would be in order...even if we have to keep our eyes constantly peeled for enemies while we dine."

Wary, he scans the trees around us, and I can tell he's thinking what I'm thinking: *Someone's out there.*

Mutual fear of death isn't exactly romantic, but I'll take anything I can get at this point.

I look up to see Atticus staring down from a branch about twenty feet above us. "Our watchdog will keep us safe," I tell Finn, nodding up toward the bird. "Watch-*owl*, rather. He'll let us know if anyone's coming. Won't you, Atticus?"

In response, the owl lets out a low hoot, ruffles his remarkable metallic feathers, and flies off to patrol the surrounding woods from the sky.

Finn and I bide our time consuming our delicious breakfast before he stashes the large pack once again, this time covering it with dead leaves and fallen branches. "We'll be faster on our feet if I'm not lugging it around," he tells me, wiping his palms on his pants.

I nod, buckling my sheathed blade around my waist and slipping my cloak on over my clothing. Finn, too, puts on the cloak he brought—this one made of what looks like liquid silver. His hood is pulled up, his face all but invisible, and for the first time, I understand what people see when I'm cloaked. If I spotted him out of the corner of my eye, I would likely think I'd seen nothing more than the shadow of a leaf twisting in the breeze.

As we begin our hike, Finn slides a finger along the silver bracelet on his right wrist and a cobalt blue digital display lights up. He raises it to his mouth and speaks quietly for a moment before lowering it again. I hear enough to know he's reciting the memorized coordinates from my father's note—an impressive feat, given that he only ever set eyes on them once.

"I can't believe you've had those in your head this whole time," I tell him. "That bracelet—it'll guide us to the specific location?"

"It will. It's an impressive bit of design—like the Inhibitors you've seen before, only more advanced. Your friend Rys developed it."

"So, you two really *have* become allies, then?"

"We didn't have much choice. We've sort of been forced to bond out of mutual affection for you."

I want to tell him Rys feels no real affection for me anymore—that every benevolent act is nothing more than a means to assuage his guilty conscience. But maybe he's right. Maybe there's something left in Rys' heart.

After all, he was once like a brother to me, and there was a time when I would have taken a bullet for him. A relationship like that doesn't just wither and die—not without a fight.

Staying close together, Finn and I walk for some time. I try to enjoy the hike, reminding myself how many times I've fantasized about this exact scenario—his closeness, the pleasure that comes with knowing that at any moment I can grab him, pull him close, kiss him.

But in reality, our adventure is tense, cautious, and frustrating as we try to avoid being skewered on this or that angry branch jutting out like a blade.

We hike for an hour at least through thick woods until Finn's bracelet finally lets out a faint *ping* sound. He slips his finger over the digital display, silencing it.

Atticus, who's stalked us from the sky for the duration of our walk, perches on a nearby tree limb and watches.

"Well," Finn says, pivoting around to scan the woods, "apparently we're here."

"All I see are trees."

There's nothing in our line of sight but a dense forest of maple, aspen, cottonwood, and a lone, ancient-looking oak tree, its roots embedded deep in the ground.

"Are you sure you had the right coordinates in your mind?" I ask, frustrated. "Not that I doubt your memory..."

"Quite sure." As if to prove himself right, he recites them to me, and each digit perfectly matches the set of numbers I memorized.

"My father wrote the note before he died. That was at least seven years ago. The coordinates may have meant something back then but nothing now. Maybe what Piper told me on the first day in the woods is true. Maybe the Consortium is just...gone."

For all I know, the man who died last night was toying with us all when he shouted his final words.

Maybe the Consortium *doesn't* live, after all.

"I guess that's possible," Finn says, sounding dismayed. But he's still scanning the area, his eyes focused like he's trying to solve a complex puzzle.

"We probably shouldn't get our hopes up, Finn. It was a good idea to come here and look around, but I think we have to admit defeat."

A sudden movement in the trees draws my attention upwards. Atticus is fussing, flapping his wings while clinging to his branch, like he's trying to signal us.

"Do you have any idea what we're looking for?" I ask him. But instead of offering any sort of reply, he simply ruffles his feathers and launches himself into the air.

Finn takes my hand and pulls it to his lips. "If we can't find allies in these woods, we need to at least find you a better shelter than last night's—somewhere you can stay hidden for the foreseeable future, until we figure out how to get you to Kel, or Kel to you. Let's go see what we can uncover."

We hike until we come to a rushing stream bubbling its way down a gentle slope. Wordlessly, we agree to follow it until it widens and leads us to an exquisite waterfall that rushes over the edge of a rugged cliff.

About twenty feet down, the water pours into a crystal-clear pool, isolated and idyllic.

"It reminds me of the Grotto," I say wistfully.

"Except this is so much better than the Grotto could ever be," Finn replies. "For one thing, my mother isn't likely to come bursting in at any moment to interrupt us."

"Don't underestimate your mother," I chuckle, but even as I speak, a chill trails its way down my spine.

"The good news is she wouldn't dare leave the Arc," Finn says, beginning the scramble down a steep, grassy ridge toward the small pool. "She'd be too vulnerable out here, and she knows it. It's why she sends her minions to do all her dirty work."

"Minions like the ones Veer was about to hand me over to,"

I reply with a sneer. A thought occurs to me as I begin to follow Finn down. "Why do you think so many people accept the Directorate as their leaders, when we all know they're pure evil?"

Finn ponders the question as he helps me down until my feet are planted on solid ground next to the silver pond. "I think people tend to believe whatever suits the narrative of their lives."

"That's a bit cynical, isn't it? You're basically saying we all wear blinders, even when we know the people in charge might be doing horrible things."

"That's *exactly* what I'm saying."

I'm about to protest when I stop myself. Much as I want to tell him he's wrong, I know deep down he's not. There are people suffering every day in the world, but we choose to look the other way, to live in denial. In the days before the Blight, I recall watching adults walk past homeless people lying in the streets, ignoring them like they were nothing more than pieces of crumpled, discarded paper.

"It's a coping mechanism," I say, half to myself. "If we thought constantly about all the terrible things, we'd..."

"Lose our minds," Finn nods. "Look at the Serfs, the people who live in the Arc's lower levels. They knew the Directorate was leaving a whole lot of people in the Mire to suffer and die, and they were okay with it. But it took the loss of their own wealth to finally inspire them to get angry."

"We're kind of a pathetic species, aren't we?" I ask with a sigh.

"I don't know about pathetic. I think it's more that we're all about self-preservation, so we become naturally adept at turning a blind eye to everyone and everything else. We do what we need to keep ourselves and our loved ones healthy and happy. But we also have a massive weakness."

"Which is?"

"We like to feel superior—and the Directorate made the Serfs believe they could have something no Dreg could have: a place inside the prestigious Arc. They were convinced that surrendering their wealth in order to live in Utopia was worth it, because..."

"Because the rest of us were left outside to die."

"Yes." Finn runs a hand through his thick hair. "You *were* left to die. But you didn't, Ash. For years, you kept your mother alive. You provided for her and managed to keep her safe, even when every other adult in the Mire was dead. That's something you should be proud of. I'm sure she was proud, too."

"She'd be more proud if I found a way to get Kel back," I reply, my voice shaking. "But I abandoned him. If I'd been there in the Mire—if I hadn't left—maybe they wouldn't have taken him. Maybe he'd be safe at home now, too."

With pain palpable in his expression, Finn takes me gently by my shoulders. "You didn't abandon your brother. If you'd stayed and let them kill you—*that* would have been abandoning him. You're out here risking your life for him. You're looking for allies, for help not just for Kel but for others, too. Everything you do is selfless, Ash. You *could* run a thousand miles away from here and start a new life on your own. You could escape all of this. But you don't, because you know there are people who need you."

"What if there's no help to be found?" I ask, a sob catching in my throat. "What if..."

Finn pulls me close, his strong arms somehow holding back the tsunami of tears threatening to flow down my cheeks. "There is always help. There's me. There's that weird robot owl of Rys'. And I'm willing to bet there are even people in the Bastille who would be willing to help you." His grip tightens when he adds, "There's Rys, too."

"You really think he's on our side?"

Finn nods. "I don't like the guy much. But he knows more about what goes on in the Arc than anyone. He's been playing both sides, and I have to admit, he's extremely good at it. But he didn't send Atticus out here to hurt you. The truth is, he's the greatest weapon any rebellion could have. He's got the Directorate eating out of his hand. They trust him."

"Do *you* trust him, though? What if he's feeding us false information to lure us into betraying ourselves?"

"It's possible," he says, nodding up toward Atticus, who's come in to land overhead like a watchful vulture. "If he wanted to, Rys could record everything we say right now to use against us. It's possible that an army of Directorate Guard is headed here right now to take us both to the Hold. But let me ask you this—after everything you've been through, do you think Rys would betray you again?"

I don't hesitate before shaking my head. "No. Not in a million years."

Finn kisses me. "Good, that's settled then. We have a very sketchy ally who has an unhealthy obsession with birds. Now...how about a swim?"

23

THE POOL

LEAVING OUR WORRIES BEHIND, we spend several luxurious hours swimming in the crystal-clear pool at the waterfall's base, its refreshing contents washing away almost every worry that's fed on my soul for days.

Neither of us has a swimsuit, of course—only our underclothes. But Finn has never been self-conscious, and much of the timidity I used to feel in his presence is long gone. I've been through too much to concern myself with frivolous matters like my body's imperfections, though admittedly there's still a shy teenage girl inside me, aware that Finn and I still have a good deal to learn about one another. On some level, we're still reserved. Guarded, even.

Perhaps it's our quiet way of protecting ourselves from more pain. But my attachment to Finn runs deep. Every second spent with him is another second when my feelings flourish and grow. He's taken root in my soul, in my mind. He'll be part of me for the rest of my life, regardless of what may happen to us both in the days to come.

For now, he's one of the few people in the world who both makes me smile and gives me hope.

A few people out of billions.

I watch him in the water as he dives under then pushes himself upright, his face to the sky as he slicks his soaking hair back. He's beautiful inside and out on a level I never imagined possible, and I don't know what I'd do if I lost him.

But the idea of saying those words out loud terrifies me.

My adoration betrays a weakness, a profound need that I'm not sure I'm willing to admit to him or anyone.

If his mother or any other Directorate member ever found us out here like this—if a drone flew over us right now, exposed as we are to their menacing red eyes—we would both be dragged unceremoniously to the Arc and punished.

His punishment would likely consist of a simple grounding for a few days.

Mine, on the other hand, would be death.

When we climb out of the water and lie down in the sun sometime in the afternoon, I command my mind to steer away from ominous thoughts. As if hoping to reassure me, Finn lays a warm hand on my lower back. I turn onto my side and ease over to him to put my hands around his neck, pulling him close to kiss him.

But before I can, I notice Atticus flying in low circles above us, his mechanical eyes trained on us as if he's waiting to see how far we're planning to go.

"Rys!" I call out, laughing. "A little privacy, please!"

Atticus makes a sort of grunting sound before flying off over the woods. I'm not sure if Rys is keeping watch over us out of a sense of protectiveness or jealousy...and the truth is, I don't much care.

When we're alone, I press myself to Finn again, and this

time I kiss him, aware that each second that passes is one second lost forever. I'm desperate to absorb every sensation, every tingle of every nerve in my body, so I can revisit this moment in my thoughts and dreams in the days to come.

"It's so frustrating," I moan as Finn kisses my shoulder. "So unfair that you have to go back there."

"I know," he says, pulling back to slip a fingertip over my cheek—a gesture I'll never tire of. "So many things are unfair, Ash."

So many things.

I don't know if I'll be alive in a month. I don't know how or when we'll find one another again after we say our goodbyes.

All I know is I don't want to lose him before I've truly been able to claim him as my own. I find myself strangely envious of the "Maidens" in the Bastille, the girls who are so excited about their coming marriages. The prospect of a long life with a partner is one I may never experience. All I have are these few stolen moments and the knowledge they'll come to a crashing end sooner, rather than later.

But those girls won't have Finn. They won't have the luxurious gift that comes with staring into his eyes, kissing his lips, feeling his hands on their skin. They'll never know his kindness.

For now, at least, he's mine alone.

I content myself with a multitude of soft, sweet kisses, Finn's arms cradling me, his breath stroking my skin. In the simple act of burying my face in his neck, there's a sweet intimacy, a reassurance that we need each other now as much as we ever did.

Holding onto one another as if we're terrified we'll be

separated by some unseen force, we fall asleep beside the pool in the late afternoon.

It's when the trees' shadows have begun to grow long across the water that a bright light penetrates my eyelids like a laser beam.

I sit up to see that Finn is already standing, his back facing me.

Atticus, flapping wildly in the sky, is issuing a series of high-pitched cries.

But the warning has come too late.

24

CAUGHT

Leaping to my feet, I reach for Finn's hand and pull myself close to him, feeling horribly vulnerable without the protection of my uniform.

Stepping out of the woods in a semicircle before us is what looks like a small army, their high-powered guns trained on us.

One of the weapons is equipped with a blindingly bright strobe light intense enough to prompt me to throw a hand in front of my eyes. I can't focus on a single face, nor can I make out the uniforms our enemies are wearing.

Only one thought sears its way through my mind:

The Directorate has found us.

"Who are you?" a man's voice calls out from the shadows beyond the penetrating light.

"Who?" I whisper, an echo of Atticus' warnings. "He doesn't know?"

I squeeze Finn's hand and he returns the silent gesture, an acknowledgment of what the words mean.

They aren't here for us.

"I could ask the same of you," Finn says, his voice deep, commanding.

"You could, but you don't have a weapon drawn, while we have many," the disembodied voice says. "So I'd suggest you answer before one of my people accidentally blows your head off."

"Fine. My name is Finn Davenport."

"And the girl?"

"Her name is of no relevance to you."

"I beg to differ. There's a female Candidate's uniform lying the ground by your feet, which means she's been inside the Arc. I'm afraid that makes her relevant."

"She's not there now, though, is she?"

The man drops the rifle to his side, its flashing light fading quickly to nothing. My eyes take a few seconds to adjust as I try to focus on the faces before us. There are seven of them, as far as I can see. Four men, three women.

Their clothing isn't that of the Directorate Guard, though they're too far away for me to make out any details.

"Two of our men went missing several days back," the man who seems to be in charge tells us. "They were patrolling on the ridge above the hell-town a group of traitors call the Bastille. Running into you here and now seems like an unlikely coincidence after that, don't you think?"

"Those were your men?" I say, ignoring the look of silent warning that Finn throws my way. I step forward, too intrigued to keep my mouth shut. "Those men tried to kill me, for the record. Or at least, to hurt me badly."

"They must have had good reason to. My people don't raise their guns without cause."

The man steps toward us. He's average height, with a shaved head, a round face, bronze skin, and dark eyes shadowed by thick brows. He's wearing a light-colored jacket, and as he comes closer, I spot a symbol on its left chest pocket.

A circle, crossed by two swords.

"That symbol..." I breathe, my hand raised to point toward him. "It's..."

"You know it?" the man asks. "How?"

"My father," I sputter. "I...I'm Ashen Spencer."

The man's eyes widen, his lower lip quivering. For a second, I'm convinced he's about to cry, but he composes himself and nods to someone behind him.

"We'll bring these two with us," he says, and before Finn or I can utter another word, two men have leapt at us, grabbed us by the arms and begun escorting us away from the waterfall. One of the women gathers our things from the ground and carries them as she and the rest of the group walk behind us.

I don't know if these people are friends or foes. What I *do* know is that I wish to God I had my uniform on right now, so I could break free and tell them we're not going anywhere until they tell us exactly what they plan to do with us.

Finn says nothing, though he throws me a look that practically screams *Let's not do anything stupid* as we march along with the small band of men and women.

As we hike, the leader tells us he has questions.

"Have you both been in the Bastille, then?"

"I have," I tell him. "Finn hasn't."

"Well then, Ashen Spencer, you're probably aware of some of what's going on in that place. I need information, and I can't risk you running off into the mountains. So I apologize for dragging you through the woods, but you may soon understand our reasons."

"Do you think you could at least give us ten seconds to put our clothes on?"

The man snickers. "Sorry, but no. Ten seconds can be an eternity out here. We can't take unnecessary risks. You'll have plenty of time to get dressed once we're inside."

A moving shadow draws my eye to the trees above us, and I glance up to see Atticus flying silently overhead. I wonder what Rys is thinking right now, if he's hatching a secret plan to free us from these people's clutches.

"I understand," I say, pulling my eyes back to the woods around us. "Look, you can keep me prisoner as long as you want. But Finn can't stay here—if the Directorate finds out he's gone, they'll..."

The man levels me with a stern look of caution. "You don't get to make the calls out here. This may once have been your father's domain, but it's not yours. Not until you tell me everything I need to know."

Silenced and frustrated, I trudge along next to Finn, pushing our way through thick underbrush as thorny brambles slice at our bare skin and our feet. After a time, landmarks around us begin to look familiar:

A rock formation Finn and I spotted on our hike this morning. A row of birch trees we noted for their pristine bark.

And finally, the oak tree that looked so out of place earlier in the day—the one that stands at the exact coordinates my father charted on the note he left behind.

When our party stops, I look up once again to see Atticus perched on a thick limb high above us. *Good. At least he knows where we are, just in case...*

The leader turns to offer up another warning look before grabbing one of the oak tree's thick lower branches and tearing it upwards. At first, I'm confused, convinced he's snapped it clean off. It only takes a moment to realize the branch is attached to the trunk by a thick iron hinge, and where its base met the tree a few seconds ago is a hidden keypad, its digits faded and dull.

The man inputs a four-digit code and turns our way. "We change the code frequently, so don't get any ideas."

"We wouldn't dream of it," Finn says.

The tree's broad trunk cracks, its bark spreading open like a thick curtain parting just enough to allow a full-sized adult to squeeze inside in a crouch.

"What the hell..." I whisper even as I feel Finn's calming hand on my back. "This has to be the place my father was trying to guide us. *This* is the stronghold?"

"Looks like it," Finn replies under his breath.

"Oliver Spencer, along with a talented team of engineers, designed this tree, as well as its entry point," the leader tells us. "That was many years ago, back when he saw what was coming. It's thanks to him that so many were saved. Thanks to him that the Pit was constructed."

"Pit?"

"You'll see," the man says with a mischievous smile before he crouches down and disappears into the oak's trunk.

25

THE PIT

FINN and I follow the man into the tree, the rest of the party on our heels as we enter a dark, twisting stairwell barely wide enough for a single adult. I breathe a quiet sigh of relief—for too many reasons to count—that we left Finn's pack hidden in the spot where we spent the night. Until we know we can trust this strange group of subterranean rebels, I have no desire to supply them with Finn's creations.

A series of dull lights flicker along the curving walls as we descend, illuminating our way just enough so that none of us plummets down the stairs to a broken ankle, or worse. Finn's calming hand remains on my shoulder until we reach the bottom, where our leader guides us down a long, dirt-packed corridor.

Our surroundings smell of musty dampness—not surprising, given that the structure we're standing in was literally built into the earth.

We advance until we reach a door made of wood with what look like cast iron hinges and an iron handle. It reminds me of something I might see in a dwarf's home in a Fantasy novel—something crafted crudely by a blacksmith, in stark contrast to the Arc's modern touches, or even the Bastille's ski-lodge aura. This strange underground world is alluring and oddly welcoming, and it takes me a few minutes to realize why:

It reminds me of my father.

His paintings of landscapes had a roughness to them, a sort of hurried quality that gave his work the illusion of movement, of wind blowing through trees, of water rushing along creeks and rivers.

The Pit is rough-hewn in the same way, but sturdy and solid, like it's been here for an eternity and will last an eternity more.

So, this is the so-called "stronghold" Veer and the Duchess have sought for so long. The secret rebel hiding place Piotr mentioned once in a training class.

Which means the man who took us prisoner and his group of armed rebels, as threatening as they seem, are the very people the Duchess fears so deeply.

When the leader finally pulls the wooden door open, I'm surprised to see the space on the other side is large and open with white, plastered walls, lit with a combination of torches and overhead electric lights. People in casual clothing are milling about the large room, drinking some kind of tea and chatting among themselves.

It's the first time in years that I've seen such a large group of people looking genuinely relaxed and happy.

When we enter, the Pit's denizens stop and turn our way, looking more curious than hostile.

The chamber is warm and welcoming in its way, and in another life I might even have rejoiced at the thought of spending a night or two here with Finn. Right now, though,

I'm unsure whether it will be the last place either of us ever sees.

The leader commands Finn and me to take a seat on two ratty-looking leather armchairs by an unused fireplace embedded in one wall of the chamber. The chairs were no doubt once gorgeous and comfortable, but now they look like they've been half-devoured by famished raccoons. Mercifully, a large wool blanket sits folded on each of their seats, so we wrap them around our mostly naked bodies before seating ourselves.

The leader positions himself in front of the fireplace, arms crossed, and several of his people surround us. A few of them have firearms at their hips, but none are drawn, at least.

"My name is Illian," the man finally says. "I'd like to welcome you both to the Pit. It's part of a massive underground system of tunnels and chambers that stretches for hundreds of miles in every direction. This section is home to what's left of the Breckenridge faction of the Consortium."

"Breckenridge?" I repeat, turning in my seat to look around at the surrounding group. "You all used to live in the Bastille?"

"It wasn't always the Bastille," Illian says bitterly. "Before the Directorate began killing our people, before they erected their confining walls, it was a beautiful place. Of course, that was before some among our ranks betrayed us. Before the *Split.*"

"Split?"

"Come, now, Ashen. You told me you've been inside the Bastille. You must know something about all this."

I shake my head, drawing the blanket tighter around my shoulders, more for a sense of protection than warmth. "Like I told you, the Bastille's people said the Consortium was gone—

they told me there was a battle and that people died. Veer made it sound like the people who live there now are all that's left."

With a shudder, I recall the words shouted by the man in the Piazza just before he was slaughtered.

"There was a battle, yes. A bloody one. About that, at least, Veer told the truth. It all began when the Arc was still under construction and the Directorate was destroying neighboring towns, looking for materials they could use to build their so-called paradise. Veer and I, among others, had disagreements about the Consortium's future. She wanted to start her own small government, one that could co-exist with the Directorate—one that fell outside the Consortium's mandate, its goals.

"Maybe it wouldn't have led to so much death if not for the fact that she ultimately wanted to wipe us off the map. We were once allies, she and I. There was a time before your father died when we hunted for this place together. But those days have long since passed. In the end, Veer sided with the Directorate, and she's far more loyal now to them than to us."

"I know. She was ready to turn me over to them, along with one of your men."

"*One* of our men, you say," Illian repeats. "And the other?"

I swallow, terrified of the consequences if I reveal what happened to the second prisoner.

"There's a guillotine in the town," I say quietly. "The man with the dark brown hair...they..."

"Rafe." Illian's hands ball into fists, and he lets out a cry. "Monsters, all of them. Oh, they purport to be highly moral, to be a bastion of ethical perfection. But they thrive on chaos, on pain and suffering. Veer wants nothing but control. She manipulates her people. Brainwashes them. Persuades them to abide by her will, claiming it's all for the greater good. The sacrifices the people of the Bastille make for her..." Illian paces for a moment before turning my way again. "Tell me, when do they intend to hand the other man—Torrel is his name—over to the Directorate?"

"In two days," I reply. "But for all I know, they may have already done it."

He shakes his head. "No. Veer loves pomp and circumstance. If she announced a date, she'll stick with it. Besides, she's no doubt trying to extract information from him as we speak. But our people don't talk. They'd sooner die."

One of them already did.

Illian scrutinizes me for a few moments before asking, "How did you—a Candidate—escape the Bastille?"

I look at Finn, wondering how much I should divulge. He shakes his head almost imperceptibly, and I can tell what he's thinking.

Don't tell them about Atticus.

"There was a ladder," I reply. "One that brought me to the top of the wall. I climbed down the vines on the other side and ran to the woods."

"All this without getting shot. Impressive." Something in Illian's expression tells me he doesn't entirely believe me. "You are both highly valuable to the Directorate, no doubt."

With that, he looks at Finn, appraising.

"In different ways," Finn concedes. "My mother is one of them. She's the one they call the Duchess."

"I see." Illian clenches his jaw for a moment before adding, "No one here will turn either of you over to them, or to the Bastille. The worst fate you'll suffer at our hands is to be sent into the mountains to starve. But that won't happen—not if you do exactly as I tell you."

26

ON THE INSIDE

"ASHEN SPENCER," Illian says. "You say you were there when Veer captured my men."

My eyes move to the floor. I don't want to lie to this man who seems to admire my father, who wears the symbol of the Consortium. But how do I reveal to him the part I played in his men's capture without getting myself killed?

I brace myself before I speak. I can feel Finn's body language, his silent warning hanging in the air.

I look at him sideways, issuing a faint smile of reassurance.

It will be all right.

"I was…" I finally manage. "I was the one who took them down."

A look of quiet rage flashes across Illian's face, but it quickly subsides, like he's forcing all emotion from his mind and heart for the sake of a tense peace. "I see. You, a girl of what, seventeen, took down two of my best men."

I nod.

Illian lets out a quiet laugh.

"I wouldn't underestimate her if I were you," Finn snarls.

"Oh, I'm not. I believe her. I have a knack for knowing if someone is lying to me, and I have no doubt that Ashen here is telling the truth. Honestly, I'm a little embarrassed."

I pull my chin up to look him in the eye. "In my defense, I thought they were Directorate Guard. They were wearing the uniforms. They shot at us—if I'd known..."

Illian raises a hand to indicate he has no interest in more excuses. "Where were you when this happened?"

"At the ski chalet above Breck—above the Bastille. The ridge you mentioned earlier."

"Ah. It's all beginning to make sense now."

"What is?"

Illian steps over to lean against the mantel. He stares into space for a moment before saying, "Did you see anything in that chalet? Anything that might have been of interest to Veer?"

"There were video screens in one building, showing footage from a lot of different locations. Views of the Bastille, of cities around the country. But we weren't there for long before your men showed up."

"That's all you saw? Video feeds?"

I begin to nod when a faint memory works its way into my mind. "When we took your men down the mountain, Veer headed back into the chalet. She said she was looking for something."

"Damn it!" Illian curses.

My stomach tightens when I see the look in his eye. Why *did* Veer return to the chalet alone? What was she looking for?

"My men were up there for several days, in search of intel," Illian says. "They'd managed to break into the system, and Veer must have known it. It's why she went up that day. Probably why she brought you, too. To gain your trust, to use you."

"I suppose she did use me in the end. I saved her son's life."

"Son?" Illian asks, seemingly surprised.

"His name is Peric."

"Peric," he repeats, his face turning pale, like he's just seen a ghost. "Not her biological son, then."

"You know him?" I ask.

"I…knew his parents." He says nothing more, and I'm left, as usual, with more questions than answers. Changing the subject, he adds, "Those men you helped capture—they were looking for something we need. Something that could help us take the fight to the Directorate. Were we to acquire it, we could win this war."

"War," Finn says, leaning forward, his bare chest exposed between the folds of his blanket. "How can there be a war coming? There are so few of you down here. You *have* seen the Arc, right? You know what you're up against."

"I'm well aware of what we're up against. But for every Directorate member—for every one of their loyal, mind-controlled soldiers, there are in fact many of us."

Finn lets out a laugh. "No offense, but I think you might need to brush up on your math skills."

"Our math skills are actually quite good," says a man I haven't seen before, who steps up to Illian's side and turns to face us. He's tall and rosy-cheeked, with light brown, floppy hair and a mischievous grin. He puts an elbow on Illian's shoulder and stares down at me. "The Directorate knows we—the true Consortium—are still out here. They want us dead, of course. But they've been unable to kill us because they can't figure out how the hell to find us. The thing you should know is that this isn't the only underground stronghold. There are many others—partly thanks to your father."

"But why…" I begin. "Why would my father have thought

to even build something like this?"

"Twenty or so years ago, before you were born, your father worked as a scientist."

"I know about that. At least, a little. I know he worked with the Duke—Finn's father."

"Oliver Spencer had a gift of foresight. He saw the rumblings of an oppressive government in the making, and he knew the dangers—partly because of a certain biological weapon he was helping design."

"I know about that, too."

Illian nods. "Your father knew it was important to maintain a system to help people escape, stay in contact with others, or simply stay alive. There was a time when he had every intention of bringing your family here, hoping to find your way to a better life. What you've seen of the Pit only scratches the surface. There's a massive network of tunnels and rooms in this section alone. We're not quite a city, but a small town. And thanks to your father and the allies who built this place in secret, we're all still alive."

Finn looks around, eyeing the corners of the room where we're sitting. "This place looks like it hasn't been altered in years," he says. "How do you survive down here? What do you even eat?"

"We manage," the floppy-haired man says with a snicker. "We have some solar power for the lights and other necessities. The evergreens in this immediate area are man-made. Their needles absorb energy that's then rerouted through our wiring. Unfortunately, they don't provide nearly the power we'd need to thrive."

"Still, that's amazing," Finn says, impressed. Some of the guarded chilliness he's exhibited until now is melting away, and I can tell he's as confused by our strange hosts as I am. It's hard not to like them...yet it's entirely possible they're nothing more than liars who intend to kill us.

"Come on," Illian's partner says. "We'll show you around."

As we rise to our feet, I say, "Our clothes—could we at least put those on before we go on a tour?"

Illian nods to a woman standing behind us, who brings us our things. I stand, letting the blanket fall to the floor before I slip on my uniform and drape the cloak over my arm. I can't help but notice, though, that no one has handed me my dagger.

"Those screens at the chalet," I ask when we're both dressed. "The ones showing the Sectors and Manhattan—whose cameras were those?"

"Originally, they belonged to the Directorate. But for a time, we had control over many of them. There's other information in those systems—coded intel, data left behind by the Directorate. Blueprints, plans for Arcologies and their tech systems. Needless to say, we were hoping to get our hands on them. I suspect that Veer has shut the whole thing down by now."

"I see," I reply as the two men guide us toward a narrow door to the side of the fireplace. "So, what's going to happen to us?"

"You ask a lot of questions," the man says as he opens the door, giving Illian a sideways glance and raising his eyebrows as if to say *She's annoying, isn't she?*

"I just want to know if Finn and I are going to live to see morning."

"Oh, you'll be fine," the man replies, guiding us down a dark hallway and up a set of sturdy wooden stairs. "The last thing we'd ever do is hurt Oliver's daughter."

When we've reached the top of the stairs, we turn right

and head into a large room filled with electronic equipment. Holographic screens, half-disassembled drones, cameras, most of which are deactivated.

"This is amazing," Finn says, stepping forward. "I had no idea the Consortium had so much tech..."

But Illian stops Finn with a hand to his chest. "Sorry. But if either of you intends to return to the Arc, this is as far as you both go. We can't have you bringing the Directorate intel, even if you're two of the good guys."

"Right," Finn replies with a nod. "Fair enough."

"The woods are equipped with hundreds of our cameras," the floppy-haired man tells us, gesturing toward one of the screens, which shows treetops, clouds, and not much else. "My name is Kurt, by the way."

"What good are cameras against drones?" I ask, adding, "Kurt."

"They allow our concealed sharp-shooters to see them and take them down before they get too close to the Pit's entry point, for one thing." With that, Kurt marches over to a table against the far wall, picks up what looks like a small rocket launcher, and strides back to us. "These puppies are very handy when drones come calling. We've taken down over fifty in the past couple of years. Drives the Directorate nuts."

"Sorry to sound naive," I half-laugh, "but doesn't the Directorate have an army? Like, planes and things? Couldn't they bomb you off the face of the earth if they wanted to?"

"Not without bombing their precious allies in the Bastille," Illian says. "Veer has been catering to their every whim for years."

"I'm honestly shocked the Directorate values Veer's life enough to care."

"It's not Veer's life they value," Illian says mysteriously. "It's what she harvests in that town of hers that they want."

"Harvests?"

"A topic for another time, when we know each other a little better."

"So, why are we here?" I ask. "Why did you bring us to this place? Why are you telling us so much, if you have any doubts about us?"

Illian and Kurt exchange a glance. "Oliver Spencer was a friend," Illian says. "A *good* friend. If you're his daughter, then we can trust you. And if you managed to find your way out of the Arc then the Bastille unscathed, you're as impressive as your father was. The thing is..."

Kurt reaches out and puts a hand on Illian's arm, shaking his head just enough to stop him saying anything more.

"Look, we have no desire to imprison you here," Kurt says. "Quite the contrary. The problem is, we need our man back. We don't abandon our own, nor do we want the Directorate torturing them for sport."

"I'm not sure you can get your man back," I say. "The Bastille is well guarded. You must know that."

"Regardless, we'd like you to free him."

"*Me*?" I ask, choking on the word. "Even if I could find my way to him—which would mean breaking back into the Bastille unseen, which is pretty much impossible, even with help—your men *shot* at me. They would have killed me, if I hadn't had..." I stop short of mentioning the unique gifts provided by the uniform I'm currently wearing. "Look, who's to say he won't try to kill me again the second he lays eyes on me? He watched his friend die—he has no reason to trust me, and every reason to despise me."

"You were with the enemy, invading territory the Consortium had staked out as its own," Kurt says. "Our men didn't know who you were. Tell Torrel Illian and Kurt sent you, and he'll know you can be trusted."

I go silent for a few seconds before saying, "Even if I decide to help you, it's not like I can just walk through the front gates. The snipers will see me coming from miles away."

It's a lie, of course; I can use the cloak to conceal myself. But I have no desire to return to the Bastille. No desire to lay my eyes on Veer or the others again, to put myself in harm's way. I'm safe now, with Finn by my side...however temporarily. I also have my brother to think about.

So another near-death experience isn't exactly at the top of my priority list.

"Ashen," Illian says quietly, taking a step toward me. "You are, quite literally, our only hope. I have no idea how you really escaped the Arc or the Bastille, but I do know you haven't told us the entire truth. You're the only vague chance we have of getting our man back without anyone on either side dying. Please—use whatever means you have to bring him back to us. It's our one chance to gain the advantage over the Directorate."

I shake my head. "Veer's people are hunting me. If they catch me, I'm as good as dead."

"She's right," says Finn. "You *can't* ask her to do this. You don't know what she went through in the Arc—what the Directorate did to her. You have no idea."

"You're right, we don't," Illian says with a sigh. He looks toward a painting on the far wall, of a landscape. The sun seems to be rising, light just beginning to filter through a bank of diaphanous clouds. "We ask only that you consider it. If you want us to trust you—if you want to fight the Directorate, to support a cause greater than yourself—please, just consider helping us."

"And if I don't?" I ask.

Illian glances at Kurt, then locks his eyes on Finn and me. He seems sad, rather than angry, which sends a wave of guilt shuddering through me. "It would be difficult to justify letting you both go, after everything," he says. "Given everything you know—the location of the Pit, the things we've told you. It would be too dangerous, too imprudent."

"The thing is, it doesn't matter," Finn says with a sneer. "If Ash gets killed, *nothing* matters."

Silently, I reach for his hand.

"Why don't you both take some time," Kurt says, "and think about it? You can go get a bite to eat—I'm sure you must be hungry. You can discuss your options."

"Options?" Finn laughs. "Be stuck here in the land of darkness forever, or—?"

"The land of darkness will soon become a land of light, if you help us," Illian tells us. "There is more at stake here than the fate of our man. An item that could change everything for us, for you. If there's a chance they found its whereabouts... Well, let's just say our army would increase exponentially in size and scope."

"Unless your men were hunting for a cloning device, I don't think you're being entirely realistic," Finn retorts, his tone sharp.

"Not quite a cloning device. But in the end, the result will be the same."

Without another word, Illian has two guards lead us to what seems like a mess hall. It's a large room with row upon row of folding metal tables set up, surrounded by matching metal chairs. There's a coldness to the place, a sort of desolate sadness. And as we enter, I realize it's not just the dull grayness that's bringing my mood down.

It's the people.

Faces turn to look at us, their skin pale, eyes veiled as though a filter has settled over their irises.

"What's happened to them?" I ask quietly.

"It's a degeneration of vision known as the Gloaming," Illian says. "It happens when you live in darkness for long stretches. As you've seen, we don't get much light down here. Most of our residents will regain their vision if ever they're able to live above ground, though. It's only a matter of exposure."

"The people we saw when we first came in didn't have eyes like that," Finn says. "You two don't."

"Some of us regularly leave the Pit to patrol, to scan the woods from the treetops. We get regular exposure to sunlight. Those who live deep inside the Pit aren't so lucky. But they're safe here, and they're willing to trade their vision for security."

My heart aches for those who are trapped down here. More victims of the Directorate's cruelty, prisoners of a system put in place to protect only the powerful.

Some of the people turn to face Finn and me as we sit down silently. I spot a woman with a young girl—maybe five or six—by her side. The girl has dark hair, but her skin is paper-white, her eyes a dull gray. She stares at me and smiles, but I get the impression that she's not seeing me as I see her, crystal-clear and perfect. To her, I'm nothing more than a shadow in a dark room. A ghost.

It's in the moment when I lock eyes on the girl that I know in my heart I've finally found my father's allies.

Down here in the dark are the people who will save the world.

The Consortium lives, after all.

27

A DANGEROUS MISSION

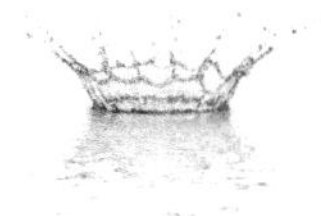

WITHOUT ANOTHER WORD, Illian leaves us seated at our table, and Finn and I stare at one another, faint torchlight flickering around us.

"Ash," Finn says, "we could leave here without risking our lives."

"I know," I reply softly. "It's just..."

"These people would let us leave eventually. They don't seem like the kind to punish us for wanting our freedom. They're not killers."

I nod. "You're right. They're not."

"You're actually thinking about returning to the Bastille," he says, reaching out and taking my hand. "You're really going to help them, aren't you?"

"If I don't, they'll keep us here. Possibly for days. Your parents will figure out you're gone. They'll come looking for you, and I don't want to think what they'll do when they find you. It puts you in danger. It puts everyone inside the Pit in danger, too."

"They won't find me. Look, they haven't found this place

in all these years—"

I put up a hand to stop him saying anything more. "It doesn't matter. I need you back in the Arc. The selfish part of me wants you out here in the wilderness with me forever, of course. But we both know that's impossible."

I can tell he wants to protest, to argue. But he relaxes his shoulders as if surrendering to my will. "You're a good person, Ash. Too good, sometimes."

I pull my eyes over to the mother and daughter seated some distance away. "My father cared about these people. He knew what was happening—he knew what the Directorate was up to. He wanted to save the Consortium from the fate that was coming for all of us."

"And now that he's gone, you want to do it yourself."

I nod again. "I know you think I'm insane."

An all too adorable smile creeps over Finn's delicious lips and he lets out a deep chuckle. "Not at all. Insanity would be leaving them here to rot instead of helping. You're the opposite. You're so sane that you're going to get yourself killed."

"You know I can do this," I whisper, pressing myself close to him. "I can get back into the Bastille. I *need* to get that man—Torrel—out, before...before Veer or your mother kills him. Look—it's our best chance at getting the Consortium on our side. If there are as many of them as Illian says, they're our best chance of defeating the Directorate."

"It's a noble pursuit, Ash. But how the hell do you plan to do it?"

"Atticus. He helped me once before. He can be my eyes. I have the cloak, the uniform you made for me. If I can get in unseen, I can get the prisoner out of there. I know I can."

"So your plan is to put all your faith in a mechanical owl

and a couple of pieces of fabric." Finn sighs. "Well, the good news is I'm coming with you."

"What? No, you can't!"

"You think I'm letting you go into that madhouse alone?" He sits back, crossing his powerful arms over his chest. "You obviously don't know me very well, Miss Spencer."

He has a point, I suppose. He has a cloak, too. He's strong, and smart.

Still, the idea of both of us risking our lives doesn't sit well with me.

"Fine," I finally exhale. "You can come."

"Okay, let's say this plan—which, by the way, is *very* iffy—succeeds. What happens after we get the prisoner back here? Will you stay in the Pit?"

"I don't know. My greatest wish is to get Kel back. If I have to hide out here while I figure out how, that's what I'll do. In the meantime, we should plan on heading to the Bastille tonight, long after dark."

"Well," Finn sighs. "At least that gives us the rest of today to enjoy each other's company."

"What are you thinking?"

"I think we find Illian and Kurt. We tell them we're both going to risk our lives to bring their man back alive. And then we ask them if there's somewhere you and I can be alone together in the meantime. Because if we're both going to die tonight, I don't want to be separated from you for a second."

"I like that plan."

Illian and Kurt don't seem particularly surprised when Finn and I fill them in on our intentions.

"We'll send a couple of our people to accompany you, in case of problems outside of town," Illian tells us.

"Understood," I reply.

"As for accommodations," Kurt adds with a clap of his hands, "we'll have our people show you both to one of our nicest rooms. I'm afraid we're not a luxury hotel, but we do have a few residents who managed to salvage some bedding from a few of Breckenridge's better hotels before all hell broke loose."

"Indeed," Illian agrees. "You two should rest. You have a long night ahead of you, and I don't want you distracted."

He speaks like a man in charge—a true leader. But he's not frightening like the Duchess or Veer. He doesn't scream "tyrant" when I look at him. He seems reasonable, calm, caring. He genuinely wants what's best for his people.

My father would have liked you, I think as I smile at him.

I mean...except for the fact that in a few hours, you're sending his daughter to her likely death.

One of Illian's men—Duncan is his name—leads us by torchlight through the Pit's labyrinthine halls until we come to one that seems a little more hospitable than the others. Its walls are evenly packed with large gray stones, giving the space the air of a homey cottage. The floor is tiled with flat layers of slate, and the doors on either side of the hallway are painted in various bright colors, each with a number on its surface. Without asking, I can tell these are residences of those who dwell inside the Pit.

We stop at number eighty-three, and Duncan opens the door for us. Inside is a double bed with soft-looking white linens, a set of wooden side tables, and a tidy dresser off to one side.

"Thank you," I say shyly when Duncan has asked if we need anything else. "I think we just need a shower and some rest, honestly."

"Showers are down the hall. Room ninety," he says, eyeing us both. "There's a series of private stalls. You'll find towels there. We do manage to wash them, so you'll find them quite clean."

"Great. Thanks," I say, desperate to end the conversation. All I want is to be alone with Finn again. To press my head to his chest, to breathe in his scent. *The calm before the unstoppable storm.*

When Duncan has left, Finn and I head to the shower room. As I slip into one of the private stalls, I close the door behind me to hear Finn humming as he showers on the other side of the partition that divides us. I can't help but smile. He sounds so relaxed, so calm. How is that possible, given what we're about to do? The Bastille's forces will be only too eager to take us both down.

I take a deep breath and force my mind toward hope instead of dread. If I give up on the notion that I can help the Pit's residents—if I surrender to despair—then I have only myself to blame when things go badly.

The water that comes dribbling out of the shower head is luke-warm, at best, and the pressure leaves a good deal to be desired. I suppose the lack of a heating system means I can't expect much more. But it still manages to invigorate me, to make me feel refreshed, renewed, and I'm grateful.

When I'm done, I wrap a large red bath towel around my torso, pick up my uniform, and slip out to find Finn standing in front of one of the sinks with a small paper envelope in his hand.

"What's that?" I ask, eyeing the package.

Finn pulls it open and taps one end. Two strips of what looks like chewing gum fall into his hand, and he offers me one.

"Toothpaste, developed in my lab," he says. "It starts off as a solid then melts in your mouth. It'll get your teeth cleaner than any brush could."

I take the offered piece gratefully, and once I start chewing, I finally begin to feel fully human again.

"It's amazing," I tell him with a laugh. "Thank your lab for me, will you?"

"I would, if mentioning your name in the Arc weren't enough to get me killed."

"Ah. Good point. You know, it's so strange to think in the Arc, I had everything I could want. Great food, hot showers. You. But…"

"But you're happier here, with dirt walls and no light."

"Happier? In a way, I guess. I can live without the great food and hot showers. But I don't like the idea of losing you."

"You haven't lost me." He rinses his hands, then, taking me by the waist, pulls me close. "You have me today. Tonight. And one day soon, if we're both very lucky..."

"Forever," I say.

"Forever."

It's a concept I can't quite grasp, too good by far to be true.

When I was small, "forever" was a day, two days. As I grew older, it became the length of time until my next birthday. Then forever was how long my parents would live.

Forever came to a crashing end.

Now, there's no such thing. Time passes in swift, often

calamitous moments that I either savor or dread—moments of danger, of uncertainty. Moments when I wonder if I'll ever have a family again, if I'll live to see eighteen.

Still, in the instant when I stare into Finn's eyes and listen to him utter the word, I feel forever in a single, delicious burst of light.

Today is our forever.

But even forever has an end.

28

QUEST

AT MIDNIGHT, a knock at the door wakes us both.

Already dressed, we bolt out of bed before the door opens. A second later, Illian is standing in the doorway, his features barely visible in the dim light.

"Are you ready?" he asks, his eyes on me.

"We are," I reply.

"There's been a change of plans," the Pit's leader says, shooting Finn a stern look. "He stays here."

"What? Why?" Finn asks, his voice raised. "That wasn't what we agreed on!"

As I look Illian in the eye, I reach for Finn's hand and squeeze.

"He wants an insurance policy. A promise that I'll come back with their man instead of taking off into the woods with you."

"Of course we'll come back!" Finn insists. "You can't keep me here! What if…"

"What if I die?" I ask, turning to him. "If I die, at least it'll be with the knowledge you're still alive. It's okay. I'll be fine."

I look into his eyes, my heart pounding. I want to put on a brave face. But the truth is, I don't know if I can do this without him. I could be killed by Veer's people, or by a summoned drone. Knowing Veer is fully in league with the Directorate means she has access to their weaponry, their technology.

It renders her more dangerous than I ever thought possible.

Some small, weak part of me wants to tell Illian I've changed my mind, that I refuse to go. That I can't bear to risk my life—not if it means never seeing Finn again, or leaving Kel without a sister.

But instead of voicing my plethora of fears, I simply smile. "I'm ready," I say, turning to Illian. "I'll do my best to get your man back. I promise."

"Thank you. I know you will."

"Ash…are you sure about this?" Finn asks.

I nod. "We have a war to fight. If I don't do my part, I won't be able to look my brother in the eye."

Finn pulls me to his chest and holds me, kissing the top of my head. "You're a madwoman. You know that, right?"

I nod. "Mmm. I know."

When I tell him I'm ready, Illian leads us down a series of hallways until we reach the spiral staircase that will take us to the surface. At its base, I turn to Finn and kiss him.

"You'll be all right," he says, but I can tell he's working hard to reassure himself. "Watch for Atticus. He'll help."

"Atticus?" Illian asks.

"An owl," I reply. "He's the main reason I managed to escape the Bastille."

"I don't know why, but I believe you. Well, if you have a helper owl, so much the better."

Without another word, I turn away from Finn, a lump in my throat as I climb the narrow staircase to its top.

When we emerge through the door in the old oak tree, two of the Pit's residents are waiting for me—a man and a woman, each dressed in khaki garments that look like they were swiped years ago from an army surplus store.

"This is Mura and Darryn," Illian says, handing me the dagger his people confiscated earlier in the day. "They'll be accompanying you to the Bastille and helping you to get the prisoner back here."

I nod, grateful to have company, at least for part of the task ahead.

Though it's dark out, the moonlight makes the woods feel brighter than the Pit is, and I'm relieved to find myself out in the open again.

"Is there anything you need?" Illian asks.

I wrap my fingers around my dagger's hilt and pull my cloak around me.

"I'd like to take a quick detour, if it's all right," I say.

"Detour?"

"Finn brought a bag from the Arc, with more cloaks like the one I'm wearing. They'll help Mura and Darryn."

Mura scoffs. "I don't think wearing a purple bedsheet will help me out there," she says, eyeing the long garment wrapped around my body.

Silently, I reach for the pressure point that activates my cloak, and once again, I disappear from view. The woman's mouth, which was pulled into a sarcastic grin, gapes open.

"You're full of surprises," Illian says. "Yes, by all means, please grab anything you think will make this mission a success."

A hoot in a nearby tree draws my eyes upward, and I spot Atticus perched on a branch, watching us.

"Strange, that owl," Darryn says. "I swear it's looking right at us."

"He is," I tell him. "He's going to help us. Aren't you, Atticus?"

He lets out a low *hooo* and ruffles his metal feathers before taking off in the direction of the hidden backpack.

The walk to the bag's hiding place doesn't take long, and seconds after we've arrived, I've extracted cloaks for each of them, as well as a bandolier covered in throwing knives, which I strap diagonally across my torso.

"My old friends," I say with a grimace, recalling Piotr's classes in the Arc. The memories aren't exactly fond ones, but I can't deny I learned to fight under his tutelage.

When the other two have activated their cloaks, we begin the hike to the Bastille.

I don't know how long it takes—an hour, maybe more—before Mura alerts us that we're getting close. When I spot the tall cement wall surrounding our destination, I guide our small party along the southern side, taking care to remain tucked in the woods to avoid the snipers' keen eyes.

"I count five of them up there," Mura says, pointing to the top of the wall. "How exactly do you plan to get in without getting shot?"

During our hike, I contemplated my options, running through every possible scenario in my mind. Climbing the vines that creep up the outer wall would likely result in death.

The door Veer brought us through to head to the chalet is securely locked from the outside.

Which leaves only one option.

"I'm going through the front door."

"No way," Darryn says with a shake of his head. "They'll take us prisoner the second we're inside."

"About that. From here on, there's no *we.*"

"What do you mean?" Mura asks, a look of fear in her eyes, like she's afraid I'm about to stab them both.

"I mean you two need to stay out here. They're more likely to spot three of us than one."

"She's right," Darryn agrees, and I'm not sure if I only imagine the relief in his voice.

I pull my eyes up to the trees. "Rys—are you there?"

A low hoot is followed by "I'm here, Ash."

Atticus flaps down to land on a low branch just over our heads. Out of the corner of my eye I see Mura and Darryn exchange a look, but I have little desire to delve into a deep explanation as to why an owl is speaking to me.

"I need something," I tell Rys. "I can get in—but you need to help me once I'm there."

"That I can do. Just say the word."

Leaving the others behind, I step out of the woods toward the road leading to the front gate. Deactivating my cloak, I raise my hands and shout, "Hey!"

Almost immediately, a set of bright lights hits the ground in front of me, then shines directly in my face.

Without a doubt, this is the most reckless thing I've ever done in my life.

"Who are you?" a man's voice shouts.

"Ashen Spencer," I tell him. "I've come back to the Bastille. Surprise."

I hear muffled talking, then the town's large doors fly open. I step through, my eyes on Atticus, who's currently soaring over the wall.

The second the doors shut behind me, two guards leap over to grab me by the arms. "Veer will be very interested in seeing you," one of them says. "Unfortunately, she's out at the moment."

"Out?" I ask. "What, like on a date?"

"Shut it," the man says, squeezing my arm hard enough to make me wince.

"We'll put her in the cells until Veer's ready to deal with her," the other guard says. "No need to wake Piper and the rest of them."

Atticus is flying large circles in the air above us, awaiting my signal. The snipers on the wall are meant to take down drones, but they don't seem to notice him. I suppose he looks a little too much like a *real* bird.

Either that, or I'm a little too interesting.

With little resistance, I let the men drag me toward the Bunker until we enter through its front door and begin our descent.

When we reach the cells in the Sub-Bastille, one of the guards opens a cell door and pushes me inside. I go fake-stumbling across the room before turning back to him.

"What, no food?" I ask. "Not fair—I'm a little peckish."

"You should have thought about that before you came back here." The guard takes a step toward me. It's meant to be a threatening gesture, but I snicker at him, mocking.

He takes one step closer before I grab him, twisting him around and yanking my knife out of its sheath to press it to his throat.

A trickle of blood drips down the man's neck as he whimpers.

"You two forgot to disarm me," I say with a chuckle. "Not too bright, are you? Now, the prisoner. The one Veer plans to hand to the Directorate—where is he?"

The second guard looks terrified. For a second, I'm convinced he's about to back away and lock us both in the cell together, but instead, he simply points at the hallway.

"Show me," I growl, pressing the blade deeper into my prisoner's flesh.

The other guard steps back into the hall, his hands raised as if he's convinced I'm going to shoot him, despite my lack of a gun. I ease toward the door, pulling my hostage with me. But when I reach the hallway I turn, shove him back into the cell, and leave, slamming the door behind me.

"Now," I say, turning back to the first guard, my knife aimed menacingly at his chest. "Show me the prisoner."

"In here," he tells me, gesturing to the cell across from the one I was in.

"Open it," I command.

He fumbles with a ring of keys on his belt until he grabs hold of the right one. He shoves it into the lock and turns, his hand shaking.

"Good. Now, unlock an empty cell," I tell him once the door is slightly ajar.

"Excuse me?"

"You heard me."

He does as I command, but before he can step in, I ask for the key ring, which he hands over reluctantly. I push him inside and lock him in before heading next door.

The man we captured is sitting on the floor, dressed in

nothing but torn shorts and an undershirt. No shoes, no other clothing.

"Are you all right, Torrel?" I ask.

He nods, but looks terrified.

"I'm not who you think I am," I assure him. "I'm here to help. Illian and Kurt sent me—I need to get you back to the Pit."

"You…you know about the Pit? But how…"

"They can explain everything later. We need to go. Now, before Veer comes back."

The man follows me down the hall, and we ascend until we reach the door that leads out to the Main Street.

It's eerily empty.

Perfect, I think.

Shushing Torrel with a finger to my lips, I scout the air for Atticus, who's perched on a nearby rooftop. "There's a door in the outer wall," I whisper-hiss. "Veer took us through it to get up the mountain—do you remember?"

Atticus lets out a soft hoot and takes off to fly in the direction of the door.

I don't know the eleven-digit code. I have no idea if there's any way to pry it open.

But we have to try.

Torrel follows me down a narrow alleyway, then across a street and down another alley until we see the imposing wall before us.

"Stay in the shadows," I whisper, kicking myself for not having brought him a cloak. "As much as you can."

We're about to emerge from the shadows to make a run for the wall when a silhouetted figure steps out in front of us.

"I can't let you do this," a feminine voice says. *"Ash."*

29

PURSUIT

"CYNTRA," I whisper. She's standing in front of us, her face twisted in an expression of rage. "I need to get this man out of here. He can't stay—Veer will give him to the Directorate. They'll kill him."

"Of course they will," she retorts. "He's a member of the Consortium."

My heart fractures in my chest as two men emerge from behind Cyntra. Each of them is holding a handgun, and each gun is pointed directly at my head.

"You've known all along that the Consortium was still out there," I say, "haven't you? You lied when you acted like it was a thing of the past."

"I've suspected there were still members out there," she says with a strange little laugh. "We all did. But the two prisoners you brought were the first real evidence I saw of it. They're an endangered species, you know. And with any luck, soon they'll be extinct."

"Which is why you should let this man go. He hasn't done anything to you."

"He wants to take away my future. He and his rebels want to destroy everything that makes the Arc great."

"Keeping this man prisoner—turning him over to the Directorate—that won't ensure a happy future for you, Cyn."

Cyntra lets out the same high-pitched giggle I've heard so often from her throat. A sound that used to be charming, and has turned grating, malevolent. A pretty set of bells, meant to deceive. "You're wrong, though. My future is in the hands of the Directorate. Don't you get it? If you take this prisoner away, you're condemning this whole town to a fate worse than death. Veer has promised the Directorate a trophy—a man who knows where the Consortium stronghold is located. What do you suppose they would do to her if they found out she has nothing?"

"You're willing to sacrifice his life to keep the Directorate happy?" I ask.

"Are *you* willing to sacrifice Veer's life just to defy them?"

I ponder the question for a moment. She's not wrong—the Directorate will lose their minds if Veer doesn't give them their promised sacrifice—a man who could lead them to the stronghold they've sought for years.

They may kill Veer. Worse, they may kill everyone in the Bastille.

But if I don't get Torrel away from here, the Directorate will get hold of us both. They'll torture him—and me—in hopes of gaining the location of the Pit. And if either of us caves to their abuse, many people will die.

"I'm sorry, Cyntra," I say, my eyes on the sky. "I'm afraid I can't give you what you want."

"You have knives," she replies, her voice poisonous. "These men have guns. Don't be stupid. I'm not going to let you do this. I'm not letting you ruin my chances of becoming an Aristocrat."

"*Aristocrat?*" I ask, shocked, my eyes landing on hers. "Is that who Veer is planning to marry you off to? Is that your dream? To be imprisoned on the high levels of the Arc, to look down on thousands upon thousands of people because your husband is rich? Wow, Veer really *has* brainwashed you, hasn't she?"

"No she hasn't!" she retorts, raising her chin haughtily. "I'm perfectly capable of thinking for myself."

"Sure you are," I tell her, stepping toward her. The guards cock their guns and take a step back, positioning themselves to fire. "Well, I guess is it. I don't know who can possibly save me now." With the last few words, I raise my hands to the sky.

Cyntra pulls her head up, but too late.

Atticus is already swooping down, his heavy metallic wings beating at the air as he makes contact with the first of the two guards, who goes crashing, his face bleeding, into Cyntra.

The other gets off a shot but it winds up in the wall of the building next to me. I leap at him, knocking the gun out of his hand and pushing him to the ground. While Atticus thrashes in the air, keeping Cyntra and the other man down, I land a blow to my victim's face that knocks him unconscious.

"Run!" I shout to Torrel, who's standing in a state of shock behind me. As he takes off sprinting, so do I.

"There's a kill-switch," he calls out. "In the door ahead. A safety mechanism that opens it in case someone needs to escape."

"Where?"

"Hidden in a beam to the door's left."

"How the hell do you know that?" I ask breathlessly as I

dart toward the door, looking over my shoulder to see Atticus is still battling his two rivals. *Good boy.*

"I used to live here," Torrel says. "This was my home for a time—years ago, when the Consortium occupied this town."

Without asking anything more, I find the beam he was talking about. At eye level is a small compartment just big enough to slip my hand into. I force my fingers in and feel around until I find a small lever, which I click downward.

The lock-wheel spins and the door snaps open away from us.

"Go!" I shout even as I twist around to see two figures running at us while Atticus dive-bombs their heads.

Cyntra is in the lead, a guard hot on her tail, while the owl does a sort of swooping mid-air dance between them.

In a final burst of energy, I charge through the door, slamming it behind me. I have no idea if the others know about the release lever, but I can only hope they don't.

Seconds later, a series of bright spotlights bursts to life, intense beams of quasi-daylight hitting the ground around us. The pings of gunfire echo off the trees in front of us, and a bullet slices into the ground inches from my right foot as I sprint.

Behind me, Torrel lets out a grunt. I turn to see him falling chest-first to the ground. Twisting back, I pick him up and help him to his feet, wrapping my cloaked arm around his shoulders.

When the gunfire mysteriously stops, I dare a look back only to see Atticus flapping at the snipers' heads.

"Come on!" Mura's voice yells from somewhere ahead.

Once we've stepped into the woods, she does a quick assessment of Torrel's injury, which it seems is a mere graze to his left forearm.

"I'm okay," he insists. "It just threw me off balance."

"Let's get back as fast as we can. These woods will be crawling with Veer's people in no time."

I pull my cloak off and wrap it around Torrel.

"But you're visible," he says, his breath heavy.

"It's okay," I tell him. "You need it more than I do."

With that, we begin our run back toward the Pit.

Our ears are met with screams and shouts of pain ringing through the air behind us. The cloaks, combined with Atticus' unrelenting attacks on anyone in pursuit, mean we manage to remain hidden until our pursuers lose any trace of us.

When we arrive, breathless, at the oak tree, it's Mura who lifts the limb and inputs the code to get us back into the Pit.

We escort Torrel down the stairs and to the first chamber, where we find Illian, Kurt, and Finn waiting for us.

Finn leaps to his feet and has his arms around me before I can say a word.

"You were sure I was going to die, weren't you?" I half laugh, half weep.

"Not at all. I have complete faith in you."

"Liar."

He pulls back, cupping my face in his hands and examining me to make sure I'm not hurt.

"I was a *little* worried. I don't know those people in the Bastille. All I do know is that I don't like them." Gently, he pushes my hair from my face. "Are you really all right?"

"I'm fine. Torrel got nicked, but he should be okay." I close my mouth and look over to where Illian and Kurt are talking to him.

Illian is interrogating him, a look of worry in his eyes. "Did you get it? The information we need?"

Torrel shakes his head. "We tried—but they showed up just as we'd broken into the system."

"Damn it," Illian curses. "Without the Quantum Source, there's no hope."

"You're telling me Ash risked her life for this man, and he has nothing to offer you?" Finn growls.

"He has *life* to offer," Illian replies. "Intellect. Loyalty. If those are of no value to you, then you're more similar to your mother than I'd hoped."

"I'm *nothing* like her."

"That's right," I interject, taking hold of Finn's arm. "He's nothing like the Duchess. Everyone, please—settle down. No one died tonight; that's what should matter."

Finn grinds his jaw for a moment. I understand his anger—I'm feeling it, too. But Illian is right. Torrel has a right to live, just as we all do.

"What's a Quantum Source?" I ask, hoping to steer Finn's mind away from rage and toward more useful emotions.

"I know what it is," Finn says, his voice calmer now.

"You do?" Kurt asks.

"Of course. There are tons of them in the Arc. They power my father's entire business. The King's corporation manufactures them. Rumor has it that there's an entire stash of them on the three-hundredth level—in the Royal Grounds. They're hidden, but...Why exactly do you need one?"

"Um...Finn, Ashen, you two need to come with us," Kurt says, nodding to one of the men to take care of Torrel. "There's something we need to show you."

30

HOPE

KURT and Illian guide us silently along a series of narrow, chilly tunnels. Illuminated only by the lanterns each of them is carrying, the route feels claustrophobic, even frightening at times. But we move quickly, and by the time we're through, I've convinced myself they have good reason for taking us on the strange adventure.

Finally, we reach a door that Illian unlocks using a device he pulls from around his neck. It looks more like a puzzle piece than a key.

He gestures to us to enter the pitch-dark space ahead, which I do reluctantly, consumed by a sudden lack of faith.

My life has taught me recently that trust is a dangerous game.

But as I push my way through the dark with Finn by my side, Illian and Kurt both follow, their lanterns in hand. In a dance of shadows, the space around us springs to life.

Above us is a surprisingly high arched ceiling, and a few feet away I spot what looks like the edge of a platform of some sort. I take one step, then another, taking care not to fall over the edge. Illian joins me, holding the lantern low enough to light the floor before us.

Looking down, I spot a thin metal rail running along the earth several feet down, leading as far as the eye can see into the darkness of a broad, arched tunnel.

"What is this?" I ask.

"What does it look like to you?"

"A rail—like on subway tracks...only there's just one."

Illian nods. "That's exactly what it is. A single rail. And about a mile down this track is the train that used to cruise along it at high speed."

"But..." I'm staring, stunned, into the darkness. The intricacy of this place reminds me of the Arc. The effort, the years that must have gone into its secret construction—the cost of it—are unfathomable. "It's not one of the lines that leads into the Arc, is it?"

"No," Illian assures me. "Those in the Arc don't know about this system. This track leads to another Consortium stronghold, one near Santa Fe. There are lines and trains running all the way to the east coast of the United States and up to Canada."

"How..." I say, trying to push back the hope that's growing inside me. "How many Consortium members are out there?"

"There are millions throughout the country," Kurt says.

"I'm confused. I met a man in the Arc—a prisoner—who told me the Consortium was broke. How did an organization with no money build all this?"

"There *was* money at one time," Illian replies. "Enough, anyhow. I don't know if you remember when the Blight first hit—"

"I do," I interrupt.

How could I forget? My father's death was like an explosion at the beginning of it all.

"It wasn't just our city that it hit, and we weren't the only ones who were walled in like caged animals. It happened all over the country, Ashen. Not always the same way—but in each case, Arcologies were built."

I nod. "I've seen the one in Manhattan."

"Your father…he knew what was happening. He'd seen it coming; he knew the Directorate's intentions. He sent out warnings to every corner of the country, to every ally. Because of him, many of us were able to communicate for a time, before the cell towers went down and the world went dark and we lost our ability to communicate with the other strongholds. Traveling over land wasn't an option because of the Directorate's drones, hunting us from the earliest days. So, the Consortium members with power, with money, began construction on our underground world. It went on for years, before our lives went dark."

"You're really saying there's hope? That we could band together—millions of us?"

"I am. We may have lost touch, but I know for a fact that there were once well over two million of us spread between the Atlantic and the Pacific. And I can only imagine there are many more by now, after all that's happened. If we can organize ourselves, we may stand a fighting chance against the Directorate."

"But you said yourself, we have no resources. That means no way to fight. They used biological weapons against our people before. I've heard they're developing more powerful ones, even. What's to stop them doing it again?"

"Nothing except for the truth. We believe in the power of words, rather than brute strength and weapons. My hope is to gather forces to my side—enough of them to take on the enemy. To reveal the truth to the people who trust the Directorate."

Good luck taking on the Directorate with nothing but words, I think, but I don't say it. Instead, I go silent.

"The thing is," Illian adds, "after years of limited resources, we lack the power to run the train—to communicate with the Santa Fe stronghold or any other members of the Consortium. If we could get this train moving, we could communicate with every stronghold accessible via the underground. Supplies could be passed back and forth. Weapons, entire armies. You name it."

"And to power the train, you need…"

"A Quantum Source," Finn says.

"Okay, can someone explain to me what that is?" I interject.

"It's like a large battery," Kurt explains. "One that never runs out. One of them would not only allow us the use of the train, but we'd be able to power the entire Pit. My people would have light. They could begin their recovery after years spent living in darkness. We'd be able to grow food down here. Our lives would change drastically, to say the least."

When Finn issues him a skeptical side-eye, Illian chuckles.

"I know, the Pit looks like nothing more than a big, damp rabbit warren. But before darkness set in, this place was glowing with technology. There used to be holo-screens showing us other parts of the country. Comms systems. Massive amounts of information are concealed in this place—tech you can't see under the current circumstances—but none of it is available to us without adequate power. If we could get it up and running, the place would look like a subterranean version of the Arc."

I look at Finn. "How hard would it be to get hold of one of these Quantum thingies?"

"Difficult," he says with a grimace. "The three-hundredth level is the best guarded in the Arc. The King is paranoid, and the level is basically a maze of holographic images, which makes it extremely difficult to navigate. But it's not impossible. The bigger problem is the weight. Quantum Sources aren't exactly light. They're not the sort of thing you can just tuck into a backpack and carry here, even if one of us managed to get our hands on one without being caught."

"Then we'll have to find another way," I say.

"Well, then," says Illian, whose smile is broader than any I've ever seen on his face, "I believe we have the beginnings of a plan in place. Now, let's get out of here so you two can get some rest."

As we make our way back along the narrow tunnels to the large chamber where we left Darryn, Mura and Torrel, I say, "There's something I need to understand."

"What's that?" Illian asks.

"The Bastille. What is it about the people in that place the Directorate likes so much?"

Kurt and Illian exchange a brief look. "What do you know of the young people in the Bastille?" Kurt asks me.

"I know when the girls turn eighteen, there's a sort of coming-of-age ceremony."

"Yes. The Finishing Ceremony."

"You know about it?"

He and Illian nod. "They marry the young women off after choosing 'suitable' husbands for them. Those husbands are Aristocrats who live inside the Arc. Look—the Bastille isn't just a strange little town that's magically protected from the

Directorate. It's a prison where humans are grown, harvested, distributed. Boys and girls alike."

"Why would Aristocrats want the Bastille's teenagers for wives when there are millions of people inside the Arc?" I ask, still puzzled. "What's special about them?"

When I see Illian and Kurt hesitate, I say, "Oh, come on. I just risked my damned life to bring your man back. If you don't trust me by now…"

"It's not that," Kurt says. "You…might want to sit down for this."

31

SECRETS AND LIES

TENSE AND SILENT, Kurt and Illian guide us to a nearby table, where all four of us take a seat.

"Veer is all about survival," Illian finally says, elbows on the table, fingertips pressed together as he chooses his words carefully. "She'll do anything to keep her people alive. That, at least, I have to grudgingly admire about her."

"Okay. But what does that have to do with—"

"You know the truth about the Cure," Kurt says. "Yes?"

I nod. "I know it's not so much a cure as an antidote."

"Right. An antidote to a biological weapon unleashed on so many in the Mire and across the country. Nevertheless, what they call the 'Cure' is effective. It serves its purpose. Anyone who's had it administered will, for a time, be resistant to the weapon known as the Blight."

"I'm still not sure I..."

Illian raises a hand, tacitly telling me to be patient.

"You may have noticed you didn't receive the Cure when you entered the Arc, Ashen."

"No," I tell them. "But eighteen-year-olds are supposed to get it if they complete their year of training."

"Have you ever met an eighteen-year-old Dreg who's received it?"

I ponder that for a second before shaking my head.

"They don't," Kurt says. "Because the Directorate discovered some time ago that the Cure has one extremely undesirable side effect."

I look at Finn to see if he has any idea what Kurt's talking about, but he looks as confused as I feel.

"I've known a lot of people who've taken it," he says. "My parents, for starters. They're healthy."

"In a manner of speaking," Illian says. "I'm sure they are. Then again, they're not a young married couple. Your mother has had her children already."

"Okay," I say, "now I'm completely lost."

"The Cure has one permanent side-effect: Sterility. It's why there are so few children under ten in the Arc."

My breath catches in my chest, and I feel Finn tensing next to me.

In my weeks in the Arc, I saw tourists wandering through the marketplace on the Escapa level. Adult members of the Aristocracy dancing and enjoying themselves. I tutored Merit, Finn's ten-year-old brother.

But I'm not sure I ever once saw a baby or a toddler.

"At first, the Directorate didn't worry much about it," Kurt says. "After all, overpopulation in the Arc is a legitimate concern. But over the course of years, an awareness began to set in that the population could wane and die eventually. Which means a weakening of the forces that make up the Directorate, the Aristocracy. If word got out to those in the lower levels..."

"They don't know?" I ask. "How can they not? Surely some of them must have tried to have children..."

"They're offered excuses," Kurt says. "Reasons for their failure that sound legitimate. Stress, change of environment, you name it. They're told to keep trying, and all the while, the doctors know it's impossible. Which brings us to the Dregs and to the Bastille."

"They started inviting seventeen-year-olds in," I say pensively. "People like me. But they trained us as soldiers, not as future spouses."

"Trust me. If they'd determined you were loyal enough, they would have found a way to breed you. Their goal is to create a society of loyalists—people like those in the Bastille, who quietly revere the Directorate. Or Dregs who are compliant enough. Have you ever noticed the Chaperons tend to work in teams of two? One woman, one man?"

"I have," I reply. "What are you saying?"

"The Chaperons are part of a large experiment. Each of those pairs is eventually forced to..."

Illian stops short of saying the despicable word, so Finn completes the thought for him. "Breed," he says with disgust.

Illian nods. "Chaperons are fit, healthy, young, and eventually will be used as breeders, yes. But in the meantime, there's the Bastille. Veer made a deal with the Directorate a few years back. She was concerned her people would remain vulnerable to attack. She'd heard through her spies about the infertility issue in the Arc, so she promised the Directorate she'd scratch their backs in return for the same."

"I'm slightly terrified to ask what that back-scratching entails," Finn says.

"I think I saw something," I reply. "A place called the Evaluation Center. They were drawing blood from a girl...and there was a mother with her young son. She looked heartbroken, like..."

"Like she was going to lose him," Illian nods. "Because she *was*. In exchange for the Bastille's ongoing safety, the Directorate demands a certain number of lives. Married women are allowed to give birth there, to raise their children for a few years. But then they're expected to surrender them—if Veer commands it. They're taken by the Directorate to be 'distributed.'"

"Distributed? You make them sound like products manufactured in a factory."

"They are, as far as the Directorate is concerned."

"But if all the children are taken—and all the teenagers—who will be left?" I ask. "The Bastille will end up in the same situation as the Arc."

"Perhaps. But should that happen, the Directorate would simply wipe them off the face of the earth, as they've done with so many other towns. One day before too many years have passed, the Bastille will be rubble, unless we win the coming war."

"How did I not know about any of this?" Finn asks, stupefied. "My family lives on one of the top floors. How has no one ever talked about what's happening?"

Illian eyes him with sympathy. "It's the Directorate's great shame, I suppose. They're monsters, but even they know the repercussions they would suffer if word got out about this."

"This still doesn't explain what Cyntra was talking about," I interject. "She said she was hoping to 'become an Aristocrat.' If she marries someone in the Arc, wouldn't he be sterile, just like all the others?"

"Not every Aristocrat is sterile," Illian says, shooting Finn a look. "For example, how old are you?"

"Nearly eighteen," he replies.

"Were you given the Cure?"

Glancing at me, he shakes his head. "They figured it was unnecessary. At least, that's what they told me."

"They're not wrong. But their reasons weren't entirely honest. There are many your age in the Arc. Many under twenty, none of whom have had the Cure. The Directorate is counting on you all to provide them with the next generation. *You* are the breeders."

"So Cyntra is being sold as a brood mare, and she's happy about it," I scowl. I can't help thinking about how attracted she is to Peric—how much she seems to dote on him in spite of his indifference toward her. I wonder if he, too, will be sent to the Arc to marry some Aristocrat or other.

"So all the parents in the Bastille just…agreed to this plan of Veer's," I say.

"They didn't have a choice," Illian tells us. "Veer knows without this deal, the Directorate would blow them off the map. The children born in the Bastille are all that's keeping the town from being reduced to rubble."

"Human shields," Finn says under his breath.

"Basically, yes."

"How do you know all this?" I ask Illian. "How could you possibly know things most of the Arc's residents don't even know?"

Illian and Kurt exchange a cryptic look, and Illian nods assent before Kurt speaks.

"Believe it or not, I was once part of the Directorate," he says. "When things first started up, years ago now. I was involved with a man who was one of them. A wealthy businessman. His name was Marcus, and he helped fund the initial building of the Arc. There was a time when I thought his cause was noble—that he and his allies were truly saving us from this hideous illness that was taking so many people down. I lived with him in the Arc. I'd had some military training of my own, and I even helped train the first Patrols—the ones you would have seen in the Mire. I helped with surveillance, too."

"How did you end up here?" I ask. "We were always told no one has ever escaped the Arc."

"I didn't escape," Kurt says, reaching for Illian's hand. "Not exactly. I went out with one of the daily patrols—we were surveilling the woods on this side of the city, looking for any sign of this Pit—of the Consortium's hiding place. I strayed from the Patrol and next thing I knew, a very attractive man had a gun to my head."

Illian lets out a quiet laugh. "I still don't know what possessed me to bring you here," he says. "Most foolish thing I ever did."

"Excuse me? It was the smartest thing you ever did!" Kurt laughs. "You'd all be lost without me."

"True."

"Okay," I say with a snicker. "Obviously there's a long, romantic story here."

"I was Illian's prisoner for weeks," Kurt tells us. "But over time, I began to share information with this not-so-tall drink of water. I gained his trust—told him I was disillusioned by the Arc's denizens and the Directorate's cruelty. I knew what they were doing to Dregs. I knew about the training—the killings. The Trials, too. I'd seen it all with my own eyes. I told Illian I wanted out. Of course, by that time, he was totally smitten with me and wouldn't have let me go for anything in the world."

I look over at Illian, who doesn't contradict Kurt's story.

"He was a valuable ally," he says sheepishly. "He knew where the surveillance equipment was—all the Directorate's cameras and screens that were still active in the mountains. Don't get me wrong—I didn't trust him as far as I could throw him, not at first. But we learned to trust one another when we went out one day to look at the screens and I nearly fell off a cliff."

"It was like something out of a movie," Kurt chuckles. "I grabbed his hand and told him to hold on. It was so ridiculous I wanted to laugh...but the truth is, I was weeping at the thought of losing him. I pulled him up—I have no idea how I found the strength, but I did. After that, he knew who I was. He knew I'd never let him go for anything or anyone."

Without thinking, I reach for Finn, taking his hand in mine. It's heartening to hear a love story that's not marred by cynicism or tragedy. One with a happy ending...or at least a *happy so far.*

I let out a quiet, suppressed yawn, and Illian says, "You must be so tired." He rises to his feet and adds, "Thank you, Ashen, for what you did for us. I had no real doubts about you, but tonight you proved you're your father's daughter. Thank you for saving Torrel from torture and torment. I'm only sorry Rafe didn't make it."

I can't think of words to respond, so I simply nod, offering up a weak smile to the two men on the other side of the table. I can't imagine making any choice other than the one I made. I know what the Directorate would have done to Torrel, what they would have put him through for their own bloodthirsty enjoyment.

As Finn and I head to our bedroom, I find myself thinking about those I left behind in the Bastille, and what the Directorate might do to them, now that I've stolen their prize.

32

LOSS

FINN and I return to the room where we spent the day. When we're sealed inside with the door closed, he turns my way, his expression grim.

"What is it?" I ask.

"It's time," he tells me.

"You have to go? Now?"

He nods, his jaw tight. "I've been out of the Arc for a long time. Every hour I'm not back is one when they may begin to suspect something."

"It's all right," I say, trying my best to put on a brave face. "We'll see each other again."

But from the look on his face, I can tell he's thinking the same thing I am:

Maybe we won't. Maybe this is the end for us both.

Unlike the girls in the Bastille with their planned lives and arranged marriages, Finn and I don't have the luxury of foresight. There are no guarantees for either of us.

The one thing I know is that his mother and her band of murderers will never cease to want me dead.

"Ash..."

I stare at him for a long moment, trying to read his eyes. I've never seen him like this. There's a grief in his expression that's contagious and begins ravaging my insides.

"You're saying goodbye to me for good," I half-whisper. "Aren't you?"

He shakes his head. "Not for good. Never for good. I'm too selfish to do that. If I don't have hope—if I don't believe I'll be with you again—there's nothing to fight for. But the Directorate wants you dead. In the Bastille, twice now, you've narrowly escaped with your life. And no matter how I try to rationalize, to justify loving you, staying with you—the truth is that I'm bonded by blood to the bad guys, whether I like it or not. I can't escape them... but you can."

The tears come, and I let them flow. "You *can* escape them, Finn. And you should. Your mother may have given birth to you, but you can walk away from her. From your father. Family is more than just blood."

"I know. But I have a brother, just like you do. Merit needs me. I can't leave him."

I swallow, choking back a sob. "I know."

He takes my hands and brings them one at a time to his lips. "I'm trying to be realistic," he says.

"I don't want reality. I've had too much of it. Too much chaos. Too much violence. I want a fantasy. I want you."

With that, he smiles at last, takes my face in his hands, and presses his lips to mine.

It's a kiss I hold onto with every tenuous fiber of my being, memorizing each sensation, implanting this moment in my body and soul...in case it's the last intimate moment we ever share.

When I pull away, I say, "The Consortium is vast. You heard Illian. We can fight. We can win this war."

"Maybe." Finn issues me a sad smile. "I want to believe that more badly than you know."

"So believe it," I command. "Believe it. For me. Please."

He nods. "I do. I will. There are two people I truly love in this world. My brother and you. I will do everything I can to protect you both."

"I know."

I press myself to his chest and wait to feel his arms envelop me before allowing myself a deep exhale. "I don't want you to go...but I know it's for the best."

"If I want to survive long enough to see you again..."

"I know."

We stand there for minutes—or maybe it's hours—holding each other. "Will you come with me part of the way?" he finally asks. "At least back to the bag we left hidden? You should bring it back here."

I nod. "Of course I will. I think Illian and Kurt trust me enough to let me go for a bit."

I'm so tired I can barely keep my eyes open, so I take Finn by the hand and lead him over to the bed, where we lie down, knowing our rest will be brief. He strokes my hair, I rest my palm and cheek on his chest, listening to his steady heartbeat.

"Do you think your parents intend to marry you to one of the teenage girls from the Bastille?" I ask. "To be a...*breeder*?"

Finn lets out a low chuckle. "I have no idea," he tells me. "But I can't quite imagine it. My mother is a snob, as you know. She would never want me to marry a..."

"*Dreg*," I say, filling in the silence. "Right. I suppose those girls are too much like me. Too low-class for your mother."

"Fortunately, my mother has no say in my choices."

"Try telling her that. I'm sure she'd beg to differ."

We lie still for a time, simply listening to one another breathe, before Finn finally sighs. "All right. It's time."

My eyes cloud with tears but I wipe them away quietly and push myself to my feet. "Let's go, then. No sense in delaying the inevitable."

When Finn and I find Illian, he tells me he wants to send Mura and Darryn with us. "For your safety," he insists. "Not to keep tabs on you."

Finn nods solemnly. "I'd feel better if I knew someone was with you on the way back here," he says. "Not to mention that there are a few items in the pack I think our friends could use."

Raising an eyebrow at Finn, I smile. He's always got a trick up his sleeve. I haven't entirely taken stock of the bag's contents, but if whatever is in there can help our new allies, I'm all for handing it over.

When Finn has said his goodbyes, the two Consortium members accompany us through the woods, rifles over their shoulders. As Finn and I move along ahead of them, a thought occurs to me.

"Atticus," I say quietly.

"What about him?"

"I haven't seen him since he was fighting off the snipers in the Bastille. I know he's just a machine...but I'm a little worried about him."

"You care about him," Finn says. I glance over to see if he's laughing at me, but he's not.

"I just want to know he's okay," I say with a nod. "He's

saved me more than once."

"I'm sure he's fine. But I'll admit I'd feel better if he showed himself."

"Me too."

When we've found our way to the concealed backpack, Finn extracts it from its hiding spot, reaches into one of its multitude of pockets, and pulls out a small metal tin before handing the pack to Darryn to strap to his back.

"Take care of it," Finn says. "Its contents are more valuable than you can imagine."

"We'll make sure Illian gets it," Mura tells us, and as if taking a hint, the two of them begin hiking back toward the Pit.

"So," Finn says, turning my way. "I guess this is it."

I chew on my lip and nod, determined not to burst into tears.

"I'll be careful out here," I promise for what feels like the hundredth time.

"I know you will." Finn puffs out his chest. "After all, you wouldn't want to get killed and miss out on *this*."

"I know you're kidding," I chuckle, grabbing him and pulling him close, "but you have no idea how desperate I am to make sure I see you again, and soon."

"Oh, I have some idea," he replies, brushing a lock of my hair behind my ear before kissing me tenderly. His lips will always be an escape, his touch a refuge. One that I don't want to surrender for anything.

But I have no choice, and after a time, we pull apart as if an invisible force is tugging at each of us from different directions.

"I have one last thing to give you," he says, holding a hand out. In his palm is the small tin he removed from the backpack before our escorts left.

"What is it?"

He pries the tin open, revealing two small white items, each the size and teardrop shape of a kernel of corn. He hands me one.

"This fits in your ear and is virtually invisible when you have it in," he tells me. "You activate it by pressing here..." He shows me a dark spot at the base of the one he's holding, which lights up when he touches it. He then slips it into his left ear. "We'll have to use them sparingly. But at least we'll be able to stay in touch."

"You've thought of everything," I grin, mirroring the action.

When he says, "Once I hear anything, I'll let you know how Kel is doing," I feel his voice deep inside my head, vibrating its way through my entire body.

I could get used to this.

With one more kiss, Finn tells me he can't delay any longer.

I hate letting him go. But as I watch him turn to make his way toward the Arc, every instinct tells me I'll see him again very soon.

33

SHOCK

When I reach the oak tree, Mura and Darryn are waiting for me warily, their eyes scouting the woods for signs of Directorate Guard or the Bastille's soldiers. We make our way silently inside and as darkness engulfs us, I breathe a quiet sigh.

Finn was right. This strange underworld—this damp, dark abode—feels more welcoming than the Arc or the Bastille ever did. I don't feel imprisoned here. I don't feel like every second is one where I'm being scrutinized or mentally tortured. Every person who resides between the earthen walls of the Pit has one goal in mind: to return one day to a life above ground, where we can be safe and happy once again.

When Mura, Darryn and I find Kurt and Illian, Darryn hands over Finn's pack. It contains at least twenty cloaks—enough for every member of the Pit's Patrol.

"Quite a remarkable young man, that one," Illian says with a smile when he sees them.

"Yes, he is," I reply.

It's not until the following night, after I've eaten a late

dinner with Illian, Kurt, and a few other "Pitters," as they call themselves, that I return to my room and hear a faint pinging sound from the earpiece Finn gave me.

"Ash," his voice says softly when I've activated it. "Are you there?"

"I'm here. Are you all right?"

"I'm home," he whispers. "Can't talk. This place is under heavy surveillance, and I don't know what listening devices might have been set up in my room—who might be eavesdropping."

"Understood. I'm just glad you're okay. I won't ask too many questions right now."

Finn snickers. "I know that's hard for you," he teases.

"You don't know the half of it."

We say our goodbyes, promising to talk again soon.

That night, for once, my sleep is peaceful and blissfully free of nightmares.

Over the next few days, I remain in the dark of the Pit. I help to cook and clean whenever I'm needed, and at each mealtime I sit with Illian and Kurt to discuss plans to get our hands on a Quantum Source.

"What we need," Kurt says during dinner one evening, "is someone on the inside of the Arc—someone with access to the Royal Grounds. Getting in will be difficult, but getting the Quantum Source out will be even more so. Getting *many* of them out will be all but impossible."

"Many?"

Illian nods. "It's our best hope of resurrecting the Consortium's various strongholds, of bringing our organization back from the brink of destruction. If we could get power to even a few of the other strongholds, we could begin to assemble our army."

"I know someone," I say, my pulse pounding with excitement at the prospect. "He's resourceful, to say the least. If I could talk to him...if we could come up with a plan..."

"Who is he?"

"A...friend. Sort of, anyhow. Rys is his name."

"Do you have any way to contact him?"

I hesitate for only a moment before I open up to them about the truth behind Atticus' creator. About how adept Rys is at infiltrating the Arc's communication systems, blocking signals, how skilled he is at playing both sides. I assure them that I trust him at this point to do whatever it takes to bring the Directorate down.

"He sounds like exactly what we need," Illian says.

"If I could head out to the woods, maybe I could find Atticus. I've been concerned about him since we brought Torrel back. Down here, it's impossible to know if he's okay. He's my one link to Rys."

"Well, then. I think it's time we gave you access to our codes so you can come and go."

Illian reaches into his pocket and hands me what looks like a small glass rectangle. As I touch its surface, it lights up with a series of four digits. 4-2-7-1.

"The current code," he tells me. "It changes every few hours."

"Thank you for trusting me with this. Do you think..."

"You'd like to head up now."

I nod. "If it's all right."

"Just make sure you're cloaked. Veer's people could be patrolling the woods."

After agreeing to his terms, I make my way—alone this time—to the surface and the oak tree's exit point.

I haven't heard from Finn since two mornings ago, when he let me know he was on his way to his lab. He warned me that his mother's paranoia was increasing, that there were Directorate Guard soldiers stationed just outside their residence.

I wonder with a smile if it had anything to do with my freeing Torrel from the Bastille's prison.

I activate the earpiece when I'm outside, but there's no reply on the other end when I whisper Finn's name.

Pulling my cloak close around my face, I venture into the woods, my eyes scanning the treetops for Atticus. I call his name quietly, but at first there's no response. It's half an hour or so before his familiar *Hoooo* finally greets my ears, and I peer up to see him perched on a branch high above me. His eyes flash red in warning, and I push myself back against a tree trunk, worried that he's telling me there's someone near.

My hand goes to the hilt of my dagger and I extract it slowly, waiting.

But no sound of snapping twigs meets my ear. Instead, Atticus flaps down to land at my feet, pulling his face up to mine. His eyes fade to a light blue shade.

"Are you all right?" I ask quietly. "Rys, are you in there?"

"I'm here," Rys' voice replies. "Atticus is a little banged up, but nothing a little maintenance won't fix."

"Good. Listen, Finn's back at the Arc, and I—"

"Ash." My name pierces the air like a bullet.

"What is it?"

"Something's happened."

Adrenaline sets me suddenly on edge, and dread fills me.

"Is it Finn? Has something happened to him?"

"No. It's Kel. Someone took him last night."

"Took Kel? What do you mean? Wasn't he in the Davenport residence? How the hell could anyone have taken him?"

"As far as I know he was there, yes, under lock and key. But a message came across the Directorate Guard feed around midnight that he had been taken. I don't know how, or who could possibly have broken in without being tracked. It's baffling, to be honest. To defy the Duchess like that...it's insanity."

An intense nausea overtakes me. Kel, my baby brother, was removed from one of the most secure, most closely watched residences in the entire Arc. The thought is a horror. Only someone powerful, someone with extraordinary resources at their disposal, could have done such a thing. But why? To what end?

"I don't know what to do," I say, my chest throbbing. "I have to go back to the Arc. What if..."

"Stay there. Wait."

"I can't, Rys! I can't just stand here like an idiot while my brother..."

"I said wait."

The words come to me in Rys' voice, but this time, instead of filtering their way through the mechanical owl, they flow through the air around me.

I spin around to see him making his way toward me through the trees. He's dressed in his dark gray uniform, a backpack strapped to his shoulders. "I took one of the Directorate's vehicles most of the way," he says. "Along the old roads leading toward Breckenridge. Damned thing broke down a few miles off, though. I've been jogging through these woods for the last couple of hours, hoping to find my way to you."

I've seldom been so relieved to see anyone in my life. My first instinct is to hug him but I tighten, remembering all the reasons I have to hate him.

You led them to my mother. She would still be alive if not for you. Kel would be safe at home.

Ignoring my chilly glare, he pulls the bag off his shoulders, drops it to the ground, and opens it. "I knew you'd want to go back when you heard the news," he says, "so I brought you a disguise." With that, he extracts two powder-blue Chaperon outfits. In addition, he pulls out a device that looks like the silver bracelet Finn was wearing when he escaped the Arc. "I've programmed this Inhibitor to replicate the type of implant you sliced out of your arm. It will convey to any and all systems that you're a Chaperon who's worked in the Arc for two years—despite the fact that she doesn't actually exist."

"Won't the cameras still be able to read my face?"

"No." Rys shakes his head. "I mean, yes, they will. But the data conveyed by the bracelet will override any facial recognition and reroute the system to your invented identity. Look, it's not a permanent fix, but it'll be enough to get you inside. From there, we'll figure out how Kel was taken, all right?"

I nod, my lip trembling, relieved beyond words to have him guiding me back to the Arc. "I don't know why you came all the way out here like this. But thank you."

Rys lowers his eyes when he says, "Ash, look—I know I screwed up. I never meant for your mother to get killed or for Kel to be taken. But I want to help. I want to make up for all the pain I've caused."

I nod again.

He can *never* make up for it.

But maybe he can help me begin to heal.

"Atticus!" I blurt out.

"What about him?"

"Can he tell Illian's men what's happening? They'll come looking for me if I don't go back to the Pit—I don't want to put them in any danger or cause panic."

"Of course. I'll make sure they know." Rys pulls his left sleeve up. On his arm is what looks like a white bandage, but the second he flicks his fingertip over it, it begins to glow with iridescent blue symbols.

As soon as Rys has conveyed an instruction, Atticus spreads his wings and takes off, banking toward the Pit's location.

"He and I have mapped the locations of their treetop cameras," Rys tells me. "He'll convey a digital message to your friends."

As much as I hate to admit it, I'm stunned, as always, by my former friend's talent.

When he's ready, we begin our hike in silence. More than once, I contemplate using my earpiece to try and signal Finn, to let him know we're on our way. But I know he'll only tell me to stay away and say I'm risking my life needlessly. He'll tell me not to come back, that he'll figure out a solution himself.

Much as I'd love to hear Finn's voice, I don't have the time or the energy for that argument.

"Once we're in, I'll have eyes on every part of the Arc," Rys tells me after we've hiked for some time. "I have access to micro-drones, cameras, you name it. I will find out where Kel's gone. It may take a little time, but I'll do it. I promise you that."

"Good," I reply. "But...how exactly are we going to get into the Arc?"

"From Sector Eight. We both know the way in—the old

drainage pipe. From there, we'll head for the train. It's our best chance."

I follow, my heart heavy as Rys leads the way through the woods like he's walked this route a thousand times. He's risked everything, coming out here to find me, to bring me back. If I find Kel alive, it will be thanks to him.

For that, at least, I'm grateful.

34

INTO THE LION'S DEN

AFTER STOPPING to rest during the darkest hours of the night, Rys and I get up and trudge silently toward the Mire. I don't know how far we've hiked—how far it is from the oak tree to the city's outer border. All I do know is that the soles of my feet are burning, my head is throbbing, and I'm exhausted.

During our hours together, we keep our conversation to a minimum. But I tell him about Illian's desire for a Quantum Source—about Finn's revelation that the King stores them on the three-hundredth level.

As usual, the news doesn't seem to surprise Rys, who tells me he has some idea where the storage area might be.

When I finally spot the Arc looming immensely against the backdrop of sky and ruins in the distance, my chest seizes into a tight knot.

Hovering impossibly several stories above the ground, it used to blow my mind. Now it looks like an ugly lead weight, polluting the scenery in stubborn defiance of gravity.

A despicable miracle.

Rys and I hike the woods around the city until we come

to the old drainage pipe that will take us into our old stomping ground. I stop at its entrance, my heart in my throat. The sight makes me want to crumple to my knees, the familiarity of it too raw, too reminiscent of Kel and my mother.

"The last time we were here..." I say quietly. But I don't complete the thought.

"I know. Things were different then. Ash, I wish we could go back in time. I wish..."

He doesn't finish expressing his regret. He's said the words more than once; there's no sense in repeating them.

"Me too."

I'm about to step into the pipe when Rys stops me with a hand to my arm. "We need to change our clothes. You can't walk into Sector Eight looking like that. Even if you *do* have a magical cloak. You're a moving target."

The idea of dressing in the powder-blue uniform of a Chaperon is soul-sucking, but he's right.

Chaperons are programmed automatons, drugged beyond the capacity to think for themselves. Humans who are barely human, devoid of emotion or of anything that makes one feel alive. The Directorate has robbed them of their very essence, just as it's tried to do to me and to the other Candidates by forcing us to kill against our will.

But they haven't broken me.

Yet.

I'm doing this for Kel.

I will wear the blue uniform as long as I need to.

I head in among the trees and strip off Finn's miraculous suit. It feels like I'm peeling off my shield, the protective second skin that's kept me from harm for so long. But the feeling of air on my bare flesh—of a strange, vulnerable sort of freedom I haven't felt since the day we discovered our pool in the wilderness—*is* sort of wonderful, I have to admit.

Craving a brief taste of Finn, I surrender to temptation, remove the small earpiece he gave me, tap it, and place it back in my ear.

"Are you there?" I whisper, but there's no reply.

After several more attempts, I hear nothing on the other end.

I resolve to try again when we're inside the Arc—*if* Rys brings us to a place where we're not being watched, that is.

"Ready?" Rys asks when I finally emerge from the woods.

I hand him my uniform and cloak, and he stashes them in his bag. "As ready as I can be. Meaning I think I'm about to throw up."

"You'll be okay," he says in a deeper than usual voice. "You're with me."

I glare at him. It's the sort of thing the old Rys would have said, something I may once have found charming and silly.

But I'm in no mood for silliness—or charm, for that matter.

"Seriously, though," he says. "I do have a cunning plan. We'll be all right."

"I'm glad you have so much faith in yourself, because I don't."

"Well, maybe by the time this is all over, you'll have just a smidge."

He leads me into the corrugated pipe and we crouch down, painfully making our way toward the distant daylight at the other end.

When we finally emerge, Sector Eight greets us like a graveyard. I look around warily. Not a leaf is twitching; no birds sing. Nothing is moving, not even the air. It's like someone flipped a switch and killed the neighborhood where Kel and I grew up.

I watch the houses as we wander past them, wondering if any of the children who once inhabited them are still alive.

My question is answered when after half a block or so, I spy a small head peeking out of the second-story window of a gray house. The girl looks about eight. Her eyes are wary, her face thin.

"I wonder why the Directorate doesn't take the kids," I say softly. "Why they don't bring them into the Arc and raise them like they do with the kids from the Bastille."

Rys doesn't look surprised when I say the words, and I remember that Atticus offered him a bird's eye view of the goings-on in that strange town. "The kids in the Bastille are quietly indoctrinated from a young age to love the Directorate," he says. "Not to mention that their parents weren't murdered in front of their eyes. They haven't suffered like the Mire's Dregs have, with little to eat and no electricity, so they're still wide-eyed and optimistic. The Directorate sees them as ideal candidates. The Dregs in the Mire, to their mind, are tainted by their trauma. Much better suited for combat, for killing. Some, of course, become Chaperons—and if they're compliant enough, the Directorate will eventually expect them to breed, too."

"So you know all about it," I reply.

He nods. "I'd heard rumors over the weeks, but I wasn't sure until you—and Atticus—saw it first-hand. It seems the Bastille isn't the only town of its kind. There are many, scattered around the country, walled in and isolated. Prison-towns where the residents are convinced they're some kind of Chosen People. Because of the towns, the Directorate is planning a massive influx of brainwashed children and teenagers over the next few years, if things go their way. They intend to strengthen their numbers, to show the Arc's 'lesser' residents how successful the Aristocracy has been at bringing children into this world. Of course, it's all an illusion. A lie. But no one has to know that, right?" He utters the last few words with a thick layer of sarcasm.

I clench my teeth and huff out a breath. "Bastards," I mutter. "I can't believe they—"

I'm startled into silence by two figures stepping around a street corner a hundred or so feet ahead of us.

"The Patrol," Rys mutters. "They've changed their route since last time we were here."

"Crap," I mutter. "What do we do?"

"Follow my lead. And whatever you do, *don't* be yourself."

"Myself?"

"Emotional."

I want to swear at him, which I suppose would only prove his point. If I show any emotion, there's no way the guards will believe I'm a Chaperon. So I put on my best poker face and walk stiffly next to Rys, shoulders back, chin up.

One of the guards holds up a hand as we approach.

"I didn't think any Seventeens were being brought into the Arc today," he says. "What are you two doing here?"

"A Seventeen on Beale Street declined his invitation to the Introduction Ceremony," Rys tells him, his voice measured, calm. "We were sent to try and persuade him to accept. Unfortunately, we failed."

The guard reaches for the gun at his waist, his jaw tensing, and looks like he's ready to charge straight in and murder the made-up teenager Rys is talking about. "Where is he? Which house? We'll take him in."

"No need. The Duchess is sending a fleet of micro-drones for him."

"Really? That's not standard protocol."

"It's an experimental measure—it's new. They're using a compound that will simultaneously end his life and melt away all evidence that he ever existed."

"Well, that's...gross," the other guard says with a shrug. "Thanks for your service, I guess."

Rys nods, as do I, and we keep walking. After we've gone twenty or so feet I begin to turn to look back, but he shakes his head and says, "Don't."

When we've rounded two bends in the road, he finally says, "They bought it."

"How do you know?"

"I just know. All right, Ash—now comes the fun part."

35

SECTOR EIGHT

Rys leads me to a neighborhood in Sector Eight that I know well. We used to play here when we were children—there was a small park on one corner with a playground that now looks haunted and grim, its metal jungle gym a rusty mess of jagged steel.

Down the street is a garage leading to what used to be an underground parking lot. Without a word, Rys heads straight for its door, which is sealed up tight.

"Is this..." I begin to ask, but stop myself. If it's the entrance to the Arc's underground train, there is probably surveillance equipment monitoring any movement. The Directorate may not be able to identify me by my facial features, but if they hear me asking stupid questions, I may set off a few alarm bells.

Rys pulls out a small disc-like device I've seen before called a Disruptor, and slips his thumb over its silver surface. The door begins to slide open to reveal a tunnel that slopes sharply downwards.

"Wait until we're inside, then we can talk. I'll disable the listening mechanisms in a few seconds," Rys whispers.

I nod almost imperceptibly, follow him in, and my chest sags with relief as I hear the door slide closed behind us.

"The Directorate Guard's surveillance team is supposed to monitor the feeds," Rys says as we walk along, lights flaring to life along the tunnel's walls. "But the watchers in charge of staring at the Mire usually fall asleep halfway though their shift. It's the guys who patrol the Arc's halls we need to worry about."

With a shiver of apprehension, I nod. "So what next?"

"We take the train toward the Hub under the Arc. That's when the tricky bit begins."

"Getting past the guards, you mean."

"Yup," he says as he remotely unlocks another door, one I went through on the day I first headed to my Introduction Ceremony. This one takes us to the platform where the pristine white train is waiting for us.

"I have a plan," Rys tells me. "But you're going to need to trust me again. Can you do that?"

The train's doors slide open and we step inside.

"Do I have a choice?" I ask, only half joking.

"Not if you want to find Kel."

"Then I trust you, Rys."

He nods solemnly and heads over to the far side of the white train car. It's similar to the one where I met Diva, the stylist who did my hair and makeup on my first day in the Arc and I find myself wondering what ever happened to her. She was one of the first denizens I met, and I have to admit that I enjoyed her company. There was something sincere about her, something kind. There's no way she was aware of the incessant cruelty of the Directorate.

Rys opens a panel in the wall and inputs a series of numbers and symbols. "Hang on," he calls out, and I grab hold of a chrome handle on the wall as we begin our rapid acceleration.

When the train has settled into its top speed, I turn to Rys. "We only have a few minutes. So I need to say something."

"Go for it."

I swallow. "Whatever your feelings about me—however little you may think of me—I need you to protect Kel if something happens to me. I need you to promise you'll find him and get him out of the Arc."

"Ash..."

"I'm serious, Rys."

"I know. And so am I. I could never think little of you. How could you even say that?" He steps over until he's standing just in front of me, slips a hand onto my cheek and gently lifts my face so I find myself looking into his eyes.

Shocked, I pull away. The gesture is too intimate, too familiar.

Rys is almost a stranger to me now. Maybe in another time—before all the mayhem entered our lives—something could have happened between us.

But not anymore.

He frowns. "What I'm trying to say is that I care about you, Ash. I'm sick every time I think of the part I played in your mother's death, in Kel's abduction. But I need you to know I'd do anything for you. I mean it."

"So prove it," I say, my voice tight. I offer up a forced smile. "Show me. Help me."

"I will, in every way I can."

"Thank you."

We spend the rest of the trip in silence, my heart racing as I anticipate our arrival in the Hub. But before we reach it, Rys heads to the far end of the car, opens another panel, and inputs another code, which brings the train to a screeching halt.

"What are you doing?" I ask.

"You and I can disguise ourselves for the cameras, but the guards in the Hub are top-level. They know that no Chaperons took a train to Sector Eight earlier today. Which means…"

"No Chaperons should be *returning* from Sector Eight."

"If the train arrives with us on it, we'll set off a million different alarm systems."

"So what now? Where are we?"

"A few hundred feet from the Hub. We'll take tunnels in, then hop on a service Conveyor. Those aren't generally monitored closely, because they're largely out of use. They were once for moving furniture into residences, but no one's done that in years."

With the press of a button, he opens the door and we slip down to ground level. Almost immediately, the door seals itself and the train starts flying back toward Sector Eight.

The tunnel is dark, lit here and there by what look like emergency lamps, and we make our way along until we come to a steel door. Rys manages to open it with nothing more than the small Disruptor he carries in his palm, and we enter. The space lights up as we step inside, startling me into a faint panic.

"Don't worry. There shouldn't be anyone in here," Rys assures me.

I nod, skeptical that re-entry into one of the best-guarded buildings in the world can possibly be this easy, and follow him down a series of corridors until we come to the broad doors of a Conveyor.

Again, Rys gets us in without a hitch, and I breathe a slow sigh of relief to think maybe things will be all right after all.

It's only when we arrive at our destination—a hallway on one of the Arc's lower floors—that my hope fades.

36

INFILTRATION

When the Conveyor's doors slide open, we're greeted by two Directorate Guards, standing alert before us as though they were awaiting our arrival.

"What are Chaperons doing on the Service Conveyor?" one of them asks. He's tall, with straight brown hair, broad shoulders, and a face that screams *I love violence.* He takes a step toward me as if to see if I'll react.

When Rys doesn't respond, I do. "That information is Classified. All you need to know is the Conveyor is being considered for a prisoner transport, and we're here to assess it."

"Prisoner transport?" the man says. "This is the first I've heard of that plan."

"The prisoners are members of the Consortium," Rys replies, his voice low. "They can't be brought into the Arc via the regular routes. We don't want to cause a mass panic if civilians were to see them."

"Why the hell would Chaperons know about this and not us?" the other guard asks.

Rys and I exchange a quick glance and I clear my throat. "The Directorate doesn't want the prisoners harmed," I reply, my voice a deliberate monotone. "The Directorate Guard members such as yourselves are powerful…and in an altercation, risk hurting, or even killing them. Those at the top felt we could provide…a calming presence."

"I see. That makes sense, I suppose," the guard says, pulling his shoulders back like he's pleased to be reminded he's a living god.

"Well, if there's anything we can do to help, let us know," the second guard says.

"Of course," Rys replies. "Now, if you'll excuse us, we have a meeting to get to."

The men part reverently and we pass between them, neither of us daring a breath until we're well out of earshot.

"Holy pants," I say under my breath. "I don't know how we did that."

"Quick thinking on your part. Well done."

"Now, maybe you can tell me where we're going?"

"To a secondary surveillance area. It's a backup room in case the main monitors ever go down."

He guides me through a large, open room filled with figures in gray uniforms who look like cleaning staff. As we enter, they're laughing and joking with one another. But the second the first set of eyes hits us, a grim silence falls over the chamber. Its occupants stop talking, backing away toward the walls as if out of some quiet, angry fear.

It's hard for me to stay silent, to keep my head up, my eyes focused on the door at the room's far end. I want to assure them we're just like them—Dregs who understand their struggles. But I know perfectly well that all they see are uptight, willing servants to the Directorate.

The Arc's eyes and ears.

Traitors.

Most of these people don't know Chaperons are injected with a chemical that makes them compliant and robs them of their agency. They don't know the Directorate has turned so many former Dregs into prisoners inside their own minds.

I make a silent vow that I'll make sure they know everything soon enough.

But for now, I have a brother to find.

Carrying on the Chaperon act, I accompany Rys to a small, dark room behind an inconspicuous locked door. Inside is a long, curved desk, above which are dozens of floating screens showing various parts of the Arc. I recognize the Escapa—the vacation level where tourists flock to go shopping in "foreign" markets, stay in posh hotels, or eat at exotic restaurants. On other screens are the Royal Gardens and the Ballroom where the Introduction Ceremony took place.

Every single vaguely public area in the Arc flashes on and off the screens, showing themselves for only a few seconds at a time.

"What are we looking for?" I ask.

"Kel, for starters," Rys tells me. "He was taken two nights ago. So we're going to search through the footage from the patrol drones."

"There are three-hundred levels in this place," I protest. "Thousands and thousands of residences, Conveyors, hallways..."

"And we'll look through each of them, if that's what it takes."

"You managed to hide my face from the cameras using tech to block signals. You don't think whoever took him would do the same?"

Rys seals his lips and shakes his head.

"Why not?"

"Because I don't think whoever took him has access to that kind of advanced technology. The only people who do are the Aristocrats and the Directorate. I have a suspicion Kel was taken by someone much lower on the social ladder."

My brow furrows at the suggestion. "Seriously? Who would do that? Who *could* do it? He was in the care of the Duke and Duchess. They have top-tier security in their place. Micro-drones. You name it."

"Maybe Kel wasn't *in* their place when he disappeared," Rys says.

"Okay, now you're seriously confusing me." But I shut my mouth and watch as he navigates to a corridor on level 298. I immediately recognize the Duke's front door, flanked by two Directorate Guard soldiers.

"This was at eleven p.m. two nights ago," Rys says, flicking a finger over the seemingly static image to accelerate its progress, and I watch as the numbers showing the hour fly by, the guards shifting on their feet as they stand at attention.

Around 12:30 a.m., the guards leave, making their way to a Conveyor down the hall.

"Well, that's interesting," Rys says.

"Where are they going?"

"Their shift probably ended at midnight. I imagine they got impatient waiting for the next guards to show."

"Not the most effective security system, are they?"

"No. And I'm beginning to understand how Kel managed to escape."

"Escape?"

"Just watch. I have a theory, and your little brother may just prove me right."

A few seconds later, I watch as the residence's front door opens and two figures emerge. They're small and thin, but I recognize them immediately.

"Kel and Merit," I breathe. "They just…left? The Duke and Duchess must know about this, surely? They must have seen this same footage."

"Agreed," Rys says pensively. "It doesn't make sense."

He manages to navigate through a series of video feeds following the boys down the same hall the guards had walked a few minutes earlier. Once they disappear, Rys switches to another camera's views, and I can see my brother clearly now, joking around with Merit inside a Conveyor.

My eyes well with tears as I watch my brother smile happily. I can't believe I'm thinking it, but it seems the Duke and Duchess have treated him well.

We watch as the Conveyor comes to a stop and the two boys exit.

"Where did they go?" I ask, straining to see.

"Not sure. Looks like…Wait, that can't be right."

Puzzled, Rys leafs his way through the floating screens, searching for the two boys. But I can see that he's as lost as I am.

"What is it?" I ask.

"I can't access the other camera in the Conveyor." He speaks quietly, and I can tell his mind is racing. "This explains why the Duke and Duchess can't find Kel. Someone's deleted the data showing where they got off."

"Wait a minute—what about Merit? *He's* not missing, right? So that means he must have gone back to the residence."

"He did. From what I heard, he told his parents some bad people took Kel."

"Bad people?" I ask, panicked. "Why is this the first you've told me about that?"

"I didn't want to worry you, Ash. He's a little boy—they say dramatic things, invent stories. They lie. We don't know for sure that he was telling the truth."

"But if there's even a remote possibility of it..." I retort, trying not to let my mind imagine the worst. "Isn't there anything we can do?"

"I can't resurrect deleted footage," Rys says sheepishly. But after a moment, he perks up and adds, "But I *can* figure out where that Conveyor is likely to have stopped."

"It could have stopped on any floor. I don't see how—"

"Give me a second," Rys says, rewinding through the footage of the boys. "Each Conveyor is precisely calibrated. The internal camera was locked on your brother and Merit. They were moving for exactly..." He pauses the feed to do the calculation. "Two minutes and eight seconds. The Conveyor they entered on the 298th level would therefore have stopped on...level twelve."

"Twelve? Why the hell would they go to twelve?"

"I don't know. They're kids. They probably thought it would be a fun adventure."

"What's on that level, anyhow?"

"Mostly Dregs who work in the Sanitation Department. Some Wealthies have residences down there, but most choose not to live that low in the Arc, for status reasons. There are quite a few small Dreg residences for people a little older than us—the ones who made it through training but haven't managed to move up in the world—they mostly work as Chaperons or hope to become Directorate Guard, but some will end up spending their lives dealing with the Arc's waste."

"Can we look at the footage from the hallways on that level?"

"Already on it," says Rys, who's scrolling through a series of video feeds. But at first, all I can see is what looks like a thick fog.

"What is that?"

"Someone set off a particulate bomb, so the patrol drone's cameras would be unable to focus on anyone's features. Clever."

Finally, I catch footage of a figure in a light-colored uniform, making its way toward the boys. *A woman...or maybe a teenage girl?*

She stops to speak to them, then seems to be guiding them down a hallway. She's silhouetted and fuzzy, but the fog isn't thick enough to prevent me from seeing her stop in front of a door at the end of the hall. The footage then stops abruptly, and all we see is blackness.

"Where does that door lead?" I ask.

"A residence. I'm not sure whose."

I'm already pulling my clothing out of Rys' bag when I say, "Let's go."

"Ash, what are you doing?"

"Putting on Finn's uniform. No way am I going in there without some kind of tactical advantage."

Rys sighs. "Fine."

"Turn your back, then," I command, and he does so with a look of irritation.

Within thirty seconds I'm dressed, Finn's cloak around my shoulders, the silver bracelet still on my wrist.

We make our way out of the room to the nearest Conveyor and head to level twelve.

"How did the Directorate not think to look for him on this

level?" I whisper as the doors slide open. "Why didn't they do what you did and figure out the timing from the Conveyor's feed?"

"Because they're idiots. They're so used to being the heads of a surveillance state that they're completely useless when their surveillance fails them. Look—no one breaks the law in this place. Stealing a child is unheard of. The Directorate Guard, for all its seeming competence, isn't experienced when it comes to true crises."

"Watch it. That kind of talk could get you killed." I almost laugh. It's nice to hear Rys talking smack about the Directorate. There was a time not so long ago when I was convinced he would never turn against them.

"It's all right," he says, holding up his wrist to show me his silver bracelet. "I've got this set to scramble anything that runs through the Arc's feeds. All they're likely to hear—if they're listening—is gibberish."

We proceed down the hall until we come to the door we saw in the video, and I stop in my tracks, my pulse pounding in my veins.

"Are you sure about this?" Rys asks.

I nod. My heart is in my throat, my breath tight in my chest. "I'm just hoping Kel's actually in there."

"Me too. So, are you going to knock, or…?"

"No. The only advantage we have is surprise, and I intend to use it. No knocking. Stand back."

Rys does as I ask, a look of mild amusement on his face as I inhale a deep breath.

The door looks solid, and I'm not convinced I can possibly break it down, even with the help of Finn's suit. But I close my eyes and remind myself to have faith in my own strength.

Kel is in there. He needs you.

I turn sideways and thrust my entire weight against the door, which gives in easily, flying open to reveal a small, empty living room, lit by a lone lamp on a side table. I leap into the hallway at the room's far end, jogging until I spot a small bedroom off to one side, its door open wide enough that I can see a silhouetted figure sitting in a chair by the bed.

"Ash?" a meek voice says from the shadows.

But the voice isn't Kel's.

37

SURPRISE

THE SEVENTEEN-YEAR-OLD GIRL seated in the chair is one I haven't seen in many days.

One I never thought I'd see again.

The last time I laid eyes on her, she was talking and laughing her way through one of our Training Sessions, seemingly carefree after shaking off the trauma we'd all endured.

But now she looks exhausted, a shell of her former self, as if that trauma has finally caught up with her.

Lying by her feet is my brother, Kel, whose chest is moving slowly up and down as he snores softly. He used to nap like that on the floor of his room, curled up like a small cat into a ball.

He always *could* sleep through anything.

I pull my eyes to the girl and say her name.

"Kyra?"

She rises to her feet. "I heard they took your brother," she says, an underlying anger lacing the words. "I heard what happened to you—that they tried to kill you. I knew..."

She pulls her eyes down to Kel.

"You knew they'd kill him eventually, too. But how did you..."

"I'm curious to understand that, too," Rys says from behind me.

Kyra holds up a small device that looks like a Disruptor. "A man with gray hair came to me a few days ago. I don't know who he was—he said something about being a scientist. That he met Ash in the Hold. He gave me this, and something to mess with my implant so they wouldn't be able to trace me."

"The man in the cell next to mine," I breathe, nodding. "I thought he must be dead by now."

Kyra shakes her head. "He escaped, somehow. Honestly, he seemed like a bit of a mad genius. He said something about hearing the Directorate had gone after your mother, your brother. He gave me this silver thing, and told me we have friends in the Arc. He said the boys would come to level twelve that night, and I needed to be ready to greet them. I don't know how he did it—how he got them down here, how he avoided the guards, the cameras, everything. It was all pretty nuts, honestly. But something about him seemed trustworthy, so I listened and followed his instructions."

As Kyra speaks, Kel finally stirs, pushing himself up slowly to a sitting position. He looks up at me for a moment, confused.

"Am I dreaming?" he asks, rubbing his eyes. "Ash?"

I leap forward and fall to my knees, reaching for him, pulling him to me and kissing the crown of his head as my tears flow into his hair. "It's me," I weep. "I can't believe I found you."

"Me neither!" He pulls away, beaming, before throwing his arms around my neck.

"Merit told his parents bad people took you. Does he know where you are?"

He nods. "He does, sort of. But he promised not to tell—he said he knew you and I were in danger. He said he'd make up a story. He likes Kyra—he doesn't want her getting into trouble. And he said he likes you, too."

I can't help but smile to think of Merit and Kel having the frank discussion that led to this moment. "So, you knew Kyra was a friend of mine?"

"She said she knew you. She told me things about you…" Kel looks over at her. "It sounded like you two were good friends, so I trusted her."

"We *are* friends," I tell him, hugging him tight again as I look into Kyra's eyes. "Thank you. You risked your life. You —*Oh my God.*"

"What is it?" she asks.

"What about training? Piotr must wonder where you are. He'll sic his dogs on you if—"

"Even if they could find me, I don't think I'm high on anyone's priority list right now. The Directorate's gone extra-nuts lately, and there's other stuff going on, too. Piotr's been super-preoccupied, ranting about rebels and stuff. But yeah, he'll probably have the class tear me limb from limb when he does get his hands on me."

I shake my head. "No way. I'm not letting him anywhere near you." Something occurs to me, and I look up at Rys. "We can't let them find us. The door…I think I might have destroyed it. What if..."

"I'm on it," he replies. "I'll make sure it doesn't look like anyone broke in."

"*Rystan?*" Kel says, his eyes moving to the doorway.

Rys turns back to look at him. I can see the sadness in his eyes as he recalls the last time he saw my brother.

The day the Directorate killed our mother.

"Did you help Ash get here?" Kel asks, his tone innocently devoid of accusation.

"I…did. But she could have done it on her own. Your sister is very brave and extremely smart."

"I know," Kel says with a yawn and a stretch. "She always has been. I just wanted to say thanks."

I watch a tear streak down Rys' cheek as he nods and turns away once again.

Kel, Kyra and I spend the next few minutes catching up, even as Kel drifts off repeatedly. Kyra tells me I've become a living legend in the Arc, that people in the lower levels have started whispering rumors about the girl who disappeared, about the Directorate's abuse of Candidates.

"No one knew where you went," she tells me. "If you were alive or dead. We all figured the Directorate had you in their clutches, because how could you possibly escape? But here you are, alive, without a scratch on you."

She stares at me, a look of pride in her eyes. But I see pain, too.

I know as well as anyone where it comes from. I was there when Luke was killed, when Maren drowned. I feel Kyra's pain like it's my own…because it is.

There was a time when I thought she'd managed to push it away, to numb her insides.

But I'm glad to see she's still human.

"There's so much more happening in here and out there," I tell her, my voice tight. "So much none of us knew—about the Cure, about what's happening in the world beyond the Arc.

We have allies, Kyra. A lot of them. I'm going to help assemble an army."

"An army? There are enough people on the outside for that? I thought all the adults were dead."

"The truth about the Blight—the Cure, everything…it's complicated. But there are millions of people in this country living outside the Arcologies, ready to fight for what's right."

"It doesn't matter," she replies with a sudden tightening of her jaw. She shakes her head like she's trying to force an angry thought from her mind. "Even if they're out there and willing to fight, they can't get into the Arcs. No one can. Except *you,* apparently."

"If I can, anyone can. But it'll take time. We have to be organized. This won't be a war fought with sticks and stones by angry outsiders. The Directorate has allies on the outside, too, so we need to plan."

Kyra lets out a tired sigh, and I realize I'm feeding her far too much information. She's an exhausted fugitive, a lost soul. She's in no shape to contemplate war or anything like it. All I can think when I look at her is that she needs a long rest.

"The allies," I tell her, "they have a place in the woods. It's hidden from sight—the Directorate doesn't know where it is."

"Sounds like heaven."

"It's not, exactly. But it's not bad."

Rys steps back into the room and says, "All done."

I nod. "Did you manage to fix the door?"

"Like new. Mostly. You…kind of dented it, Miss Formidable."

"You broke the door, Ash?" Kel asks, opening his eyes. "You've gotten super-strong!"

"What can I say? I really wanted to see you, Little Man."

Kel lets out a glorious giggle, and for the briefest moment, I feel at peace.

But as Rys and I exchange a *what now?* look, I realize I haven't thought that far ahead. Not once did I consider what I'd do when I found my brother, how I'd sneak him out of the Arc. I suppose it's too much to hope I could just shove him under my cloak and make my way back out.

"Could we sleep here tonight?" I ask Kyra. "Just for a few hours?"

"Of course."

"I don't know if that's such a great idea," Rys protests. "They're still looking for Kel. They *will* find him eventually, even if it means breaking down every door in the Arc."

"Let's just shut our eyes until first thing in the morning," I plead. "Then we'll get out of here and go back to the Pit. I'm too tired to do it now—I just need a few hours of peace."

Rys still looks concerned as he glances over at Kel, but he finally nods. "I have to get back to my residence. But I'll come check on you in the morning and do my best to make sure you get out of here in one piece."

"Thanks."

Kel, wide awake now, jumps to his feet, leaps over, and throws his arms around Rys' waist. "Thank you for bringing my sister back, Rystan," he says in his sweetest little boy voice.

Rys looks once again like he's going to burst into tears, but he holds it together long enough to tell my brother, "I'm not sure I deserve you thanks. But I'm very glad you're happy… Little Man."

38

MORNING

WHEN KEL and Kyra have gone to sleep, I try once again to contact Finn.

"Ash?" a voice on the other end says when I've activated the communication device.

"You're there," I breathe.

"You sound surprised," he chuckles. "Were you expecting someone else?"

"Let's just say I worry about you…" I stop myself, unwilling to reiterate what a monster his mother is. "I've found him, Finn. I'm with Kel now."

"Wait—you're in the *Arc*?"

"Yes. Rys brought me here. And before you say anything, there's nothing you could have done to stop me."

"No, I don't suppose there is. I'm just glad you're both safe."

"Are your parents at home?" I ask, relieved not to have to jump head-first into an argument about my insane lack of judgment.

"Yeah. My mother has been losing her mind over your

brother. If I didn't know any better, I'd swear she was actually worried about his well-being."

"More like she's worried about her prize being stolen," I mutter.

"Maybe. But Merit seems really attached to Kel. He's pretty upset. At least, he's putting on a good show."

"You've spoken to him?"

"A little. Though my mother insisted on being in the room at the time, so he didn't tell me much other than what he's already said—that some bad people took Kel. But if you're with him right now, that can't be true...right?"

I fill him in on what's been going on around here, on Kyra's role in all this and my hope that I can get Kel to the Pit.

"I'm glad you're with them," Finn says. "Because my parents are watching me like hawks. It feels like..."

"Like they suspect something?"

"Yeah. Speaking of which, we probably shouldn't talk like this for too long. I have a bad feeling..."

"Has something happened?"

"Not exactly. I'm using my Disruptor to block surveillance devices, but I think my parents have something new in place—something to override the interference. I'm worried they know I've been in touch with you."

"Oh, God," I whisper, eyeing the door like they're about to rush in and take all three of us down. "Do you know that for sure?"

"No. It's just a hunch. My mother's so uptight with Kel disappearing—she's become even more psychotic than usual. It's like she suspects literally everyone in the world."

"Then we should stop talking. But first thing in the morning, I'm going to take Kel back to the Pit, and I need to get

Kyra out of here, too. Do you think you could bring a cloak for each of them?"

"Of course."

I tell him where to find us, and we agree that he'll come by at eight a.m. "Any earlier would arouse suspicion," he says. "I'll head to the lab first—that way my parents won't ask questions. I'll come to you with everything you need, I promise."

When we disconnect, I exhale, lean my head against the wall, and close my eyes, letting my exhaustion take me at last.

At eight the following morning, I find myself on the couch in Kyra's temporary abode, awaiting Finn's arrival.

8:10 rolls around, and there's still no sign of him.

Then 8:15.

When I click the earpiece he gave me and whisper his name, there's no reply.

I tell myself Finn must have some other sudden commitment. His parents have insisted that they have breakfast together, or he has to look after Merit, or…

No. I don't want to think about any more "or"s. He has to be fine. He *has* to make his way to me.

I need to have faith in that much, or I'll lose my mind.

At 8:45, a knock finally sounds at the door. But when Kyra cracks it open, it's Rys' face that greets her.

"I came to see if you need any help," he says when he's stepped inside, but when his eyes meet mine, I can tell he senses my quiet panic. "What's happened?"

"Finn was supposed to come by this morning at eight. I don't know where he is. The earpiece is broken or something."

"Let me see it," he says, holding a hand out. I give it to him and he examines it, handing it back a moment later. "It's fine. Finn's just disconnected from his end—probably out of caution. You should try it again in a little while."

I glance over at Kyra and Kel, who are sitting on the couch. Kel seems relaxed, but Kyra has a look on her face that tells me she knows what consequences will soon come for her.

"I have to get them out of here," I whisper. "Kyra will be killed if the Directorate finds her. And Kel..."

"I can get them out," Rys says under his breath. "I'll make sure they get where they need to go."

"Won't people notice your absence?"

"I won't be gone long. I'll run and grab two Inhibitors and some clothes, then show them the way out of the city—that's really all I can do. I'll give Kyra directions to the Pit's entrance then come back. Atticus will let the Pit know these two are on their way. Your friends will probably send a party out to find them—and hopefully they'll get to them before the Bastille's people do."

I nod. There's nothing more to say. I can't leave the Arc yet, not until I know Finn is all right. But keeping Kel and Kyra here for a second longer is too risky.

Within ten minutes, Rys has left the apartment and returned with supplies. Kyra gathers her things, and thanks to Rys, she and Kel dress in nondescript street clothes that make them look like they belong on one of the middle levels of the Arc.

"You're not coming?" Kel asks, a look of dismay on his face as I guide him to the door.

"I am," I assure him as I drape my cloak over his shoulders. *He'll need it more than I will.* "Just not this second. I have to make sure my friend is okay. But I'll follow you two very soon, I promise. In the meantime, the people in the Pit will look after you and keep you both safe."

Kel shoots me a skeptical look but lets out a sigh and shrugs in a way that somehow manages to make me laugh. Our father used to react the same way whenever our mother won an argument.

I hug him hard before doing the same to Kyra. "Be safe," I whisper to her. "Watch for the owl. He'll have your back."

She nods as she pulls away, issuing me a smile that doesn't quite manage to mask her pain. The road ahead for Kyra is far longer than a simple path through the woods. It will be years before she heals...*if she ever does.*

I can only hope our allies in the Pit will manage to restore a little of her faith in humanity.

When we've said our goodbyes, I turn to Rys. "Look after them," I say, a note of warning in my voice.

He nods. "I'll come see if you're still here when I get back. But I sincerely hope you aren't. You need to leave the Arc as soon as you possibly can."

"Agreed."

When the three of them have left, I pull out my earpiece and give it another try. This time, I hear a connection, followed by the encouraging buzz of background noise.

My heart springs to life in my chest as I whisper, "Finn?"

At first, I'm met with nothing but a strange, malevolent chuckle.

It's a full five seconds before a woman's voice says, "Ashen Spencer. What a pleasant surprise."

39

ENEMY

"HOW NICE IT is to hear from you again," the Duchess says, her voice shaded with a smugness that renews my desire to murder her. "I'm afraid my son is indisposed at the moment. It seems—*would you believe it?*—that he's been fraternizing with the enemy."

My skin scorches with undiluted rage and fear combined, and I'm barely able to force my lips to form the words, "What have you done with him?"

"Oh, don't you worry. He's right here. He's fine. Aren't you, dear?"

"Ash!" Finn's voice shouts. "Don't—"

I hear a thud, followed by a flurry of activity.

"I warned you and my son to stay away from each other some time ago," the Duchess finally says. "It seems you're both terrible at listening. I suppose the good news is that you're still in the Arc…aren't you?"

I wait only a second before replying. "Yes."

"Good. If you ever want to see Finn again, I'd suggest you

come to the Arenum at six o'clock tonight. It was amusing to watch you fight Randolph the last time you graced us with your presence. I'm sure the battle will be even more entertaining this time."

This time.

She's going to make me fight again.

I open my mouth to speak, but she's gone. All that meets my ear is silence.

I wonder with a swell of nausea if the Duke is aware of what his wife is up to—that she's using Finn as a pawn, a weapon against me. A human lure.

Then again, I'm not sure he'd care.

My breath catching in my throat, I glance over at the clock projected on the room's far wall. 9:07 a.m.

For the next several hours I'll be confined to this small residence, pacing my way back and forth as I hold in screams of rage and torment.

A tiny voice in my mind tells me to run. To escape the Arc.

That's what Finn was trying to convey to me:

Don't listen to her.

Do not sacrifice yourself for me.

But I have no choice. I know in my gut, in my soul, that the Duchess' people will kill him—or at least torture him—if I don't show up.

I find myself watching, hoping, for Rys' return. At this point, I'd gladly take *any* human walking through the door and putting me out of my misery. I need to speak to someone, to unleash the hurricane of emotion twisting inside me.

But as the hours tick by, there's no sign of him. I can only hope he's managed to get my brother and Kyra safely beyond the wall of Sector One. If I find they've been harmed, I swear I'll kill someone.

When 5:40 finally hits, I strap my sheath around my waist. I'm dressed in my uniform, hopeful that whatever adversary the Directorate is about to throw at me, I'll find a way to survive.

For Finn. For Kel.

For me.

I leave the residence, no longer worried about being seen by the Directorate's multitude of cameras. *Let them study my face. Let them know where I've been concealing myself. Nothing matters anymore.*

The entire Directorate Guard could descend on me and it wouldn't make a difference. Whatever happens, I will stand before the Duchess in a few minutes. I'll look defiantly into her eyes, challenging her.

Whatever happens, I will not let her make me feel like a lesser being.

I arrive at the Arenum at six o'clock exactly. Two men of the Directorate Guard stand outside its doors, blocking my way.

"I've been summoned," I tell them with a sneer.

They exchange a look, and for a second I wonder if they're going to challenge me. But they pull apart without a word, and the doors swing open.

I step out and proceed down the aisle toward the dirt-floored space that I've come to despise almost as much as I hate the Duchess. *The place the Wealthies come to watch Dregs die.*

To my surprise, though, the Arenum is empty.

I've just made my way to the center of the fighting ring,

my eyes searching the surrounding seats, when a figure emerges from the shadows on the far side:

The Duchess.

Dressed in a long red gown, her hair impeccable, her makeup flawless.

She's a beautiful, poisonous asp, waiting to strike.

"Well?" I say, shrugging my shoulders in quiet challenge. "I'm here. Where's Finn?"

The Duchess lifts her left hand and makes a small gesture, after which two more Directorate guardsmen step into the ring, with Finn between them. On his right cheek is a cut that someone has patched up with a small piece of white gauze. The skin around his eye is raw and swollen.

Anger bubbles up inside me as I examine him, but I say nothing. I merely stare into his eyes, seeking an answer to the question, *Are you okay?*

He gives me a tiny nod and the merest smile, but when his mother turns to glare at him, he scowls.

"You'll let him go, now that I'm here?" I ask.

"Let him go?" she replies. "He's my son. I'll *never* let him go." She steps toward me, her chin high. "A mother's bond with her child is strong. Unbreakable...even after death. Wouldn't you agree?"

I sneer at her. "I can tell you from experience it's a lot stronger during life. Before the mother is *murdered.*"

Her mouth twists into a half-smile, like she's trying to work out if I'm talking about my own mother's death or my desire to slay her.

But she lets it go.

"If something were to happen to Finn—if he were to get badly hurt or, God forbid, die—" she says, "I would still love him. He will always be my firstborn. So his betrayal does not shatter our bond. It may, in fact, strengthen it in the end…if he does as I've commanded."

"Oh?" I ask with a chuckle. "What exactly is it that you've *commanded* him to do?"

"Kill you, for starters."

40

A GRIM PRICE

I STUDY the Duchess for a long moment, convinced that she's joking. She's the most depraved, cruel person I've ever met, after all.

But even she wouldn't ask her son to murder the person he loves.

Would she?

When her face offers me no answers, I pull my eyes to Finn, who seems to have been silenced by some unseen, violent force. He's straining like he wants to talk, to tell me something...but it's as though his lips have been glued shut.

The only thing I can tell from his expression is that he knows the Duchess is dead serious.

How is Finn expected to do it? Stab me? Shoot me? Drown me?

Any of them would suit the Directorate just fine.

"At eight o'clock," the Duchess says, "this place will fill with spectators. Wealthy ones, of course; the Arc's Elite—the ones who would love to see Oliver Spencer's daughter die slowly. After all, you're the only person who's ever escaped this place. We simply must make an example of you."

So, I think with an internal snicker, *she doesn't know about the others. About Finn getting out, or Kel or Kyra...or Rys?*

Good.

If it weren't for my fear that the guards would kill Finn in retaliation, I'd hurl myself at the Duchess and take her life right here and now.

"You tried to make an example of me once," I remind her with a bitter scowl. "How *is* Randolph? Has he recovered from his wound? Or did he die because your band of jackasses couldn't get to him fast enough?"

"He's just fine," she says. "Recovering nicely, thank you for asking. Now, as for the fight..."

"Fight?" I ask, my mouth agape.

"You didn't think I was just going to ask Finn to come out here and murder you in cold blood, surely?" the Duchess laughs. "A firing squad of one would be so dull. No—you two star-crossed lovers will battle it out to the death."

Now my heart is throbbing in my chest. I'm expected to try and kill Finn?

That won't happen. Not tonight. Not ever.

I look into his eyes again, and again he nods, as if to confirm his mother's words. By now, I understand why he's not talking. What could he possibly say to make our situation any less horrid?

"Finn has told me about that lovely uniform you're wearing," the Duchess adds. "I know it's impressive. I also know it's why you managed to beat Randolph. And don't worry—I won't make you surrender it. If you want an advantage against my son, please, by all means...take it. If he can't manage to beat a weak girl in a one-on-one battle, he's not the young man I thought he was, and I've told him as much. But survival instinct is a powerful thing, and I'm quite certain he values his life more than yours…as much as he may proclaim the opposite."

I want to spit a retort at the Duchess, to hurl venom at her.

But there's nothing I could say that would make me feel any better.

If I want them to set Finn free, I have to fight.

If I fight, one of us dies.

"What if I win?" I ask, though I have no intention of doing so. "What if I beat him?"

The Duchess looks taken aback for a second, but then she laughs again. "Goodness, what a hypothetical. All right, I'll play. If you win, you can go free. You may go live in the mountains with your new allies."

There's no doubt in my mind that she's lying. The chances of the Duchess setting me free are about the same as a snowball thriving in Hell.

"And if I lose? What will happen to Finn?"

"He'll go back to the life he knew before you came along and ruined it."

"Then I guess I'll have to lose."

The Duchess looks perplexed, but she finally turns to the guards and tells them to take us to the cells. "Give my son anything he's asked for. Let him dress Ashen Spencer in full body armor if that's his wish. He's already half-dug his own grave; let's see if he finishes the job."

When I remain in place rather than step toward the guards, the Duchess nods to one of them. Without a word, he punches Finn hard in the side. Finn sputters and sags as if the wind has been knocked out of him.

"I'd suggest you accompany them," the Duchess commands. "Now."

If I kill her now, I tell myself, the guards will take Finn down. He's too weak right now to fight back.

He *may* be too weak to kill me tonight.

All I know is that he has to try.

41

THE LAST

THE GUARDS DON'T NEED to drag me down the hall toward the cells. They know I'll go willingly.

I can feel the Duchess' eyes burning into my back as I walk along behind them and Finn, my mind racing with theories, with hopes, with thoughts of how he and I can possibly escape.

Surprisingly enough, they put us in the same cell when the time comes. All I can think is that this is all part of the Duchess' plan. She wants us to work together—to plan our demise as a couple. For these last moments to consist of nothing but pain, fear, and anger.

The guards escort Finn to the cell's only cot and lay him down. He groans, his hand on his chest. I rush over as the men shut the door and cup his cheeks in my hands.

"Finn," I whisper. "Can you hear me?"

He nods, but barely.

"What have they done to you?" I ask, tears in my eyes.

"I was..." he sputters, "drugged."

Okay, I think. *This is only a temporary state.*

"Can you get up? Can we get out of here? I still have a Disruptor on me, and I'm pretty sure I can take the guards down."

He shakes his head and points weakly toward his left foot.

I look down but see nothing but his shoe.

"Under my pant leg," he mutters.

When I get on my knees and feel his ankle, I understand.

They've attached some sort of monitor to him like the kind the police used to put on convicts they didn't want violating their house arrest.

"We can pry it off," I tell him. "I can..."

But he shakes his head again. This time, his speech is clearer. "If you try that, we'll both die. It's sophist...sophisticated. I've seen this sort of thing before. It's not going anywhere until they take it off just before the fight."

Tears run down my face as the words sink in. "What are we going to do?"

"I've already asked them bring you some things—including a new uniform."

"Why? You're the one who needs one."

"I'll have one," he replies, squeezing my hand and quietly pleading for silence. "But you have to listen to me—I need you to win tonight."

I shake my head. "No. No way. I'm not hurting you. I'm not...*killing* you. I can't."

"You can. At the very least, you have to try." His speech is clearer now, like adrenaline has begun to combat the drug in his bloodstream. "So hurt me. Wound me badly enough that maybe my mother or father will have a crisis of conscience. We both know if I hurt you, they'll just cheer for more until..." His voice trails off, and he shakes his head, defeated. "I can't."

"Finn, this is insane. We can't do this. We have to escape."

"It's impossible," he says with a shake of his head. "There's no way. Not anymore."

Hearing those five words of surrender on his lips is enough to send me into a fit of sobbing. He pulls himself up to a sitting position and leans over me, holding me, kissing me. "I'm sorry," he whispers. "I'm so sorry, Ash."

When I've exhausted my supply of tears, he strokes my cheek and whispers, "Kel...Kyra...did they..."

I nod, wiping at my face with my hands. "Rys got them out. At least, I'm hoping he did. They should be safe."

"That's what really matters," Finn says. He looks and sounds so exhausted, his face and body in a state of ruin.

"Yes, it is."

"Ash...we don't have a lot of time. Tonight, things are going to end for one of us."

I want to argue, to fight. I'm angry with him right now, for how easily he's surrendered to our hideous fates, for how he's accepted that one of us will simply die tonight, like it doesn't even matter.

An urge assaults me, instinct commanding me to slap him, to scream at him.

But that's just what the Duchess wants. She *wants* us to hate each other, to tear into each other like rabid beasts, leaving deep wounds that will never, ever heal.

No. It's more than that.

She craves my blood...and her son's soul.

"Tell me you mean *me*," I finally say, taking his hands in mine. "Tell me you mean things are going to end for *me*, and not for you. Please, Finn. I need you to say it."

He lowers his chin and looks wearily at my face. He opens his mouth to speak just as the door opens and two Directorate

Guard soldiers make their way in, grab my arms, and yank me toward the door.

At first I try to resist, but Finn levels me with a look of silent warning.

My eyes burning with tortured tears, I go quietly. Fine. They can bring me to whatever hideous destination they have in mind and toy with me there. I'm not sure I can summon the energy to care anymore.

All I know is that tonight, I take my last breath.

42

PREPARATION

THE GUARDS DRAG me down the hall toward a steel door, which slides open to reveal a white room with shiny walls. Its corners are slightly rounded so that they disappear, and I feel oddly as though I'm standing inside a cloud, disoriented and miserable.

They shove me inside and for a few minutes, I simply stand there and wait. For what, I'm not sure.

My fate, I suppose.

After a few minutes, the door opens again and someone walks in—a woman, wearing a form-fitting red uniform. On her face is a mask that reminds me of those the Directorate wears, only this one isn't silver. Instead, its surface swims with orange and yellow flames that dance and move as though her skin is on fire.

Her dark hair is pulled up into a series of snaking braids on top of her head, and she steps forward, seemingly assessing me, before finally removing the mask.

I look into her eyes, stunned. I haven't seen her since my first day in the Arc, since the train brought me here.

"Diva?" I stammer. "What are you doing here?"

She was the stylist who did my hair and makeup on that first day, and who first told me about the Aristocracy. She seemed so happy back then, so carefree and positive.

Right now, though, she looks terrified.

"Ashen," she says, her eyes shifting around the space, checking corners for micro-drones or cameras. On her wrist, her implant flares to life, flashing red in warning. She shakes her head in a barely perceptible movement as if to say, "I'm sorry, I can't talk."

"Do you know what's about to happen?" I ask her.

She nods.

"Have you known all this time...what they do to Dregs?"

As if petrified to make a sound, she shakes her head.

"But you know now."

She sucks in her cheeks and hesitates before saying, "They wanted me to prepare you for tonight. They said something about 'the symmetry of life.' I suppose they thought it would be...fun to have the same stylist work with you now as that first night."

She's smiling, her voice bright, but I can see in her eyes that the horror is still sitting inside her like a stone.

I whisper, "Diva, listen to me carefully—I know you can't tell me much. I know you can't help or they'll kill you. But I need you to know there are a lot of things that happen in this place...things you can't even imagine. If I die tonight, I need to know it won't be in vain."

"Let's get started, shall we?" she asks as if brushing off what I've just said. But I see a flicker in her eyes, a quiet look of acknowledgment.

She doesn't need to say a word.

"I'm going to do your hair and makeup," she tells me, her

voice strained. "The outfit they're bringing you is pretty amazing, I've heard. I can't wait to see you in it."

"I'm glad to hear it, because it'll be the last thing I ever wear."

Swallowing hard, Diva walks over to the door and slides her hand over a barely visible panel next to it, pressing a series of symbols before the floor opens up a few feet away and a chair rises from its depths.

As I make my way over to sit down, the walls alter around us, the pure white surface fizzling away to reveal a landscape of rolling hills covered in a field of flowers.

"Any requests?" Diva asks. "For scenery, I mean?"

"Yes," I reply. "I'd like to see Sector Eight."

She looks confused. "Sector Eight? But isn't it..."

"Falling to pieces? Yes. It is. And I want to see it."

Her hand shaking, Diva slips her fingers over the panel again, inputting information until we're both surrounded by the splintered houses and cracked, overgrown streets that used to be my favorite place in the world.

"I wonder if they'll take the girls who are left," I say almost absently.

"The girls?" Diva asks, but she clams up instantly, realizing she's participating in a conversation she shouldn't.

"You don't know, I guess," I tell her, turning her way. "The Directorate has begun raising Dreg girls outside the Arc to use as brood mares." I let out a laugh that sounds mildly insane. "Don't get me wrong—they're brainwashed first into thinking they have a future in here. That it'll be exciting to marry a rich man who will provide them with everything they could want. Everything, that is, except for love. Oh, and the ability to go outside. Or any sort of freedom whatsoever."

"Whatever the Directorate is doing, I'm sure it's for the greater good," Diva says in a stilted voice.

"Of course," I reply with a snicker. "The Directorate is nothing if not benevolent, right? That's why I'm about to get murdered in front of a crowd. That's why they've killed my friends and my mother. Always for the greater good."

Diva is standing behind me now, and she lays a hand on my shoulder, ostensibly to begin styling my hair. But I feel her squeeze, then I feel a tear drop onto my scalp before she pulls away.

"Ashen," she whispers. "There's something you should know."

"What's that?"

I spin in my chair to look at her, bracing for more bad news.

"Rumors started spreading a while back. Rumors about a girl who defied the King and Queen of the Arc by taking their son down. A girl who escaped, who went looking for help."

Part of me wants to tell her to stop talking, that she's saying too much and the Directorate will kill her for it.

But I need to hear this. Before I die, I need to know what's being said.

"It gave people hope. Those in the Arc who already knew what the Directorate was—former Dregs who've been through training, and others, too. Some of them have been talking. There are even some residents involved—it's all been quiet, but word has finally gotten out. Some of the Wealthies have let the Directorate know how angry they are. Some have been punished for it, but the Directorate can't imprison all of them—there are far too many."

"What are you saying? There's an actual rebellion brewing?"

Finn theorized that it was why his mother had become so paranoid, why she'd stepped up security measures. And Kyra said something, too. *So—it's really happening.*

"I'm saying you're not alone anymore," she whispers. "You—"

The door slides open and two Directorate Guard soldiers come in, guns at their hips.

When the door has shut again, the men wordlessly position themselves against the wall, hands behind their backs.

Diva and I exchange a look, and there's no doubt in my mind she knows what I'm thinking.

Do they know what we were talking about? Could they hear us?

"Now, let's get started for real, okay?" Diva asks, clearing her throat. "I still remember how I did your hair on that first day. Would you like it that way again?"

"Yes," I tell her, reaching out and squeezing her hand. "And…thank you."

She hums to herself as she begins to twist my hair. At first, I don't recognize the tune.

But as it progresses, I realize it's a song I heard many times when I was little. An old tune from a musical my parents once showed me on television, back when there was such a thing in the Mire. I remember watching a group of soldiers sing about rebellion against an oppressive government…the uniting of a downtrodden people against a common enemy.

"Does your family still live on level 250?" I ask Diva, interrupting the sweet music in case the guards, too, recognize it.

"They do," she says.

"Good," I tell her. "You should go back to them once you're done here."

"I'm not sure I'll be able…" she says, her hands trembling as she eyes the Directorate Guard's soldiers.

"Diva hasn't done anything wrong," I announce, turning to the guards. "She's doing what you asked her. If you hurt her, you will inspire the wrath of some very powerful people."

One of the soldiers steps toward me, says, "Shut up!" and slams the butt of his gun into the back of my head. For a moment my surroundings blur, but I regain my composure.

"If you don't let her go," I snarl, "I'll kill you."

"I'd love to see you try," the man chuckles. He moves closer, his eyes menacing.

But he doesn't assault me again.

Just as Diva is finishing up, the door slides open and two Chaperons march in, each carrying a plain white box. They stop before me and open the first box to reveal a folded garment that looks like it's made of fine scale, or possibly even chainmail. It's silver and reflective, and even more intricately crafted than the violet cloak Finn gave me.

As I lift the garment, I see that it isn't the only item in the box, but I lay it back down and nod.

The other Chaperon opens the second box. Inside is a metallic belt with a sheath, holding a long dagger with an intricately carved handle. I pull it out of the box, unsheathe it, and stare at the blade itself. It looks like a simple dagger—but if it comes from Finn, something tells me it's anything but.

Not that it matters, since there's no way in hell I'll be using it to hurt him.

Alongside the weapon is a pair of silver shoes with leather soles. They look comfortable, light, and flexible.

I know what Finn's doing, that he wants to give me every chance to win tonight. No doubt he's spent months on this suit, developing it originally for the Directorate Guard—of course, that was before he knew just how terrible his mother's organization was.

Holding the uniform in my right hand, I glance over at the guard who scoffed at me earlier.

"Thank you," I tell the two Chaperons as I re-sheathe the blade and lay it back in the box.

They set the packages on the ground and leave the room just as Diva commands me to stand. She slips over to the panel next to the door and activates it, and the walls surrounding us turn to mirrors.

I can see myself from every angle now, reflected on each of the four walls. My hair is twisted and tangled into an exquisite series of knots, and a sea of blue butterflies surrounds my head, just as they did once before.

"Thank you, Diva," I say quietly before turning to the two guards. "I need to change. Which means you need to leave."

"No way," one of the men retorts with a nod toward Diva. "Not without her."

"I need her to help me into my uniform. So you'll have to wait outside."

"Fine," the man says, ushering the other one out through the door. "We'll be *right* outside."

I hold my finger to my lips, telling Diva not to say another word. She's already put herself in too much danger by telling me about the brewing rebellion.

Silently, I remove the uniform from its box, strip down to my underclothing, and pull it on. It's one piece like a well-fitting jumpsuit, and at the ends of its arms are a set of gloves of the same fabric. When I slip my fingers into them, I can feel that there are pressure points on my palms. I squeeze my hands into fists, which activates the garment's cloaking mechanism. When I've deactivated it, Diva helps fasten a clasp at the back of my neck then pulls a thin sort of veil over my head, which I then draw down over my face.

Though it clings to my features, I can see through it astoundingly well.

"Finn, you're amazing," I say softly. "It's too bad this creation of yours won't save me from what's about to happen."

In that moment, I notice something else in the box—a small envelope, no bigger than a large postage stamp. At first, it looks like nothing. But when I pick it up and flip it over, I see that someone has written:

Press me into your skin, Ash.
And tonight, when you want it all to end,
cross your hands over your heart...
then thrust them out,
palms forward.

Inside the envelope is a small, flat square of paper, the color of my skin.

"What is this?" I murmur, turning to Diva.

"No idea. I've never seen anything like it. Is it..."

I look more closely and see what looks like a tiny pin no thicker than a silk thread and less than half an inch long, jutting out from the paper.

"A needle of some sort?" I ask.

"You might not want to put that anywhere near your skin. You don't know where it came from," Diva cautions, but I shake my head.

"Finn leaves me notes. Gifts. This has him written all over it. Besides, the Directorate won't kill me by poisoning me—it's not their style. If I had to guess, I'd say it's some sort of pain inhibitor. Something to make the...*end*...less unpleasant for me."

I pull the veil off my head and, parting the back of my dark hair, push the narrow sliver of metal into my skin. I barely register that it's penetrated my flesh.

I'm not sure why Finn instructed me to cross my hands over my heart when the time comes. Maybe it's a tribute to the Consortium, to Illian and Kurt and all they're fighting for.

Maybe it's a trigger for my own demise.

Whatever the case, I know he's doing it to ease my pain.

I strap the silver belt around my waist. When I curl my hands into fists, activating my uniform's cloaking ability, it immediately disappears along with the rest of me, vanishing as if it was never there.

"A cloaking blade," I murmur with a smile. "Incredible."

"Ashen," Diva says, but I shoot her a look, pulling my uniform out of its stealth mode.

"Don't say it—whatever you're thinking," I warn. "Just don't."

"You could just walk away," she tells me in a whisper. "It seems to me that's what Finn wants you to do—with this uniform, the blade..."

I shake my head. "I won't. Finn will be killed if I leave before the fight starts. I can't let that happen."

She bows her head. "Then I guess it's time."

When the door slides open, the two guards eye Diva, and for a moment I'm sure they're going to take her away and lock her up in the Hold.

But instead, they let her walk out, fixing their eyes on me.

Diva turns back when she's in the hallway. Her eyes filled with tears, she slips her fiery mask back on then crosses her hands over her heart, nodding once.

"I'll always remember you, Ashen Spencer," she says.

43

THE ARENUM

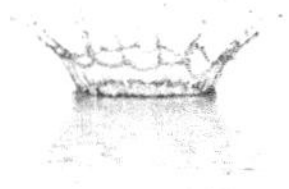

It's only a few minutes before the guards push me into the arena, my eyes scanning the crowd. I scowl as I register the masked faces of the Directorate and the Aristocracy.

You cowards.

Still unwilling to show yourselves as you call for the death of a Dreg.

I find the Duchess and Duke in the box seats, sitting on gilded thrones alongside the King and Queen. As if to defy the rules, the Duke and Duchess are unmasked, their faces stern and icy cold.

In an exaggerated gesture, I bow low toward her, though what I really want is to leap into the stands and tear her apart.

"I'm not going to do it!" I shout, my voice echoing back toward me via the speakers set up around the arena. "I'm not going to kill him."

The Duchess rises to her feet. "Then my son will kill you, and I will enjoy it. It will be a fine result."

The Duke looks vaguely troubled. *But not enough to do anything about it,* I think. *You spineless bastard.*

I stand at the arena's center, looking around until my eyes meet a familiar face—one of the Directorate Guard soldiers.

Marsh?

My former friend—the one who derived such sadistic pleasure from killing Luke on that fateful, wretched day. I'm surprised to see him in the uniform; his training can't be complete yet. I suppose his bloodlust impressed the Directorate enough to accelerate his elevation to the rank of *professional asshole.*

He stares at me, his expression hostile, and I find myself seething with hatred. How is it that a boy like him—a boy from the Mire whose parents, like so many others, were murdered by the Directorate—is now loyal only to them? How does a person turn as he has?

I'm just about to say something to him when the arena's door opens and Finn walks through, dressed, as I am, in a silver cloaking uniform. Like me, he's entirely visible, though I have no doubt he could disappear if he wanted to. Sheathed at his waist are two silver-handled daggers.

Good, I think. *We're on equal footing, at least. That means he plans to try.*

Finn strides toward me. He looks better now than he did earlier, more together, more alert.

For a moment, I think he's going to stop a few feet away, but instead, he keeps coming until he's only inches from me. With a glance up to his parents' seats, he cups my cheeks in his palms and kisses me passionately.

Almost instantly, the crowd erupts in a chorus of jeers and derisive shouts, but Finn doesn't pull away. Instead, he presses his cheek to my own and whispers, "Did you get the graft?"

"Graft? You mean the needle thing?"

"Yes, I did as you asked."

"Good."

"What does it do?" I whisper, backing away and looking him in the eye.

He smiles. "It protects us both, when the time comes."

I smile. Just as I thought—it must be some sort of anesthetic, some pain inhibitor. Finn is abiding by my wishes. He's going to finish me tonight, but he's made sure my death won't come with physical agony.

Good boy.

No—Good *man.*

He backs away, turning to face the King, Queen, and his parents. Like me, he bows sarcastically to them. "You've put us both in an impossible position," he says, his voice booming through the speakers. "I only hope you're happy with tonight's outcome."

His mother raises her sharp chin but doesn't reply.

I wonder if there's any part of her—even the tiniest morsel—that feels guilty about torturing her son. What about Merit, back in their residence? What would she tell him if Finn died tonight?

Not that it matters. Finn won't die, because I won't kill him. The crowd will be lucky if I so much as land a weak punch.

"Ashen Spencer," a voice bellows. I look up to determine that the King is speaking from behind his mask. "And Finn Davenport. You have been sentenced to fight to the death. The winner will leave this arena tonight. The loser will not."

Finn and I exchange a glance. *This is it,* I think. *This is how it begins.*

And ends.

But the King, it turns out, isn't done.

"If each of you should fail to kill the other," he says, "You both die."

His words aren't wholly unexpected, of course. But I find myself wondering how they would do it. Drones? Guns?

Will Marsh be the one to take my life?

I turn to Finn.

"I love you," I say quietly. "You know what you need to do. For Merit. For everyone."

"Yes. I know what I need to do."

"Let the fighting commence!" the King shouts to the deafening roar of cheers and foot-stomps from the audience.

I back away from Finn, my heart thudding in my chest. I've been here before, in this very arena, my feet digging into the earth.

But last time, I was fighting someone I didn't know—and the little I did know of him, I despised.

Finn, on the other hand, is everything. He's good and kind. He's protective. He wants the same for this world that I do—for the Directorate to be defeated, taken down. For the truth to come out, for the people to come to understand how they were deceived.

And Finn has a better shot at changing the world than I ever could.

We circle one another slowly. Neither of us draws our weapons. At first, we simply keep our arms by our sides and engage in a slow-paced staring contest. But after watching our deliberately sluggish dance for a few minutes, the crowd begins to hurl abuse our way.

"Pe-ril! Pe-ril!" they cry. "Slaughter the Dreg! Tear out her heart!"

Not a single person calls for Finn's death, and I'm glad of it.

Give the crowd what they want. Come on, Finn. Kill me.

But it seems he has something else in mind. He wants to put on a show.

With both hands, he signals me to come at him. I shake my head, my mouth turned down in a frown.

"Ash, you have to," he finally says. "At least try. Just try to make it look real, or…"

"Come on, Dreg!" someone shouts. The voice is familiar—one I've heard many times. "You're pathetic! You're weak!"

I look over my right shoulder to see Marsh joining in with the crowd.

No, Marsh. I'm not the weak one. I'm not the one who murdered a classmate in cold blood, or who now worships the devil who runs the Arc.

"Ash, focus!" Finn commands.

Enraged by Marsh's presence, I lunge at Finn but pull my attack up short, shoving him as gently as I can. But the new suit's enhancements are impressive and I send him tumbling backwards. He rights himself only after he's crashed into the dirt floor. He pushes himself to his feet, smiles, and nods. "That's it!" he calls out. "Again!"

I run at him and push him once more, and again, he flies backwards.

"Why isn't your suit working?" I ask. "Why is it so easy to push you down?"

He issues me an apologetic grin and a shrug.

"Finn, this isn't funny," I shout over the din of the crowd.

"I know it's not. But I'm not going to let you die, Ash. Not tonight. So I'm afraid you're just going to have to kill me."

I shake my head and cross my arms, my feet planted in the dirt floor.

"If you want me to hurt you, you'll have to come at me," I insist.

"You know I can't hurt you."

"Try."

For a few minutes, we entertain ourselves—and the crowd—with a game of cat and mouse. Finn runs at me, grabbing me and throwing me to the ground. The spectators, ignorant of the special enhancements granted by my silver suit, seem to think he's actually hurting me. They scream for more, cheering for my death, disappointed with each new breath I take.

Finn pulls his fist back and brings it down toward my chest, but I stop it with both hands, holding it for a moment as I smile up at him. "This is actually pretty fun," I admit. "Too bad we can't keep it going."

"It really is."

As predicted, it doesn't take the crowd long to realize we're teasing them. There's no blood. No shattered bones. Our weapons remain sheathed at our waists.

"Boring!" someone shrieks.

An announcement comes over the speakers, the King's voice bellowing, "If no blood is shed within thirty seconds, you both die."

As if to reinforce his promise, a small army of drones descends from the highest point of the ceiling and moves into a sort of Y-formation above us. A hundred or more red lights point in our direction, reminding us how vulnerable we really are.

"*That's* boring," I scoff, pulling my dagger from its sheath. I hold it up to the crowd, and more cheers erupt in support of whatever they think I'm about to do.

"Good girl," Finn says, his voice low. "Now, take me down."

"Not on your life," I tell him, drawing the blade across the palm of my left hand.

I hold it up to let a trail of blood run down to my wrist, showing the Directorate, the King and Queen.

"Blood has been shed," I tell them. "Satisfied?"

The King, apparently displeased, signals with his right hand and the drones begin to descend once again.

"Come at me, Ash!" Finn orders again, this time through clenched jaws. "Punch me in the face! You have to hurt me!"

I shake my head. "No," I say, tears welling in my eyes. "I can't. I won't."

"We can't *both* die. Think of Kel. Think about how much your brother needs you."

My lip is quivering as I look up to see the electronic army hovering in the air above us.

If only to keep the drones at bay, I leap at Finn, determined to make a show of my fake attack. I take him by the collar with one hand and punch him in the face with the other, careful to hold back.

My fist meets his jaw with a sickening *thwack* sound and I back away, horrified, while the crowd cheers.

"Are you okay?" I ask.

Grabbing his chin, he smiles as blood dribbles out of his mouth. "I'm great. Now do it again."

I attack him once more, throwing him down and landing another blow, this one to his chest. He's winded but still manages a smile.

After another series of improvised attacks, I look up, expecting to see the army of drones retreating, but instead, they hover close, ready to strike.

"They're not moving," I say, panicked. I pull my eyes to Finn's.

"The King wants us to end it," he replies, his voice far too calm. "He wants death."

He steps toward me, pulls me close and kisses me long and deep one last time.

"We can disappear," I say, desperate. "We can cloak ourselves, and…"

But Finn shakes his head. "The drones' guns are locked on us. The second we disappear from view, we're both dead."

The crowd, annoyed at the show of affection, chants, "Finish her! Finish the Dreg!"

"Are you ready for the end?" Finn asks. "Do you remember what I wrote on the note—about your hands?"

"I do. I'm ready." It takes all my strength to steady my voice. "Watch over Kel for me."

"You know I will."

Finn backs away and stares at me. The drones, still buzzing in the air above us, haven't made any move to attack…yet. But I know they'll kill us both if I don't finish this.

Stepping back, I look into Finn's eyes. He smiles, nodding as I recite the instruction he wrote in his note:

Cross your hands over your heart...
then thrust them out,
palms forward.

"I want it to end!" I shout, pressing one palm then the other over my chest like the swords in the Consortium's symbol. I pull my hands away and push them toward Finn, my eyes still locked on his.

His lips are still curled into a warm smile, like he's telling me not to worry…and promising me death won't be so bad.

As I shove my palms out, a flash fills the Arenum, electric

blue and blinding. A vast orb of pure light shoots through the air away from me, slamming into Finn's chest and hurling him backwards.

As if he weighs nothing, he flies through the air, slamming hard into the far wall.

He slumps, limp, to the ground.

"Finn!" I scream, sprinting to his side. I throw myself onto the ground next to him, cradling his head in my lap.

He's not breathing. There's no sign of life. I search for a pulse, but feel nothing.

"What happened?" I cry, pulling my eyes up to scan the crowd. "What have I done?"

"Ashen Spencer has won," a calm voice announces over the speakers. I push myself to my feet, shaking my head, turning to face the King.

I look down at Finn. His eyes are closed, his face motionless, pale. If I didn't know any better, I'd think he was sleeping.

But I *do* know better.

I did that. I killed him.

"There is no winner here!" I cry out. "You've killed us both!"

"Yes," the King replies. "You're quite right about that."

With a simple flick of his fingers, the drones begin their descent again.

Only, this time, there's no stopping them.

44

GONE

Moving into a menacing circular formation, the drones descend slowly toward me, their red eyes focused on my own.

"Take me, then!" I scream, my arms extended. "Kill me! Let the Directorate finally have what they want, damn it!"

Tears blur my vision, transforming the swarm of mechanical threats into one massive flying beast surging through the space above me. It hangs in the air, a dark cloud drawing out my pain.

All this, just for the pleasure of a crowd of screaming monsters.

A crowd that...

Gone silent.

Not a whisper, not a single cheer for my impending death.

Why aren't they cheering?

My question is answered when I hear a collective gasp.

I wipe my eyes with my sleeve and spin around, trying to figure out what they're reacting to.

At first, I see nothing. But when I pull my chin up, my eyes locking on the high ceiling above me, I understand.

Birds in flight.

Hundreds of them.

They attack from above, diving at the drones as a protective sparrow attacks a hawk. But these are no mere sparrows. Tearing the drones apart with fierce talons, the birds let out shrill battle cries, a violent cacophony echoing like tormented screams off the Arenum's walls.

A few of the drones manage to get shots off, and some of the metal birds go tumbling to the ground, crashing and exploding into jagged shards at the feet of the crowd.

Flapping between the drones, distracting, displacing, and throwing them off kilter, the rest of the winged army battle the enemy's mechanical forces. Disoriented, the drones smash into one another in mid-air and tumble downward.

The crowd, terrified, cowers, shielding themselves with their arms over their heads.

Shouts assault my ears:

How did they get in here?

There's never been a bird inside the Arc...none except the holographic projections in the gardens!

It's not possible!

I watch the chaos unfold, waiting, hoping for a familiar silhouette to show himself.

And then he does.

Atticus.

The silver owl swoops down from what looks like a dark gash in the ceiling high above us—the same opening the drones flew through minutes ago.

When Atticus is close, Rys' voice meets my ears, cutting through the chorus of hysterical banshees losing their minds around me.

"Ash! Follow me!"

I shake my head even as the last of the drones are dispersed and the birds move in to attack the crowd in a vicious, choreographed dance.

"I can't!" I shout. "He's…"

I twist around to see Finn, still lying on the ground, his body twisted horribly. But when my eyes land on him, I perceive the tiniest movement—the fingers on his left hand curling toward his palm.

Atticus makes his way around to hover in front of me, his glowing eyes locked on mine, and Rys speaks again. "Ash… you have to go with the owl, or they'll kill you. You can't help Finn now."

I shoot a look toward the crowd and the Directorate Guard members—even Marsh—all under attack by Rys' man-made forces. Many of the spectators are bleeding, others cowering, terrified for their lives.

But not a single face is turned my way.

I peer around Atticus to lay my eyes on Finn one last time…only he isn't there.

"His suit," I whisper. "He's…cloaked?"

The movement of his hand must have done it. But was it a conscious clenching of his fist, or a reflex after death?

"Ash!" Rys shouts, his voice piercing.

I activate the cloaking mechanism in my suit, pull the webbed veil over my face, and chase Atticus up one of the aisles and out through the open door.

The owl glides ahead of me to the end of the hall, where a panel slides open. Without thinking twice, I leap onto the waiting Conveyor and watch as the door closes, sealing us in.

I've put every ounce of faith in Rys. Every bit of trust I have left. I'm in his hands now.

"What happened back there?" I ask. "The blue light…the explosion…"

"What happened is exactly what Finn wanted to happen. It's what he had planned from the moment he knew he'd be fighting you."

"But—I was the one who was supposed to die, not him. I never meant to—"

"It was the blast that took him down, Ash. A blast you didn't know was coming."

"So he really is dead."

A sob heaves its way up my throat and I collapse against the wall, my legs limp under me.

Rys goes silent for a few seconds before he finally says, "Look—the Arc is a place of illusions and deceit…but not *every* deception is the work of the Directorate."

My voice quivers when I muster the words, "What are you saying?"

"I'm saying you just barely escaped death. Whether Finn did as well remains to be seen, but I promise you, we'll find out."

"*Remains to be seen,*" I repeat under my breath. There's hope in those words.

So much hope…

"Whether Finn is alive or dead, I think it's time to fight back," Rys tells me. "Don't you?"

Curling my hands into fists to temporarily disable my uniform's cloaking mode, I hold my arm out and Atticus, who's been hovering in mid-air, comes in for a landing. He's surprisingly light, and when his head twists around to look into my eyes, I actually manage something approaching a smile.

Finn is alive.

He ***has*** *to be.*

"Tell me what to do," I say, "and I'll do it."

"Come with me, Ashen Spencer. The war is about to begin."

End of Awaken, the Cure Chronicles, Book Two

COMING SOON: ASCEND

Spoiler-free Summary:

The Uprising is gaining ground. But supplies are scarce, and the Aristocracy is more powerful than anyone ever imagined.

Ashen's fight may be unwinnable...but the affection of a certain young man may just give her the strength she needs to persevere.

NEW! THE RAVENMASTER SERIES: ARISE

For Fans of *Recruitment* and the *Conspiracy Chronicles:* A new series is soaring your way!

In a spectacular crossover event of re-emergence inspired

by Homer's epic adventure *The Odyssey*, Kress and Brohn leave the Emergents Academy on a daring mission to confront the leaders of the Cult of the Devoted in their nearly-completed arcology in the center of what's left of Denver, Colorado.

Making their deadly mission even more impossible, Epic—the villainous, marble-skinned techno-geneticist—has turned his Hypnagogic assassins loose on them.

When Brohn mysteriously disappears in the middle of the night, Kress is forced to embark on a perilous quest through a dozen urban districts packed with brainwashers, gunmen, ghosts from the past—and even an entire neighborhood of one-eyed gangsters and their packs of wild dogs—to get him back.

Arise (Coming in October 2021)
Banished (Coming in January 2022)
Crusade (Coming in 2022)

ALSO BY K. A. RILEY

If you're enjoying K. A. Riley's books, please consider leaving a positive review on Amazon or Goodreads to let your fellow book-lovers know about them.

Dystopian Books:

The Cure Chronicles:

The Cure

Awaken

Ascend (Coming in December 2021)

Resistance Trilogy:

Recruitment

Render

Rebellion

Emergents Trilogy:

Survival

Sacrifice

Synthesis

Transcendent Trilogy:

Travelers

Transfigured

Terminus

Academy of the Apocalypse Series:

Emergents Academy

Cult of the Devoted

Army of the Unsettled (July 2021)

The Ravenmaster Chronicles:

Arise (Coming in October 2021)

Banished (Coming in January 2022)

Crusade (Coming in April 2022)

Athena's Law Trilogy:

Book One: *Rise of the Inciters*

Book Two: *Into an Unholy Land*

Book Three: *No Man's Land*

Fantasy Books

Seeker's Series:

Seeker's World

Seeker's Quest

Seeker's Fate

Seeker's Promise

Seeker's Hunt

Seeker's Prophecy (Coming in 2021)

To be informed of future releases, and for chances to win free swag, books, and other goodies, please sign up here:

https://karileywrites.org/#subscribe

K.A. Riley's Bookbub Author Page

K.A. Riley on Amazon.com

K.A. Riley on Goodreads.com

Made in the USA
Las Vegas, NV
13 November 2023

80785502R00194